Call of th

CAROL FINCH

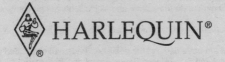

HARLEQUIN®

TORONTO • NEW YORK • LONDON
AMSTERDAM • PARIS • SYDNEY • HAMBURG
STOCKHOLM • ATHENS • TOKYO • MILAN • MADRID
PRAGUE • WARSAW • BUDAPEST • AUCKLAND

ISBN 0-373-29192-2

CALL OF THE WHITE WOLF

Copyright © 2002 by Connie Feddersen

Please address questions and book requests to:
Harlequin Reader Service
U.S.: 3010 Walden Ave., P.O. Box 1325, Buffalo, NY 14269
Canadian: P.O. Box 609, Fort Erie, Ont. L2A 5X3

This book is dedicated to my husband, Ed,
and our children—Christie, Jill, Kurt, Jeff and Jon—
with much love. And to our grandchildren—
Blake, Kennedy and Brooklynn. Hugs and kisses!

Chapter One

Arizona Territory, 1878

John Wolfe had been dreading this day for two years. No matter how many ways he turned it around in his mind, feelings of guilt and betrayal twisted in his gut like a shot of bad whiskey. He tried to ignore those tormenting emotions while he lay sprawled on a slab of rock, slithering forward like a snake so he could peer over the ledge. But the moment he saw his adopted Apache brother kneeling below him, sipping water from the trickling spring, another wave of guilt and betrayal buffeted him.

When a man was forced to turn against one of his own it made him feel like the worst kind of traitor.

Silently, John unholstered his Colt, then took Raven's measure down the sight. Dead or alive, John's commander had told him. Made no nevermind to Jacob Shore. But it mattered to John Wolfe. It mattered a helluva lot. When a man had a foot planted in each of two contrasting civilizations, walking that fine line and trying to pretend indifference was pure hell.

John had taught himself not to feel, not to react and not to care that he was as white as he was Apache. Yet seeing Raven in the valley below was like tearing open a wound that had never really healed, no matter how much he tried to pretend it had.

Well, he was here to do a job, distasteful though it was, and he'd better get at it.

"Don't move," John commanded in the Apache dialect.

Raven froze, his cupped hand halfway to his mouth. Water trickled between his fingertips and ran down his bronzed arm. The Apache raised his eyes and squinted into the bright light of sunset to locate John on the outcropping of stone above him.

John knew the exact instant Raven recognized him. Tension sizzled in the evening breeze like lightning. Slowly, Raven rose from his crouch, his body taut, his expression rife with loathing.

"So the white-eyes sent you for me, did they, Brother?" Raven spat derisively. "Ah, but who else could they have sent? Who else knows the Apache's mind and the Apache's way better than an Apache turncoat?"

Raven's words were like an embedded knife twisting in John's spine. Willfully, he ignored Raven's mutinous glower and hateful words. He kept the Colt trained on Raven's heart, wondering if this renegade still had one left after all the crimes he'd committed these past two years.

With an economy of movement that was ingrained and practiced, John contorted his body until he was sitting upright, his booted feet dangling over the ledge. His pistol never wavered from its target on Raven's heaving chest.

"I'm taking you back to the reservation at San Carlos, Raven," John told him grimly. "I can drag you by your heels or with your hands in chains. But if you ask me, it is not a good day for you to die."

"I was dying a torturous death at that pigsty of a reservation,'' Raven growled in reply. ''But you knew that feeling yourself, didn't you, Brother? *You* cut off your braids, stole civilian clothes from the army commissary and sneaked away from the reservation to turn white again. *You* turned your back on The People, on the clan that took you into its fold to feed you, clothe you and train you to become a mighty Apache warrior.''

Raven's eyes raked John up and down, with visible distaste. ''The brother I knew as White Wolf, adopted son of Chief Gray Eagle and, *my* adopted brother, has joined the ranks of my hated enemies, just so he can enjoy his own freedom. White Wolf is nothing but a traitor!''

Raven's harsh words stung like a swarm of wasps, for they were the very words that constantly buzzed in John's conscience—every waking hour of every livelong day. But John had concealed his identity and sneaked off the reservation—at Chief Gray Eagle's command. He'd been assigned the duty of battling the whites from within their own society, of becoming a buffer to protect the Apache nation.

It hadn't been an easy path for John to follow, but Raven would never understand that, refused to listen to any explanation. In Raven's eyes, White Wolf had sold his soul to the white devils in order to reclaim his freedom.

When Raven's gaze discreetly darted to the rifle lying at his feet, John cocked the trigger on his pistol. The imminent threat of death hung in the silent dusk. Raven's pinto mare pricked its ears and lifted its head from the stream, sensing the gravity of the moment.

Raven shifted his gaze from the rifle to John. ''Your aim is as true as ever, is it not, White Wolf?''

John inclined his head slightly. ''Better.''

''I do not doubt it. The legends you have inspired since you turned white have not been exaggerated, I suppose.''

"No." It wasn't a boast; it was the simple truth. But there wasn't a white man alive who knew the truth about John Wolfe's background. No one knew how or where he'd honed his impressive skills as a tracker, gunfighter, territorial marshal and oftentimes bounty hunter. The criminals he brought to justice claimed he was some sort of avenging phantom who could disappear into thin air—then reappear. His Apache training contributed to his uncanny ability, constantly tested and perfected as he dealt with the worst vermin preying on society.

Chasing down white criminals and sending them to hell where they belonged didn't weigh as heavily on John's conscience as tracking his Apache brother. Raven had foolishly joined up with two army deserters who'd stolen reservation supplies and sold them to settlers and miners in the territory. A worthless white cutthroat and a blood-thirsty Mexican who were wanted for murder and robbery rode with the gang. In order to achieve his freedom, Raven had aligned himself with those ruthless outlaws, all of whom had high prices on their scalps.

John wondered if Raven perceived his own abandonment of the Apache on the reservation as detestable as John's. Probably not. To Raven's way of thinking, no crime was quite as unforgivable as an Apache who purposely turned white.

The instant Raven glanced speculatively at his horse—obviously trying to decide if he could use the animal as a shield before a fatal shot was fired—John tossed a pebble off the cliff. The distraction served him well. When Raven reflexively shifted left, John launched himself off the stone ledge, dropped a quick ten feet and landed in a crouch. His Colt was still aimed directly at Raven's heart.

Raven smiled, but there was nothing pleasant about his expression. "You do not miss a trick, do you, John Wolfe? I remember the day my father taught us that deceptive technique of diverting attention. Do you remember? Or have you purposefully forgotten that you owe everything you are to the Apache who raised you?''

Not one minute of one day went by that John Wolfe didn't remember who and what he was—a contradiction, a man in torment who walked a path that must surely entail the white man's concept of a living hell.

''I prefer to take you back alive, Raven,'' he murmured as he rose from his haunches. ''Gray Eagle also prefers to have his son returned to him in one piece.''

John couldn't interpret the expression that momentarily settled on Raven's bronzed features. It vanished as quickly as it came. ''Then I have no choice but to return to that hellish place, do I, John Wolfe?''

John told himself not to let his guard down when Raven seemingly accepted his fate. But this, after all, was the adopted brother who had shared his life for almost two decades. They'd grown up in the same wickiup and struggled side by side to become accomplished warriors. They'd survived famine, sickness, war and captivity.

The only difference was that John had been born white and Raven was full-blood Apache. Until this pivotal moment, the differences between them hadn't mattered to John.

Now it was all that mattered.

''I will go willingly to the reservation if you will use your authority and influence with the white-eyes to reduce my punishment,'' Raven offered. ''The army deserters and thieves forced me to scout for them. They swore they would kill me if I didn't join their gang. My craving for freedom was too great, my hatred for reservation life too strong, so I agreed to help them.''

John wasn't sure if he believed Raven. The circumstances surrounding his escape from the reservation were unclear in the report John had received from his commander at headquarters in Prescott. In his line of work John had heard every excuse imaginable from cornered criminals. He'd learned long ago that a man would lie through his teeth to save his skin.

But this was not just any man. This was *Raven*.

"You know I'll do everything I can," John promised solemnly.

"No chains or cuffs. The soldiers kept me in chains when we were herded to San Carlos." His lips curled in disdain. "I bear the scars and the memories of their cruel treatment. Do you remember? I was the example to our people." His voice transformed into a growl. "No chains, John Wolfe. I would prefer to die here and now rather than to be chained up like a dog!"

Hands held high, Raven approached his paint pony, then bounded onto the saddle blanket with the grace and ease of a warrior who had executed the maneuver hundreds of times.

John realized a split second too late that he'd allowed his sentiment for Raven to override his hard and fast rules about dealing with crafty criminals. He saw the glint of steel reflecting sunlight when Raven's concealed pistol suddenly came into view. Without hesitation the Apache fired straight at John's chest, then at his left leg. The double impact sent John staggering backward, to collapse in the grass. He didn't return fire because Gray Eagle's request to bring Raven back alive still echoed in his mind.

Raven walked his pinto toward his downed enemy. Gloating triumph glittered in his onyx eyes. While John lay there gasping for breath, battling the burning sensations that spread through his thigh and chest, Raven's goading laughter billowed in the aftermath of violence.

"May you die a slow death for betraying the Apache," he jeered as he watched the bloody stains spread across John's shirt. "It seems your white heritage has failed you,

John Wolfe, for no white man can outsmart a *true* Apache.''

Raven walked his pinto over the top of his onetime blood brother. ''My father has only one son now,'' he sneered down at him. ''May you burn in your white man's hell for your treachery!''

The clatter of hooves hammered in John's ears as the world tilted sideways, then darkened like the coming of night. John closed his eyes and fought against the wave of nausea that crested over him.

Maybe this was a good day for *him* to die, he thought. And what better place to find his way to the hereafter than on this sacred ground that had once been part of the *Apacheria*. The People called this panoramic valley the Canyon of the Sun. Reverent chants were sung to the great spirits who communicated with them on this hallowed ground. In days gone by, sacrifices were laid at the base of the triple stone spires called the Altar of the Gods. The towering pillars of sandstone that rose like gigantic sentinels from the canyon floor were the Earth Mother's eternal monuments to the omnipotent Apache gods.

With great effort, John opened his eyes once more to stare at the conical stone peaks that rose majestically toward the sun. This valley, three-quarters of a mile wide and more than a mile long, was the most spectacular and awe-inspiring place he'd ever seen in all his treks across the territory. If he had to breathe his last breath here, he figured he could do a lot worse.

Vaguely, John sensed a presence in the near distance and wondered which spirits—white man's or Apache's— had been sent to witness his death.

He didn't know which deity would preside over his personal judgment day. Didn't really matter, he reckoned. Evil spirits would attend him, because of his betrayal to the tribe that had raised and trained him. Indian or white, evil spirits were probably pretty much the same, he figured. He existed in a realm a few miles this side of hell. He supposed he was destined to spend eternity doing penance for being a white man by birth and an Apache at heart.

John closed his eyes for what he expected to be the final time. To his dying day—and he was positively certain this was it—he wasn't sure if he was considered white or Apache. He didn't know which god to pray to, so he didn't pray at all. He just lay there, struggling to breathe, and wondering how many breaths he had left.

Since John had heard every excuse under the sun, heard the wild claims of innocence from the worst sinners the world had to offer, he decided he'd just keep his mouth shut and not ask for forgiveness or mercy. He was simply going to lie here and die with what little dignity he had left.

Tara Flannigan scrambled down the rock-strewn slopes of the canyon with more speed than caution. Twice she tripped, skidded and skinned both knees. She ignored the discomfort and scurried toward the man who lay sprawled beside the stream, wondering if she'd arrived too late to revive him.

Tara had been drawn to this remote area of the valley by unidentified voices, and she'd hunkered down by a cedar tree to prevent being spotted. Although the white man and Indian had been speaking a foreign tongue, she'd witnessed the tragic results of their confrontation. One man lay dead—or dying—and the other man had picked his way up the narrow trail and thundered off into the gathering darkness.

Grimacing from the pain in her knees, Tara squatted down beside the wounded man. She pressed her hand against his throat and felt a weak pulse. Alive, but not for long, she predicted. Her mediocre lifesaving skills were about to be tested to their very limits.

Hurriedly, she ripped open the man's shirt, then blinked in surprise when she saw the strange bone-and-metal breastplate that covered his chest. She'd never seen such unusual body armor. It was an odd combination that resembled an Indian war shield and medieval chain mail.

On closer inspection, Tara realized the bullet had ricocheted off a fragment of metal, shattered the bleached bone ornament and become embedded in the man's rib. Quickly, she ripped off the hem of his dark shirt and pressed it against the seeping wound.

Her gaze dropped to the pulsing wound on his thigh, and she tore the hem from her own tattered shirt to control the bleeding. When she tied the fabric tightly around his leg, the man's eyes fluttered open momentarily.

Tara's breath clogged in her throat when eyes so blue that they appeared silver stared up at her. In addition to those spellbinding eyes, with their fan of lashes, the man had a crop of raven hair, a swarthy physique and an incredibly handsome face.

This was, unquestionably, the most attractive man she'd ever encountered. His effect on her was startling. When their gazes met, time screeched to a halt and she got lost in the intensity of his unusual blue eyes.

She was still staring at him in trancelike fascination when he whispered, "An angel. Well, I'll be damned."

"I only wish I were a miracle-working angel, mister," she murmured.

When he slipped back into unconsciousness, Tara gave herself a mental shake and concentrated on the grim task at hand. "Angel indeed," she muttered. "From the look of your wounds, you could use an angel right now."

Tara glanced this way and that, trying to figure out how to transport this injured man to the farmhouse, when he likely outweighed her by more than a hundred pounds. She guessed him to be about six feet three inches—maybe four—of solid muscle. There was no conceivable way for her to drag or lift him. Though she hated to leave him, Tara had no choice but to return to the ranch for help.

She took off like a shot to retrieve the horse she'd tethered in the distance. She rode hell-for-leather through the valley, knowing every second counted. She prayed for all she was worth that the wounded man with hypnotic silver-blue eyes would still be alive and breathing when she returned.

John lifted heavy-lidded eyes to see that lovely face, surrounded by a mass of curly, reddish blond-hair, hovering over him a second time. Now, as before, the light shimmered around her golden head like a glorious halo. When she shifted, the angle of light intensified the color of her hair. It seemed as if the curlicue strands caught fire and burned with amber flames.

Long ago, in a nearly forgotten lifetime, John remembered his white mother telling him that angels were the essence of all that was pure and sweet in heaven. Who would've thought heaven was where he'd end up when he had so much blood on his hands and a trainload of guilt weighing down his conscience? With his white man's soul and his Apache heart, he'd sort of figured he'd be trapped in some eternal way station—or delivered straight to hell because he'd turned out to be a traitor to both civilizations.

While John was contemplating the hereafter, five more heads appeared above him. He studied the three male and two female faces—varying in age, but all younger than his angel of mercy.

"He's awake." This from the smallest female cherub with dark, hollow eyes and a waterfall of chestnut hair.

"Reckon we must've saved him, after all."

John shifted his attention to the adolescent male face to his right, then frowned dubiously when he realized what the kid had said. He was alive? He thought about that for a moment, then decided the aches and pains that were becoming more intense with each passing moment probably indicated that he did indeed live and breathe—but just barely.

His chest hurt like a son of a bitch. His leg throbbed like hell. Breathing was definitely an effort because pain was shooting through his ribs like an assault of poison darts.

"Medicine pouch," he wheezed, amazed that it took so much effort to speak.

A befuddled frown settled on his angel of mercy's enchanting features. "Medicine pouch?" she repeated in such a soft, wispy voice that John sighed at the soothing sound.

"On my belt," he managed to croak, in a voice that reminded him of a bullfrog.

The six faces hovering over him disappeared momentarily. Murmurs and whispers came from the right and left of him, but John couldn't muster enough energy to turn his head. He stared at the wooden rafters above him and waited.

"Is this what you're talking about, mister?"

The angel's face came into view again. She held the beaded leather pouch in one dainty hand.

"Buttons," he whispered. Gawd, the pain seemed to be spreading rapidly. There wasn't an inch of his body that didn't hurt—and badly.

"Buttons?" she parroted. "In here?"

"Yeah. Three of them." He hissed in pain when he tried to reach for the pouch. His left arm was killing him. This woman with cedar green eyes, pert nose and

creamy complexion, who had apparently saved his
wretched life, rummaged through his pouch, then held the
button-shaped objects in front of his eyes. "Do you mean
these?"

"Put them in my mouth," he requested.

She complied. He chewed, swallowed, then choked.
"W-ater."

Scrabbling noises indicated someone had scurried off
to fetch a cup of water. Moments later, John felt the tin
cup pressed against his lips, and he sipped eagerly. His
strength abandoned him abruptly and the pain returned in
full force, leaving a barrage of cold chills in its wake. He
swore the drink of water was freezing like ice in his
bloodless veins.

He waited impatiently for the peyote buttons that the
Apache used to override pain to take effect. John definitely needed something to ease the indescribable ache
spreading throughout his body.

He wondered where this brood of children who hovered
around him had come from, wondered where the hell he
was. All he knew was that he was alive—whether that
was a blessing or not. It didn't feel like much of one.
Considering the pain and misery he was enduring he figured dying would've been a whole helluva lot easier.

When the peyote took welcomed effect, John sank back
into the darkness that had become his ever-present companion.

Hours later—days maybe, he wasn't sure—he heard
that quiet, soothing voice calling to him from a long
winding tunnel. He felt warm liquid sliding down his
throat. He was vaguely aware of gentle hands moving
lightly over his chest and thigh, soothing him, consoling
him.

It'd been years since he remembered feeling a compassionate touch gliding over his flesh. He was instinc-

tively drawn to the comforting presence. He wanted to open his eyes to see if that angelic face surrounded by red-gold hair was lingering above him. He wanted to reach out and touch her, to draw from that well of beauty, purity and sweetness that seemed so foreign, yet so compelling. But he simply couldn't find the strength to move. He felt as if lead weights were strapped to each arm and leg, holding him in place. And so he just lay there, helpless and exhausted, wondering if he'd ever find the energy to lever himself into an upright position again.

"Do you think he'll ever wake up for more than a few minutes, huh?"

Tara Flannigan glanced down into Flora's small, delicate face. Because Flora was so frail and thin, her eyes looked enormous in contrast to her milky white features. The five-year-old appeared malnourished, though Tara took great pains in preparing meals to put meat on the child's bones and give her that healthy glow the other children had achieved these past two years.

"Tara?" Flora prompted when Tara lingered too long in thought.

"I'm hoping he'll wake up soon," she said as she applied fresh bandages to his mending wounds.

"But it's been four days," Flora pointed out.

"I know, sweetheart, but he suffered very serious injuries and it takes time to mend."

Despite the Good Samaritan tendencies that had compelled her to rescue this man from death's doorstep, Tara was hounded by mixed feelings. When she searched his pockets, hoping to learn his identity, she'd discovered this man called John Wolfe was a territorial marshal. She'd found several bench warrants stashed in his saddlebag on the piebald stallion that he'd apparently left tethered near the canyon rim before his confrontation with the Apache.

This man was the long arm of the law in Arizona Territory. Although Tara wasn't sure how long the arm of justice stretched—and she hoped it wasn't all the way to Texas!—there was a possibility that John Wolfe could make trouble for her and the children when he recovered.

Tara had made too many personal sacrifices, taken several daring risks to reunite the children and to locate this spectacular valley that was as close to paradise as she could get. With a bit of Irish luck and a great deal of willful determination, she had made a home in this secluded canyon. The day she and the children had ridden into the valley to set up housekeeping she swore it would take an act of God to make her move away. For her and the children, this valley was their long-awaited promised land.

Their exodus cross-country hadn't been an easy one. Tara inwardly winced, remembering the horrifying incident that forced her to hurriedly gather up these children, stow away with them on a westbound train and follow the rails as far as they went. Then, they'd set out on foot to find shelter and food, and avoid notice.

God forgive her for the things she'd been forced to do in order to make a home for the five children in this remote place.

"Tara, the broth is warm. Do you want me to bring in a cup?" Maureen asked.

Tara secured the makeshift bandages on John's chest, then glanced over her shoulder at Maureen, who waited expectantly at the bedroom door. "Yes, please, dear. It's time to spoon-feed John Wolfe again."

The thirteen-year-old turned on her heels, causing her strawberry-blond hair to sway across her shoulder blades. Tara smiled fondly as Maureen disappeared around the corner. These days, the young girl was eager to help, and brimming with vitality. Three square meals a day had improved Maureen's beanpole figure. Tara dearly wished she could say the same for the fragile-looking five-year-old who was hovering beside her.

Maureen entered the bedroom with an energetic spring in her walk and didn't spill even a drop of the steaming broth. "The boys said they're having a devil of a time with that piebald stallion that belongs to John Wolfe," she reported as she handed the cup to Tara. "The horse didn't mind being put in a stall beside our two mares, but he wouldn't let anybody but little Calvin handle him."

"That piebald is a lot of horse for a seven-year-old to handle," Tara murmured worriedly. "I don't want Cal to get hurt."

Maureen bubbled with quiet laughter. "Hurt? Not likely. It was the funniest thing I ever did see. That stallion was careful where he stepped when Cal took the reins. But when Derek and Samuel tried to brush him down he would have none of it. The boys got into a shouting match, blaming each other for making the stallion difficult to handle."

Tara rolled her eyes in dismay as she eased the spoonful of broth between John's unresponsive lips, then massaged his throat to ensure he swallowed the needed nourishment. Both Derek and Samuel undoubtedly had their pride smarting right about now, she mused.

Those two teenage boys were a handful on a good day. They were always squabbling and scuffling and getting defensive when she asked them to assume various chores. Their tempers flared at irregular intervals, and often without provocation. Tara wasn't sure what had gotten into them lately. They tried her patience more times than she cared to count.

"Oops, Zohn Whoof is dribbling," Flora said as she leaned forward to blot his bristled chin with a napkin. "He's pretty, don't you think, Tara?"

Tara smiled at the frail little elf whose distorted pronunciation of John's name never failed to amuse her.
"Men prefer to be referred to as handsome, not pretty,"
she corrected the five-year-old.

"He *is* terribly handsome, isn't he?" Maureen observed as she perched lightly on the opposite side of the
bed.

"Yes, he is, in a rugged sort of way," Tara reluctantly
admitted.

The man was sinfully handsome, extremely muscular
and practically tan all over…. She jerked upright when
that traitorous thought darted through her head, bringing
with it a visual image that heightened the color in her
cheeks. In truth, she'd seen more of John Wolfe's virile,
sinewy body while she was preparing him for her primi-
tive brand of surgery than a young woman rightfully
ought to see.

Between the anxiety of wondering if she was capable
of performing the tasks of a physician, and seeing John
in his entire splendor and glory, Tara had been a nervous
wreck. Her hands had refused to stop shaking while she
stitched his jagged flesh together, and her attention kept
drifting to the broad expanse of his chest, washboard belly
and horseman's thighs.

No question about it, John Wolfe was more man than
Tara had encountered in her twenty years of existence.

"Be careful, Tara!" Flora yelped. "You're dribbling
hot soup all over Zohn Whoof."

Tara felt another wave of heat rising in her cheeks and
she struggled to regain her composure. Stifling her arousing thoughts, she concentrated on feeding John the last
spoonful of chicken broth, then waited for young Flora to
dab up the dribbles on his stubbled chin.

"We'll let John rest while we finish our evening
chores," she announced.

Flora stared unblinkingly at their patient. "Can I wait inside with Zohn Whoof? Just in case he wakes up? I don't want him to be alone."

Tara brushed her hand through the child's shiny dark hair and smiled. She knew Flora had awakened feeling lost and alone, and had become frightened dozens of times before Tara rescued her. But these days, Flora bedded down with Maureen, who made certain she never felt abandoned.

"I don't think John will wake up for a good while yet. You need your daily dose of exercise and fresh air." When Flora pulled a face and looked as if she was about to object, Tara held up her hand to forestall the child. "But you can come check on John every half hour, just in case he wakes up."

Flora hopped off the bed to follow in Maureen's wake. Tara watched the girls go, wondering if the five-year-old had developed a severe case of hero worship for John. The girl continually reached out to touch his arm, to trace his lips, nose and cheeks while he was unaware. Maureen, too, spent a considerable amount of time staring pensively at John Wolfe. It seemed this man attracted female attention, no matter what the female's age.

Tara glanced back to monitor the methodic rise and fall of his masculine chest. She supposed she would be every bit as infatuated by John Wolfe, if not for this nagging apprehension that he could cause her and the children serious trouble. If he discovered the whys and wherefores of how they'd come to be reunited...

Tara tamped down the uneasy thoughts. No, if John Wolfe tried to separate her from the children again, it would be over her dead body! Besides, he owed her a huge favor, didn't he? She had saved his life. Surely that counted for something with this territorial marshal.

It better, she thought determinedly. If not, she would

remind this lawman on a daily basis that he was alive because she'd dug lead out of him, stitched him back together and generously taken him into her home so he could recover.

Chapter Two

"Blast it, Tara, you promised two weeks ago that we could ride into Rambler Springs with you this time," Samuel complained as he watched Tara retrieve her knapsack.

"You did promise," Derek was quick to add.

"That was before John Wolfe landed on our doorstep," she reminded the teenage boys, who had been giving her grief since she'd announced her early morning departure. "I'm leaving you two in charge."

"But who is going to protect you in that rowdy mining town?" Samuel demanded. "You said yourself that you ran into trouble last time you were there. *We* should be there to protect you."

"The incident was nothing I couldn't handle," she reassured them.

For certain, she'd dealt with much worse back in Texas. Raucous cow towns and mining communities were pretty much the same, in her opinion. Men could be such unpredictable, predatory scoundrels when they had several shots of whiskey under their belts. But Tara had spent enough time in the streets during her childhood, living a hand-to-mouth existence, to learn a few effective counters to amorous assaults. She wasn't a shrinking violet by any means, and she certainly wasn't helpless. She could take care of herself, thank you very much.

"You're treating us like kids," Derek groused. "We're almost men."

Tara slung her knapsack over her shoulder, then adjusted the sleeve of the one and only dress she had to her name. She took a moment to appraise the gangly boys, who seemed to be in some all-fired rush to become men. Tara preferred they remain children, but she vowed Derek and Samuel would become honorable, law-abiding grown-ups who were nothing like the rowdy miners and cowboys that showed little respect for women. Unfortunately, the boys were straining at the bit, demanding to be viewed as adults, and they were giving her fits—daily!

"I realize you are nearly men," she replied belatedly. "And being the responsible men you are, I'm sure you realize the irrigation channels running through our garden need reinforcement after last week's rain. The weeds around the vegetables need to be hoed and the livestock must be fed."

The boys—young men, pardon her mistake—groaned in dismay.

"All we do is work around here," Samuel grumbled sourly.

Tara was running short on time so she played her trump card, as she was forced to do from time to time. "Would you prefer to be back in Texas? Or back in Boston? Hmm?"

The boys—young men—clamped their mouths shut and shifted uneasily from one oversize foot to the other.

"You know we don't have the slightest hankering for those hellholes we've been in," Derek muttered.

"Don't say hell. You aren't old enough," she chastised.

"We're nearly men," Samuel reminded her—again.

"Right. What could I have been thinking? But please

refrain from using obscenities in front of the other children.''

"Anyway,'' Derek continued, undaunted, "we need a change of scenery. We want to protect you from those drunken bullies in that mining camp. I could accompany you and Samuel could stay here—''

"Oh no, I won't!'' Samuel objected strenuously. "I'm older and—''

"Both of you are going to stay here and that's that,'' Tara said in no uncertain terms, then surged toward the front door. "And positively, absolutely no fighting while I'm gone. Do you hear me? I don't have time to tend to another round of black eyes and bloody noses when I return, either.''

Serenaded by adolescent grumbling, Tara hiked off to retrieve the roan mare from the barn. She wished she could take the children into town more often, but she preferred they didn't know she cleaned house for two older couples, one of whom owned the general store and the other a restaurant. Plus Tara cleaned the church for the parson during her weekly jaunts to Rambler Springs. The extra money provided her with funds to support the five children in her charge.

Although their vegetables, chickens, milk cow and small flock of sheep kept the family fed, she needed money for clothes and provisions. Heaven knew those two boys—young men!—were growing by leaps and bounds. Keeping them in properly fitting boots put a sizable dent in the family budget.

Hurriedly, Tara gathered up fresh eggs from the henhouse to sell in town, then mounted her horse. She'd spend the day there, working fast and furiously to dust and sweep two homes and the church, and would return exhausted, as usual. She needed Derek and Samuel to hold the fort during her absence; hopefully, they'd honor her request not to engage in another fistfight.

What had come over those two young men? Lately,
they left her questioning her ability to handle them. And
to think they'd been such adorable children when she'd
first met them!

John felt as if he'd awakened from the dead. Every
body part objected when he shifted sideways on the bed.
Groaning, he pried open one eye, to see a small waif
hovering over him. He wondered what had become of the
flame-haired, green-eyed guardian angel that had been
drifting in and out of his fitful dreams. Although angel
face was nowhere to be seen, several vaguely familiar
faces appeared above him.

"You're awake at last!" the dark-eyed child exclaimed
happily. "Hallo, Zohn Whoof. My name is Flora."

"Hallo to you, miss" he wheezed, amused by her mis-
pronunciation of his name.

The waif giggled and her enormous brown eyes spar-
kled with pleasure. She edged closer to the bed to pat his
uninjured shoulder. "Feeling better?" she asked.

He nodded slightly. "Where am I?"

"In Paradise Valley. I'm Maureen. It's a pleasure to
make your acquaintance, John Wolfe," the older girl said
very politely.

John surveyed the adolescent girl standing to his left.
With her sky-blue eyes, wavy strawberry-blond hair and
sunny smile, she was destined to knock a passel of men
off their feet in years to come, John decided.

"Nice to meet you, Miss Maureen," he greeted her
cordially.

The girl beamed in delight, opened her rosebud mouth
to reply, then got nudged out of the way by a small boy
with coal black hair, a gap-toothed smile and a scar on
his chin. "I'm Calvin and I'm seven years old," he introduced himself.

"A pleasure to meet you, Calvin," John replied.

From the shadows, a tall, gangly adolescent boy with dark brown hair and gray eyes emerged. The boy drew himself up proudly, and John expected the kid to beat his chest like a warrior exploding into a war whoop. "I'm Samuel. I'm fifteen and I am in charge here—"

"No, you aren't. We're both in charge. Tara said so."

John glanced toward the foot of the bed to appraise the offended boy, whose sandy-blond hair hung over one blue eye.

"I'm Derek. I'm fourteen and I'm half in charge." He glared at Samuel, then returned his attention to John. "If you need anything, I'm the man you want to see."

John swallowed a smile. He supposed at one time in his life he had struggled from adolescence to adulthood, but it had been so long ago he didn't recall it. He felt a century old in the presence of these children. The nagging pain in his ribs and thigh drove home the point that the hellish experiences of his profession weren't making him any younger. In fact, he'd come perilously close to dying in his thirtieth year, thanks to the desperation and treachery of his brother, Raven.

"Glad to make your acquaintance, Derek," John said. "I do need something, as a matter of fact, but I prefer not to have these pretty young ladies in attendance."

The boys realized his discomfort immediately and shooed the girls from the room. Moaning in misery, John levered onto one wobbly elbow—and received one helluva head rush. The brightly decorated room, which boasted mason jars filled with wildflower bouquets, and curtains made of feed sacks and ribbons, spun furiously, making him nauseous.

"Here, we'll help you," Samuel offered, grabbing John's good arm.

"I'll get the chamber pot," Derek volunteered.

"Uh, you can take it from here, can't you?" Samuel asked, his face coloring with embarrassment, as Derek placed the pot near the side of the bed. "Me and Derek and Calvin will be right outside the door if you need us."

Five minutes later, the boys returned to ease John back into bed. Sitting up for only a few minutes had been exhausting. John was anxious to settle in for another much-needed nap, but Maureen and Flora arrived with a loaf of bread and some broth.

"Tara said you should eat if you woke up," Flora informed him.

By the process of elimination, John figured Tara had to be the absentee angel of mercy. "Where is Tara?" he asked.

"She rode into Rambler Springs to fetch supplies and sell the extra eggs," Samuel reported, then scowled. "She wouldn't let us go along to protect her from those rascally miners, though. Made us stay here to take care of y—"

John smiled when Samuel's cheeks turned the color of the sandstone spires in Paradise Valley. "I'm most grateful you stayed behind. Does Tara usually have a problem with the miners?" John wouldn't be surprised to hear it, considering her bewitching face and that cap of curly, reddish blond hair. He hadn't gotten a good look at the rest of her, but from the neck up, his angel of mercy was the stuff masculine dreams were made of. He should know, since he'd had his fair share of them during his recuperation.

"Sometimes Tara has trouble with the miners," Derek reported. "But she won't let me and Samuel be her bodyguards. She says she can take care of herself."

"Tara *can* take care of herself," Maureen interjected. "I saw her do it a couple of times back in—"

When Maureen shut her mouth so quickly that she nearly clipped off her tongue, John noticed the other children were staring at her in horror. Instinct and training told him that they had been instructed not to spill their life stories. He couldn't help but wonder why.

"Is Tara your mother? Or...older sister?" John asked.

"No, she's—ouch!" Little Flora yelped when Samuel trounced on her foot.

Yep, something was definitely going on here that angel face didn't want John to know about. Which brought him around to posing the question he had intended to ask earlier. "How did you know my name?"

"That's easy," Flora gushed. "Tara found your horse and searched through your saddlebags. She said you were a marshal and that we should watch what we said around you."

The other children groaned in dismay. There was definitely something going on here that a territorial marshal wasn't supposed to find out about. But how bad could their secret be, considering that they were amusing, well-behaved children? John couldn't imagine.

When he opened his mouth to fire another question about Tara, Maureen crammed a slice of bread in his mouth. Flora handed him a spoon so he could chase the bread with broth. John's taste buds started to riot. Damn, he couldn't remember eating such tasty food. By the time he slurped the last drop of the delicious broth and ate half a loaf of bread he was so exhausted he could barely keep his eyes from slamming shut.

"Tara said you needed plenty of rest," Samuel said, hustling the children from the room. "Just give a holler if you need anything else."

When the children filed out, John settled himself carefully in bed, then noticed the pallet near the south wall. He suspected his angel of mercy had camped out on the floor while he lounged in her bed. Well, enough of that. He wasn't going to inconvenience angel face more than he already had. Hell, he was accustomed to sleeping on the ground—had done it for years.

Clutching the side of the bed, John dragged himself sideways until his feet were planted on the floor. He bit back a yelp when he eased down on his tender leg and strained the wound on his ribs. Huffing and puffing for breath, he dragged himself toward the pallet.

If he hadn't felt so damn guilty about betraying Raven he'd curse that bitter Apache for shooting him to pieces. But Raven had been cornered and threatened with hated captivity. It was understandable that he'd react violently. John wondered if he would've reacted the same way, had he been in his adopted brother's moccasins.

But damn it to hell, Raven would make things a hundred times worse for himself if he continued to scout for those cutthroats who were plundering the territory. However, John refused to believe Raven had stooped to killing the settlers and miners left in the outlaws' wake of destruction.

Raven had only been desperate for a taste of freedom, John assured himself. He himself knew the feeling well. He remembered the sense of relief he'd experienced five years ago when Gray Eagle insisted that he cut his long hair, disguise himself in white man's clothes and sneak away from the reservation. But John's freedom had come at a steep price and carried a wagonload of tormenting guilt, awkward adjustments and excessive frustration.

He decided not to rehash his recent past. He was in serious pain and thoroughly exhausted. He definitely needed another nap. Everything else would have to wait until he felt better—if that day ever came.

Tara brought the roan mare to a halt beside the barn, then dismounted. She tugged at the torn waistband of her gown to conceal the damage. She refused to let Samuel and Derek know she'd encountered two drunken miners who tried to drag her into an alley.

Men! Honestly, there were times when Tara wondered why God had populated the planet with those heathens. No way was she going to allow Samuel, Derek and Calvin to grow up to behave so disrespectfully. Today's incident stirred horrifying memories of that awful night in Texas when—

Tara refused to think about that again—ever. No one would find out what had happened, she reassured herself. She was safe with her secret—unless Marshal Wolfe started digging into her past. But he wouldn't dare hold that incident against her, because she'd explain her situation with the children. Somehow she'd make him understand and forgive her for what she'd done.

Before Tara could fully regain her composure and stash away her unsettling thoughts, Samuel and Derek bounded off the front porch and dashed toward her.

"I'll tend your horse," Samuel volunteered.

"I'll carry your knapsack," Derek insisted.

Tara shook her head, helpless to understand why the boys—young men—were falling all over themselves to assist her. When Derek snatched up her knapsack, she settled her left elbow over the rip in her gown. "Thank you, boys...er, gentlemen."

"You're welcome," they said in unison.

"John Wolfe finally woke up this afternoon," Derek reported.

"Did he?" That was encouraging. Tara made a mental note to carefully inspect and cauterize his wounds if they hadn't healed properly by now. She didn't want to risk gangrene setting in. Her injured patient didn't need any setbacks, especially one as dangerous as gangrene.

When she surged through the door, Maureen was at the stove stirring the stew Tara had prepared at dawn. The aroma tantalized her taste buds, reminding her that she'd skipped lunch and was ravenous. Nodding a greeting, she headed for the bedroom to change clothes.

Quietly, she inched open the door, then did a double take when she noticed the empty bed. To her shock and dismay, John was sprawled half on, half off her pallet in the corner. What in heaven's name did he think he was doing? He was seriously injured and he needed the comfort of her bed.

Muttering silently at the sleeping invalid, Tara tiptoed across the room to shed her torn gown and don her usual attire of men's breeches and shirt. She turned her back on John to pull on her shirt, then nearly came out of her skin—and there was a lot of it showing, blast it!—when his husky voice rumbled behind her.

"So you must be Tara."

Tara clutched the shirt to her bare breasts and struggled to pull her sagging breeches over her hips. Her face flushed a dozen shades of red as she shoved one arm, then the other, into her shirtsleeves. "I didn't realize you were awake," she said self-consciously.

"You were halfway undressed before I could tell you."

Tara glanced over her shoulder to see his lips quirk in an amused smile. Those captivating silver-blue eyes drifted from the top of her head to her feet, missing nothing in between. He deserved a good slapping for waiting until she was undressed to inform her that he was awake. But Tara figured he'd suffered enough pain for one week. She'd overlook the incident—this time.

"You must be feeling better if you managed to crawl onto the pallet. But I warn you, if you split a stitch I'll be none too happy about it."

"You're Irish. The accent is unmistakable."

She spun around as she fastened the bottom button on her shirt. "And you're injured. You shouldn't have crawled off the bed," she chided as she marched over to inspect his wounds.

The moment Tara laid her hands on him she could feel her cheeks flood with color. Touching this muscular hulk of a man while he was unconscious was one thing. Tending him when he was staring up at her with those incredible silver-blue eyes was something else again.

"I noticed your dress was torn at the waist," he murmured. "Trouble in Rambler Springs?"

Tara glanced away quickly. "Yes, but nothing I couldn't handle. I'd appreciate it if you wouldn't mention it to the children."

He cocked his head sideways and regarded her for a long moment. "About the children."

Tara tensed immediately, ordered herself to relax, and then graced him with a cheery smile. "Yes, what about them? I hope they didn't disturb your sleep. They've been anxious for you to wake up."

"You wanna tell me what's going on around here?"

No, she most certainly did not! Tara flashed him another bright smile. "I haven't the faintest idea what you mean, Marshal. Now brace yourself, because I need to cleanse these wounds."

John recognized a diversion tactic when he heard one, but he let it slide because he swore Tara had peeled off his jagged flesh when she exposed his tender wound. It was all he could do to prevent himself from howling in pain.

"Your face has gone white," Tara observed. "I'm sorry if I hurt you." A frown beetled her brow while she inspected his ribs. "I'm going to have to cauterize this wound. The other one, too, I suspect. I bought some whiskey in town to numb your pain."

"Is that why you ran into trouble?" he guessed correctly.

Tara nodded. Her glorious hair shimmered in the light. John had to make a conscious effort not to reach up and run his fingers through that silky mass that constantly captured his fascinated attention.

Tara rose gracefully to her feet. "I'll fetch the whiskey from my knapsack."

"I'd rather have a leather strap to bite down on," he told her.

Her brows jackknifed. ''Do you realize how much this is going to hurt?''

''It won't be the first time I've had a wound seared. Probably won't be the last.''

''No, I imagine not, considering your dangerous line of work. I noticed a scar on your right leg that looks like a healed knife wound. There's a bullet hole in your shoulder, too. You're definitely no stranger to pain and discomfort,'' she murmured as she pivoted on her heels and headed for the kitchen.

When Tara walked out, John smothered a groan and felt his gaze helplessly drawn to the hypnotic sway of feminine hips. Hell! Wasn't it enough that he'd accidentally seen his angel of mercy stripping down to her threadbare pantaloons, and found himself staring at her bare back, wishing she'd turn toward him? Damn, she was a vision—with all that creamy skin arranged more perfectly on her feminine body than any he'd ever beheld! And in his condition, he didn't need to become aroused—but he was, damn it. He'd never be able to think of his angel of mercy without remembering the accidental unveiling of her shapely body.

John muttered an obscenity when his own unruly body stirred restlessly. This situation was entirely new to him. He'd never seen a woman naked without having her in his bed. But Tara, this beguiling angel with secrets in her eyes, was off-limits. She wasn't going to join the ranks of the women who entered and exited his life without him giving them a second thought.

First off, he owed Tara his life. In the Apache culture, that signified that his spirit became hers. Therefore, he wasn't in a position to follow up on the arousing sensations Tara ignited in him. He'd do what he could to help her with this brood of children, as soon as he was back on his feet, but he was going to keep his hands off her.

Besides, he wasn't going to be here very long, John

reminded himself. A flaming affair with Tara was out of the question. He couldn't stay any longer than necessary because he had to track down that ruthless gang that was wreaking havoc in the territory. He'd also promised Chief Gray Eagle that he'd do all within his power to ease the Apache's plight and ensure the tribe was treated humanely.

John gnashed his teeth, wondering if it was possible for one man to change the collective attitude of a white population that didn't understand the Apache's way of life or spiritual beliefs. Hell, for white society it was like trying to measure the familiar with a foreign yardstick. Furthermore, too many soldiers, settlers and miners adhered to the appalling philosophy that the only good Indian was a dead one.

No, John had entirely too many irons in the fire to become sidetracked by a beautiful woman who would, without question, be heaven to touch, to possess.

Although he had never known a woman he called only a friend, Tara could be no more than that. He couldn't allow male desire to dominate his thoughts and actions. He'd be gone from Paradise Valley as soon as he was able, and he couldn't, wouldn't, look back.

When he'd turned white again, his purpose had been twofold—to return Raven to the reservation and to use his legal authority to deal with whites that preyed viciously on each other and on the captive Apache. It didn't matter what John wanted, desired or needed personally. He was here to serve a higher purpose. These tantalizing fantasies about Tara that chased around in his mind were nothing but a futile distraction.

At that sensible thought, John slumped on the pallet. Next time Tara touched him he wouldn't allow himself to react as a man responded to a beautiful woman. That feat shouldn't be too hard to accomplish, he mused grimly. After all, she would come at him bearing a heated blade to sear his jagged flesh. *That* should be enough to discourage improper thoughts.

The creak of the door prompted him to glance up. Sure enough, the bewitching angel carried a knife that glowed red-hot. She held a lantern in her left hand, and the expression on her face testified to her apprehension and her compassion. John tried to assure himself that cauterizing a wound wasn't as painful as the initial gunshot, but he knew better.

This was gonna hurt like a son of a bitch.

"I'm sorry," Tara said, apologizing in advance.

John reached out with his good arm to retrieve the leather strap draped over her arm. "Just do it, angel face," he ordered.

"I wish you wouldn't call me that, especially since we both know this is going to hurt like the very devil."

"Okay, *Irish*. Just do your worst." John stared straight into her thick-lashed cedar-green eyes. "If I curse you, don't take it personally, since you'll be burning the living hell out of me. Deal?"

"Deal." Tara nodded bleakly, and then braced herself on her knees while John bit down on the leather strap.

"Do the leg first," he said around the strap. "With any luck, I'll pass out before you sear my ribs. I hope you sent the children outside so they won't have to hear a grown man scream bloody murder."

"I sent them to one of the springs to pick wild grapes," she said, her attention focused intently on the angry flesh on his leg. "Ready? On three—"

Tara didn't wait until the count of three. She wanted to get this grisly task completed before John tensed up. Even then, he nearly came off the pallet when she touched the heated blade to his thigh. All the while she told herself that if she could prevent gangrene and spare his leg, and his life, it was worth his suffering—and hers.

Watching beads of perspiration trickling from his brow,

seeing the tears swimming in his eyes, noting the complete lack of color in his chiseled features was killing Tara, bit by excruciating bit. John let out a pained howl that nearly blasted holes in her eardrums. His hand clamped around her wrist like a vise grip when she reflexively eased the blade away from his wound.

"Not long enough," he said through clenched teeth. "You know it. I know it. Again, Irish." His hand guided hers downward, completing the unpleasant process.

Tears floated in Tara's eyes as she watched him deal with agonizing pain. This, she realized, was no ordinary man. In the face of adversity, he was extraordinary. Had their roles been reversed, Tara was pretty sure she would've been screeching hysterically and fighting him with every ounce of strength she possessed. He, however, held her hand steady to thoroughly sear the wound.

"Damn, here I was hoping I'd pass out," John panted as he drew her hand and the blade toward his rib cage.

His intense gaze locked on hers again. He stared unblinking at her, while what must've been excruciating pain blazed through him. Unintentionally, he nearly crushed the bones in her wrist in his effort to force her to finish the gruesome task. When she would've pulled away again, he ensured that she remained steady and relentless. Tara was crying by the time he allowed her to withdraw the knife, and she practically collapsed beside him when the gruesome deed was done.

"You're one hell of a woman, Irish," he said, between gasps of breath.

"You did most of the work and endured all the pain," she reminded him as she wiped the beads of perspiration from his brow, his upper lip. "Were I you, I'd have fainted dead away minutes ago."

She was so close to him and he was so overcome with pain that he wasn't thinking clearly. That was his only explanation for what he did next. He up and kissed her right on the mouth, just like he'd told himself he was *not* going to do—ever. He was pretty sure he got lost in the sweet taste and compelling scent of her, because the next thing John knew the world turned as black as the inside of a cave and swallowed him up.

Dazed, her lips tingling, her body shimmering with unfamiliar sensation, Tara gaped at her patient, who'd collapsed unconscious on the pallet. In the first place, she couldn't believe he'd kissed her. Secondly, she couldn't believe she'd kissed him back. But she supposed if any man ever deserved to steal a kiss—and get away with it— it was John Wolfe. Considering what he'd endured, he probably hadn't realized what he was doing. Either that or he'd sought comfort in a moment of maddening pain.

Like a crawdad, Tara scuttled backward, then covered John's limp body with the sheet, which had shifted sideways during the ordeal by fire. While she cleaned and bandaged the wounds, she decided she'd treat the unexpected kiss as if it had never happened. Chances were that *he* wouldn't remember it, anyway.

It didn't mean anything. She could not *let* it mean anything, she told herself firmly. Still, the feel of his lips devouring hers with something akin to desperation left sizzling aftershocks rippling through her body.

Tara willfully shook off the tantalizing sensations and climbed to her feet. She tiptoed over to retrieve her sewing kit so she could mend her torn dress. Now was as good a time as any to repair the damage. And she'd do so as soon as her hands stopped shaking and she could breathe without John's masculine scent clogging her senses completely.

Chapter Three

During the days that followed, John's energy returned gradually. He received periodic visits from the brood of children. They came alone. They came in pairs. They came in a group. But Tara never once approached him without a chaperone of one or two children following at her heels. He reckoned the impulsive kiss he'd planted on her dewy, soft lips was responsible for her standoffish manner.

Not that he blamed her. He'd been more than a little surprised by it himself, especially after he'd sworn up one side and down the other that there could be nothing more than friendship between them. He supposed the agonizing pain of the ordeal had triggered the impulse, making natural instinct difficult to control.

He should apologize, but the truth was that he wasn't sorry he'd kissed her. She was the one taste of purity and sweetness in his violent and isolated world. He wouldn't let it happen again, of course. His Irish angel of mercy was now, and forever more, off-limits.

"You want some bread and wild grape jelly, Zohn Whoof?" young Flora asked as she sank down cross-legged beside him on the pallet.

John smiled at the cute little tyke who had already

wedged her way into his heart. He couldn't help himself. The kid was warm and giving and altogether adorable, especially when she invented her own unique way of pronouncing his name.

"Bread and jelly sounds mighty good, half-pint."

Flora slathered jelly on a slice of bread, then handed it to him. "I help Tara make the jelly. We have jars and jars of it stored in the root cellar."

John sighed contentedly at the first bite. Someone around here really could cook, and he presumed it was Tara. Of course, as far as he could tell, there wasn't much that she couldn't do well. He'd watched her come and go from dawn until dusk without a single complaint. She always had a smile and kind word for the children. Her organizational skills, he'd noted, were a marvel, and she made time for each child's individual needs.

This unique family fascinated him, even though the life they led was utterly foreign to him. It'd been years since John had felt family ties, felt as if he belonged anywhere. Not that he belonged here, of course. But this family didn't treat him as an outsider, the way most folks did when he ventured into one town, then another. Usually, people didn't engage him in conversation or venture too close. He figured most folks considered a man who was part lawman, gunfighter and bounty hunter unworthy of respect because he dealt with evil, violence and death on a regular basis.

John had pried bits and pieces of information from the younger children to appease his curiosity about Tara, though he told himself repeatedly that his fascination with her was ill-advised and impractical. He'd discovered that Tara was a passable markswoman who could put wild game on the table to feed her brood. That she harvested and processed vegetables from the garden, and had somehow managed to acquire the livestock that grazed in the canyon. He was incredibly curious to know how these acquisitions were made on her limited budget.

There were, however, two other things about Tara that he didn't know and was dying to find out—where had she acquired her unique family and where had she been sleeping since John crawled onto the pallet so she could sleep on her bed. She wasn't using the bed, he'd discovered. He figured he'd ferret the information from the loquacious five-year-old who was feeding him bread and jelly. If there was one thing he'd learned about Flora it was that she loved to talk, and most of the thoughts bouncing around in her head made their way to her tongue.

"Do you have another bedroom in the cabin where you and the other children sleep?" he asked nonchalantly.

Flora sampled a piece of bread, then nodded. "Maureen and I sleep in the other bedroom and the boys sleep in the loft above us."

"Tara has been sleeping with you, too?"

She shook her dark head. "Nope, she moved into the barn loft."

The barn loft? John cursed under his breath. That woman was making all sorts of sacrifices for him and the children. He was the one who should be sleeping in the straw. He'd slept in the great out-of-doors for years and was accustomed to it. On rare occasions, while on his forays to track down criminals, he rented a hotel room.

"Tell Tara that I'll be trading places with her," John requested.

"Can't do that," Flora replied as she wiped her mouth, smearing jelly on her chin. "Tara says she wants you somewhere that's clean and dry so you can mend properly. She also says the boys are gonna take you to the spring to bathe tomorrow. She says the mineral spring we found near one of the rock ledges will be good for you."

"Hmm, Tara sure has lots to say, doesn't she?"

"Certainly does," Flora agreed. "But most of all, and she says this is very, very, *very* important, we're a family and we'll be together forever. She says no one will break our family apart 'cause we belong to each other."

John wondered why that was the first commandment in the gospel according to Tara. Who wanted to break up this unusual family? And why did Tara instill that sense of unity and belonging in these children? It sounded a mite overprotective to him, but what the hell did he know? He hadn't been a part of a clan for over five years.

"Where did you meet Tara, half-pint?" he asked.

Suspicion filled those wide, soulful eyes. "Tara says we're not supposed to say anything to anybody about where we came from or how we got here. It's a secret."

Interesting, he mused. Maybe Tara had something to hide. If she thought he'd sit in judgment she was mistaken, because John Wolfe wasn't who folks thought he was, either. After all, he'd slipped away from the reservation under cover of darkness, without permission.

According to the Indian roll call conducted the morning after Chief Gray Eagle bade him to escape and return to white society, White Wolf didn't exist and his name wasn't to be uttered again. In the Apache culture, the name of a deceased person was rarely mentioned. As far as the tribe was concerned, White Wolf was dead and gone.

Maybe he needed to have a private talk with Tara and assure her that whatever concerns his presence provoked were unnecessary...unless there were criminal charges involved and she felt threatened by his profession as a law officer. Damn, this could get ugly, thought John. Maybe he didn't want to unlock those guarded secrets he saw flashes of in Tara's eyes, after all.

"I have to leave now." Flora popped to her feet. "Tara says I have to walk the lambs around the canyon to make 'em stronger."

John suspected these compulsory walks were designed to build little Flora's own stamina. The child was entirely too frail and thin.

"Calvin has to go with me," Flora added as she scooped up the jar of jelly and leftover bread, "just in case I have trouble managing the sheep."

Calvin, the seven-year-old with the noticeable limp, he mused. No doubt Tara ensured Calvin was getting his daily requirement of therapeutical exercise, too.

To John's complete surprise, Flora abruptly reversed direction, dropped to her knees in front of him, then flung her bony arms around his neck to hug him tightly. "I love you, Zohn Whoof," she whispered in his ear. "Maybe when you feel better you can walk the lambs with Calvin and me."

John battled to draw breath after Flora scurried off. He couldn't afford to become attached to these endearing children, damn it. Gray Eagle had given him a lifetime assignment of protecting the Apache from the whites. Plus Raven was running loose, aligning himself with a merciless outlaw gang, giving the Apache a bad name—as if the whites' publicity hadn't given the tribe a bad reputation already.

John had witnessed firsthand the atrocities committed against Indians. They'd been slaughtered like buffalo— women, children, elders and warriors alike. They'd been poisoned with strychnine, herded onto reservations and forced to sign treaties that gave white men their valuable and productive lands. In fact, Gray Eagle had been ordered, under penalty of death, to sign over several strips of land where silver and copper deposits had been discovered so the prospectors could mine the ores without sharing with the Indians.

John had done his damnedest to prevent the whites from stealing the Apache blind, but to no avail. He'd reclaimed his white heritage hoping to make a difference—

and he'd failed, time and time again. It was enough to make a grown man weep, especially when he cursed himself countless times for being born white and growing up Apache. Half the time John didn't know who the hell he was or where he rightfully belonged. And now this sweet little child, with her hollow eyes, pasty skin and delicate bones, was gushing with affection for him and looking up to him as if he were her beloved father. The kid was killing him, while he was trying to maintain an emotional distance from her and the rest of this extraordinary family.

John sighed heavily. This child and her entire family were definitely getting to him, hour by hour, day by day. He couldn't afford to become attached, because it would make leaving this valley more difficult. He'd locked away all sentimental emotions the day the Apache captured him as a child and started training him to be one of them. If he allowed all these conflicts that roiled inside him to surface he wouldn't know how to deal with them. He wasn't sure he could face a single one without his thoughts getting all tangled up with the other feelings he'd buried in order to survive all the trials he'd faced in his life.

Besides, this family really didn't have a place in his world, he reminded himself for the umpteenth time. He went about his grisly business of tracking down and apprehending vicious criminals that were overrunning the territory. No feelings allowed, John told himself sensibly, and he'd better not forget it. Life was a test of survival— *that* was the gospel according to John Wolfe.

Tara wasn't prepared for the shock of seeing her patient fresh from his bath at the mineral springs where the boys had taken him. When she returned from doing chores in the barn, he was sitting on the wooden bench on the front porch. She missed a step when her gaze landed on his face, now devoid of the week's growth of dark beard. To say that John was ruggedly handsome, with his bronzed skin, athletic physique, electrifying eyes and sensuous lips, had to be the understatement of the decade. The entire package of lean, powerful masculinity was enough to increase her heart rate and leave her feminine body aquiver.

Lord, listen to her, Tara scolded herself. She sounded as bad as Flora and Maureen, who sang John's praises the whole livelong day. Of course, Tara had asked around Rambler Springs to see if anyone had heard of Marshal Wolfe. What she'd discovered was impressive and unnerving at once. This man who braved death on a daily basis was the stuff legends were made of, according to Wilma and Henry Prague, who ran the general store, as well as Corrine and Thomas Denton, who owned the restaurant. It was true that Wilma Prague was long-winded and tended to get caught up in the tales she liked to spin, but the hearsay she'd conveyed had kept Tara on the edge of her seat. John Wolfe's feats of capturing the worst criminals in the territory were nothing short of phenomenal.

"Good morning, Irish," John greeted her, breaking into her thoughts.

"Morning," Tara murmured as she sank down on the bench beside him. "How are you feeling after your bath?"

"Revived and not the least bit anxious to spend another day indoors."

"Not accustomed to it, I suppose, considering your line of work."

He inclined his shiny raven head. "Exactly, which is why we'll be switching sleeping quarters this evening," he asserted.

That sounded like an order, and Tara had never been much good at taking them. "Excuse me, Mr. Wolfe, but I'm the one in charge of your rehabilitation. I'll decide where you'll sleep, especially when this happens to be *my* house you're convalescing in."

He merely chuckled at her flare of temper. "I've watched you and listened to you handle this passel of children with patience and gentle requests for nearly a week, Irish. In case you've forgotten, I've been shot. You're supposed to be nice to me."

"I have been for a week," she countered. "So don't push your luck."

"How is it that I've ended up at the sharp end of your tongue? Is it me in particular or men in general?" He waited a beat, then asked, "Or is it because of that kiss?"

Tara glanced over to meet his penetrating stare, noticed that quirk of a smile that did funny things to her insides. She steeled herself against her innate attraction to him. "Perhaps a bit of all three," she admitted honestly.

He stared across the grass, then his gaze lifted to the rock-capped summits of the canyon, admiring the panoramic view. "You've nothing to fear from me, Irish. There'll be no incidents like the one you recently had with the miners. As for that kiss…well, consider it a needed compensation for the pain I was suffering. It won't happen again."

Tara couldn't honestly say if she was disappointed or relieved. What was she thinking? Of course she was relieved, even if she felt as if she'd suffered another form of rejection. But allowing herself to become as attached to John as the children were already was dangerous business.

"Good, I'm glad we have that settled and out of the way," she said, flashing him a smile. "As for the sleeping arrangements, you're staying in my room and I don't wish to hear another word about it."

He smiled a mysterious smile, then shrugged. "Have it your way, Irish. I suspect you usually do."

Tara snapped her head around and frowned at him. "And what is that supposed to mean?" she challenged.

"Only that you're accustomed to controlling the children, though I admit you rule with such a gentle hand and winsome smile that they don't realize they're being bossed around."

"I suppose you're accustomed to probing and prying and sticking your nose in various places because of your line of work." Tara snapped her mouth shut, amazed that she was addressing John in such a sarcastic tone. Blast it, this man didn't fit into the nice, neat world she'd created for the children and herself in Paradise Valley, and she was having trouble dealing with him. Why was that?

He shrugged a broad shoulder, seemingly unoffended by her sassy rejoinder. "I suppose you're right, Irish. I do spend considerable time grilling witnesses before I track criminals. I'm inquisitive by nature and by habit…. So, how'd you come to acquire this abandoned homestead here in what the Apache call the Canyon of the Sun?"

Tara blinked in surprise. "How do you know that?"

"About the abandoned ranch, you mean? The boys told me. They don't seem to be quite as cautious about divulging information as you are. No doubt you instructed them to watch what they said around me. Now why is that?"

Tara opened her mouth to ask how he knew she'd instructed the children not to reveal more than necessary about their past, then figured she could already guess the answer. Flora had difficulty refraining from telling everything she knew, just to hear herself talk. So did young Calvin. He'd jabber all day if you let him.

Tara decided that telling the truth—or as much of the truth as she could—wouldn't do any harm in this instance. "I acquired the deed to this abandoned farm after the children and I happened onto it, while searching for a shelter during a storm. When I inquired about the ranch in Rambler Springs, I learned the previous owners had left during the Indian uprising six years ago. Since the Apache were confined to San Carlos, it seemed safe enough to set up housekeeping here." She peered questioningly at him. "How did you know this is sacred ground to the Apache?"

He was silent for a long moment while he scanned the panoramic valley with its towering cap rock, wild tumble of boulders, canopies of cedars, cottonwoods and pines, and its refreshing springs. Then he shifted slightly, and his solemn gaze probed hers with an intensity she'd come to expect from him. John didn't simply look at her; he examined, studied and looked *into* her, as if he were reading her private thoughts.

"If I tell you the truth about that, will you explain how you came to acquire this unique family of yours, Irish?"

She knew he saw her flinch, for his astute gaze never seemed to miss a thing. She was beginning to think the phenomenal feats, the unerring instincts and tracking skills that Wilma Prague raved about weren't an exaggeration. There was an extraordinary aura about this man—especially now that he was recovering from his injuries. He was sharply attuned to everything that transpired around him. He had a sixth sense she envied.

"Irish?" he prompted, holding her captive with nothing more than the intensity of his silvery stare. "What I'm offering here is something you can hold over my head, in exchange for something I can hold over yours. That will keep the battleground even, wouldn't you agree?"

"We are going to do battle?" she asked, smiling impishly.

"I don't know. Are we?" he questioned in turn.

She wasn't quite sure she understood what made this unusual man tick. He wasn't like her other male acquaintances. He was asking her to give him a weapon to use against her. In return, he was handing her a weapon. Why? she kept asking herself.

John studied the wary expression that claimed her enchanting features. He could tell she wasn't sure what to make of him and his unexpected offer. But he'd be damned—literally—if he told her the truth about himself without some leverage, and he had to know if he could trust her to hold in confidence what he was about to tell her. Considering what this amazing woman had done for him, he wanted to trust her, to confide something that only Gray Eagle knew.

Why he was willing to stick out his neck John wasn't sure. Maybe it was an instinctive response to the feelings Tara evoked in him. Maybe, with this life of isolation he'd been leading, he sought some kind of connection. Maybe he simply felt indebted because she'd saved his life. Maybe... John refused to delve deeper into the whys and wherefores. He'd looked a little too deeply already when it came to the feelings and sensations Tara aroused in him.

"Very well, John Wolfe, you have a bargain," she agreed. "A sword for a sword, so to speak. But I want you to remember that you wouldn't be alive today if not for me."

He grinned, amused by her insistence that he shouldn't forget he owed her his life.

"But I must have your word of honor that if you do decide to turn against me, after I answer your question, that you'll become responsible for these children," she insisted.

That was an odd thing for her to say, he thought. It suggested some deep dark secret that would make it impossible for her to care for the children if the truth came out.

John stared her straight in the eye and said, "I know this canyon is sacred Apache ground because I am

Apache. Or at least I was an Apache until five years ago, when the uprisings were contained and the tribe was herded onto the reservation. Fact is, there is no John Wolfe.''

She gaped at him for a full minute. When her questioning gaze continued to focus directly on him, he nodded in confirmation. Then, suddenly, she burst out laughing. That wasn't the reaction John had anticipated. Her riotous laughter drew the attention of the children, who were tending to various chores. The boys appeared from the shadows of the root cellar, which was in actuality a small cavern tucked beneath an overhanging rock ledge. The girls emerged from the house to stare at Tara in complete bewilderment.

Tara tossed back her head, sending the haphazard braid of red-gold hair cascading down her back. She cackled uproariously, then slapped her knee and cackled some more. To John's disbelief, she curled into a ball and rolled off the bench onto the planked porch. Still giggling and gasping for breath, she clamped her hands around her ribs and guffawed. John and the children stared at her as if she'd gone insane.

''Oh, that…is…funny,'' she said between howls of laughter.

Despite his baffled confusion, John broke into a grin while Tara rolled around on the porch, giggling and struggling to draw breath.

''Is she okay?'' Samuel asked as he jogged toward the house.

''My gosh, what's happening to her?'' Derek said in alarm.

It was obvious to John that Tara had never allowed the children to see her reduced to fits of laughter. But why his confidential announcement had caused this reaction, he had no idea. He suspected Tara usually took her responsibility for the children quite earnestly and always displayed a facade of control—whether she felt in constant control or not.

Face flushed, tears streaming down her cheeks, Tara looked up at him and erupted in another fit of giggles. Each time she peered at him the hysterical fit began all over again.

"She'll be fine," he assured the concerned children. "Go tend to your chores. Maureen, perhaps you could bring Irish a cup of water. I think she'll be needing one when she recovers from her fit of giggles."

Reluctantly, the children turned away, but not without casting several worried glances over their shoulders. Tara was down to muffled snickers by the time Maureen returned with the water.

When Tara took the cup and sipped, John waved Maureen back into the house. He looked down at the woman who was curled up at his feet. "I assume your grave secret is that you have a tendency toward madness." He was giving her a way out. He wondered if she'd take it. When she shook her head, he was confident he could trust her with his secrets.

After Tara regained a semblance of composure and slumped beside him on the bench, she glanced at him. "I'm sorry. I don't know what came over me."

"I suspect your week has been as long and stressful as mine, Irish. If I could reduce myself to busting a gut laughing, without splitting a stitch, I'd like to try it. That looked like fun."

"It was, actually. Discovering that you don't exist stuck me as hilarious. You're entirely too real to be a figment of anyone's imagination."

"There really is no John Wolfe," he repeated. "I was born white, captured by the Apache at the age of ten and rigorously trained to become one of the elite group of warriors who were sent on the most dangerous missions. I lived with my clan, accompanied them on raids against invading hordes of Spaniards, Mexicans and whites, and then I was confined to the reservation. The fact is I'll always be more Apache than white.''

"Captured?" The laughter in her eyes died.

"Rescued would probably be more accurate. My father was a drunken prospector. An Apache hunting party overtook us while he was beating me, as he had a habit of doing on a regular basis. My ability to speak English made me useful to the Apache, who were dealing with whites more often than they preferred. I was taught the Apache dialect, as well as Spanish. In turn, I was instructed to teach Chief Gray Eagle and his family to speak English. Being the only white captive in our clan, I was often called upon to translate during conferences with the army. Because of the color of my eyes, Chief Gray Eagle always kept me conveniently obscured from the soldiers because he considered me too valuable an asset to release.''

"What is your Indian name?" she asked.

"White Wolf.''

"And your white name?''

He hadn't spoken his given name in twenty years. It felt unfamiliar as it tumbled off his tongue. "Daniel Braxton.''

Why he had gotten sidetracked with particulars of his life that he hadn't divulged to anyone else, he couldn't say. What was there about this woman that drew his confidence? he wondered. He truly was treating her like a friend—the first he'd had in years.

"That explains why an Apache warrior has silver-blue eyes rather than dark ones," she said thoughtfully. "That's also why townsfolk praise your legendary skills and instincts. According to gossip around Rambler Springs, you're part bloodhound. Your success rate in tracking and apprehending criminals is incredible, bordering on supernatural.''

"It's the result of years of meticulous Apache training," he explained. "It's a culture of introspect, reflection and a life closely attuned to nature. Whites get too caught up in the acquisition of property and wealth to fully understand who they are and how they fit into the world around them.

"I cannot begin to explain the torment of knowing my white ancestors are responsible for the atrocities committed against the Apache, and vice versa. It's like straddling a picket fence, uncertain which culture is my true enemy. But I do know that if the truth is revealed, I'll be jailed and sentenced by the white courts because I was involved in retaliations against whites who committed unspeakable atrocities against the Apache."

Her expression turned compassionate. To his surprise, she reached out to touch his hand, which had involuntarily curled into a fist—an outward manifestation of his inner turmoil.

"I'm sorry, John. I promise that your secret is safe with me. I'm most thankful that I was able to save such a unique man."

An unfamiliar lump formed in his throat. She accepted his explanation, accepted him, without making judgments. He didn't elaborate on the particulars of his life story, didn't want to disturb this unexpected sense of peace and contentment that stole over him. He'd never experienced anything quite like the sensations thrumming through him. He simply sat there, surrounded by the towering sandstone walls of the canyon, absorbing the tranquility of the moment and enjoying the breath of wind stirring through the trees.

Suddenly he realized just how badly he needed this hiatus in the place Tara called Paradise Valley. Being here with her and the children, in this spectacular location, was like lingering at an oasis after a grueling walk in the desert sun.

"Now that you've revealed your truths, I'm obliged to reveal mine," Tara murmured as she withdrew her hand. "It's ironic that you're the one man who poses the greatest threat to my existence, and yet we're exchanging confidences."

She swallowed uneasily, because she'd never confided this tale to another living soul. Certainly, the children in her care knew fragments of the story, but they didn't know the whole truth.

"My parents immigrated to Boston," she began quietly. "I lost them in a flu epidemic and I nearly died myself. I had no other family to take me in and I was forced to live a hand-to-mouth existence in the streets and alleys with several other children who found themselves in the same predicament. We begged for food and picked pockets to survive...until one night when three policemen swarmed in and gathered up the strays. The older, more experienced street urchins managed to vanish in the network of alleys, but I was frail and sickly, like little Flora, at the time. I was taken to an orphanage, given a cot, a ration of food and hand-me-down clothes that were so thin from numerous washings that it was like being naked during the cold winter months."

Tara darted a glance at John. He was staring intently at her again. She swore she'd never met another living soul who listened with such concentrated absorption. He didn't even blink an eye when she admitted to stealing to survive.

"Occasionally families visited the orphanage to take children into their homes, but I was always overlooked. I guess they considered me too old to be trainable, too frail to put in a hard day's work."

"Which is why, I suspect, little Flora and Calvin are in your care. You see yourself in them, don't you?" he asked.

Tara nodded. "Flora was just an infant when her

mother, the daughter of a wealthy family, brought her to the orphanage. The woman was unmarried and feared wrath and disinheritance.

"Calvin was left alone when his parents were killed in the carriage accident that mangled his leg and scarred his chin. Maureen couldn't speak a word for the first two years she lived in the orphanage. The caretakers thought she was a deaf-mute, because she made no contact with anyone. Thankfully, she's emerged from her shell. But to this day she refuses to speak of whatever tragedy landed her at the orphanage.

"As for Samuel and Derek, they know nothing of their heritage, nor do I. They simply arrived in the dark of night as young children. They were already there when I was taken into the orphanage. You wouldn't know by looking at them now, but they were sickly, weak and shamefully unsure of themselves."

Tara took a sip of water, then continued. "When the time came, we were scrubbed and dressed in an exceptionally better set of hand-me-downs than what we usually wore. We were hustled aboard a westbound train without being informed of our destination or purpose. We stopped in nameless towns in Missouri and were herded into local churches. Like livestock on the auction block, we were presented for adoption. Many of the younger children were carted off to foster homes."

"But not frail-looking Flora or crippled Calvin," John surmised.

"No, the six of us were rejected for one reason or another, so we returned to the train and ventured into Texas. When the train pulled into a dusty cow town there, we were the only ones left. A man who owned a fleabag hotel notorious for housing rowdy drifters took in Flora and Maureen. Although they were young—especially Flora—they were put to work cleaning and sweeping. The boys ended up working for a cantankerous farmer who practiced your father's technique of controlling and disciplining children.''

"And you, Irish?" he questioned. "How old were you at the time?"

Leave it to this man to poke and pry into places she planned to skip over with only the briefest of explanation. "I wasn't quite eighteen," she told him reluctantly.

"Marrying age," he murmured shrewdly.

"Something like that," she replied, unable to meet his perceptive gaze. "I was taken in by a rancher who claimed he needed a foster child capable of caring for his ailing wife."

John hadn't liked the sound of this story from the beginning. It was growing more distasteful by the minute. The fact that Tara's expression had closed up, that she was suddenly holding herself upright on the bench, keeping a stranglehold on the cup of water and staring sightlessly at the canyon walls, alerted him that the rancher had had unseemly designs on her. An unfamiliar sense of rage swept through John, momentarily overriding the nagging pain in his rib and thigh.

"There was no ailing wife, was there?" he said through clenched teeth.

She didn't answer for a moment, didn't glance his direction. Finally she said, "There was a gravesite on the far side of the garden." She shivered slightly, cleared her throat, then continued. "There were also metal cuffs dangling from the headboard and footboard of his bed."

John felt as if someone had gut-punched him. Damn it to hell, he wasn't sure he wanted to know what came next. In fact, he refused to hear and he didn't want to imagine what Tara had endured, so he leaped ahead to spare her the telling.

"So I assume you regathered the children from their various residences and decided to make a new life together."

She breathed a relieved sigh and smiled ruefully. "Yes, the children are now my family, and I promised to make a home for them. We hopped a cattle train and followed the rails west as far as they went. For three months we wandered like nomads, feeding off the land, living for short periods of time at missions and in abandoned shacks along the way—wherever we found shelter. We gathered stray livestock that we encountered along our route through New Mexico Territory and we took temporary employment where we could, but we never stayed in one place long enough to become acquainted with anyone. We traveled into towns in separate groups so as not to arouse suspicion or raise questions we didn't want to answer."

It occurred to John that Tara might've done something in the past that made her fearful he'd cause trouble for her. In spite of that, she'd taken him into the fold and nursed him back to health. That said a great deal about her character—and she had considerably more character than most folks.

"When we happened onto this canyon, with its run-down buildings, I knew this was where we belonged. I knew that with hard work and determination I could make a real home for the children. This is the place of permanence, stability and security none of us ever had."

When she turned toward him, John could feel the intensity and determination radiating from her. "This family of cast-off children, who have been rejected more times than I care to count, will have a full understanding of belonging. They'll feel a strong sense of welcome and acceptance. They'll be confident that when they set off to find their places in this world, I'll be here to welcome them back with open arms."

When she stood up and strode off to attend her limitless chores, his gaze followed her until she disappeared into the root cellar. Tara didn't hang around long enough for John to caution her about setting her sights on this canyon as a permanent home. This part of the territory, though it had escaped violence in recent years, was becoming a hotbed of criminal activity because of the silver and copper mines discovered in the area. Gangs of ruthless outlaws preyed on prospectors and anyone else who provided easy pickings. Tara and the children wouldn't stand a chance against men like the outlaws Raven had fallen in with.

Although John knew it wouldn't be easy, he had to convince Tara to move into town where there was more protection. That was one conversation he wasn't looking forward to, especially now that he knew she'd put down roots and had no intention of leaving. No doubt he and Tara were destined to butt heads about that.

Chapter Four

Tara inhaled several cathartic breaths and stared at the rows of canned fruits and vegetables stored in the root cellar. Skirting so close to the unnerving incident with the cruel, demented Texas rancher unearthed emotions she preferred to forget. The retelling of the story had taken its toll. Flashbacks of the night when she'd fought for her life left her shaken.

When it came right down to it, she couldn't bring herself to reveal her deepest, darkest secret to John. Amazingly, he hadn't pried for details. He'd handed her a weapon that would expose him, if she chose to reveal his true identity, but he hadn't demanded the same kind of weapon to use against her. Why not? she wondered.

Tara snatched up a jar of jelly and a can of corn, then asked herself how in the world she and John had gotten so personal so quickly. They'd been verbally sparring, then wham! They were confiding in each other like life-long friends. In a way, she felt guilty that she hadn't told him the very worst of her experiences in Texas, especially when he'd held nothing back. He'd taken mercy on her, and she couldn't puzzle out why. This legendary lawman, who had undoubtedly seen more violence in a month than she wanted to witness in a lifetime, had given her an easy

way out. She could've hugged the stuffing out of him for
that.

Her respect for John multiplied, which was a shame,
because Tara had the unmistakable feeling she already
liked the man more than she should. They'd be no more
than confidants and friends. Permitting this liaison to progress any further was an invitation to heartache. Tara had
had enough of that in her lifetime. She'd suffered enough
feelings of disappointment, inadequacy and rejection
without inviting more of the same.

After giving herself that silent lecture, she lurched
around and headed to the house to prepare lunch. To her
amazement she found the children inside with John,
who'd propped himself up on his improvised crutch, fash-
ioned by Samuel from a tree limb. John was mixing up
hooligan stew—which none of the children had heard of.
A little of this and that, he said as he added ingredients
he found in the cabinet. Tara stood aside and watched
him take command of this troop of children, giving soft-
spoken orders that had the youngsters hopping to do his
bidding.

And later, while he sat at the head of the table, passing
around food with his good arm, he began spinning yarns
of an Apache legend that held the children captivated. It
was the Indian version of creation, and it held Tara spell-
bound as well. Tara wondered why John was passing
down the legends, then decided that he didn't feel comfortable speaking of his Apache upbringing while he wandered among white society beyond the boundaries of Paradise Valley. Here he could be all he was, without fear
of exposure to the outside world. In addition, she suspected he didn't want these children to grow up with prejudices against the Indian cultures. He was, she decided,
attempting to change one youthful mind at a time.

Tara had to admit that Apache philosophy was very
sound, practical and down to earth. She sensed there was

something else, something very subtle, going on here, but she couldn't put her finger on exactly what it was.

After the meal John announced that he was taking the children on an excursion around the canyon to acquaint them with some of the herbs that served medicinal and nutritional purposes. Tara protested that the exertion of hiking might cause a setback in his condition, but he shrugged away her concerns for his welfare. While the children were cleaning up after the meal, John gestured for her to follow him into the bedroom. Curiously, she watched him limp inside, then close the door behind them.

"What are you up to, O great warrior, White Wolf?" she asked without preamble.

He smiled indulgently. "Something you said earlier got me to thinking."

"I hope that isn't a bad thing—you thinking, that is," she teased.

He cocked a thick brow. "You're in an odd mood, Irish."

"What can I say? I'm an odd person." And for the life of her she didn't know what to make of the comments flying from her mouth. Maybe it was the fact that she was unaccustomed to relating to someone other than the children. With John, she felt herself assuming an entirely different role. She wondered if her attitude and response to him was some sort of strange defense mechanism. After all, the better she got to know this man the more she liked him. And that might not be such a good thing, because his presence here was temporary and her growing fascination with him might become much too permanent.

"The point here is that you mentioned sending the children out in the world to find their place and make lives for themselves. It occurred to me that I could repay your kindness by teaching them the knowledge I've gained from my Apache training. There are resources of food, medicine and means of protection in the wilds that I can show them. It also occurs to me that I can share the responsibility for these children while I'm here and give you some time to yourself.''

Tara gaped at him. ''Time to myself? What an utterly foreign concept. I wouldn't have a clue what to do with myself without children underfoot.''

''You can start by taking a nap,'' he suggested. ''On your own bed, not in the hayloft. Then try something as decadent as lounging in a chair and daydreaming.''

Her gaze narrowed suspiciously on him. ''And what is the purpose of this?''

''Getting to know yourself,'' he replied. ''It's part of the Apache philosophy I mentioned to the children. From what you told me, and what I've witnessed, you simply live to serve and care for these children.''

She stiffened defensively. ''I told you why. I want them to overcome their feelings of rejection. I want them to feel wanted, needed and loved.''

''You've accomplished that,'' he stated. ''So it behooves you to regenerate your own energy. Take a nap.''

''I quit taking orders two years ago,'' she told him. ''I didn't like it then, and I don't care much for it now.''

''Really? It hardly even shows.'' He chuckled, despite her annoyed frown.

''All right, Mr. Marshal, you baby-sit and I'll lounge around. But don't get to thinking that while you're here recuperating you always get to be the boss.''

He opened his mouth to reply and must've thought better of it because he clamped those full, sensual lips together and stared thoughtfully at her. When he hobbled out of the room, Tara sank down on the foot of her bed, wondering what she was going to do with herself for an hour or two. She was in the habit of rising at dawn and working nonstop until she collapsed in exhaustion at night. She'd never pampered herself a single day in her life and wouldn't know how to start!

"Don't plan supper," he added as he poked his head back inside the room. "I'll teach the kids to hunt. We'll return with the meal in hand and prepare it ourselves. The rest of the day belongs to you, Irish. Enjoy it."

"The whole rest of the day?" she echoed bewilderedly.

"I'm giving you a long-needed break from your routine," he insisted.

With that, he closed the door. Tara flopped back on the bed and stared at the ceiling. Take a nap? In the middle of the day...? That was the last thought to flit through her mind before she drifted off to sleep.

Although his leg ached fiercely, and it felt as if someone was trying to pry apart his ribs with a crowbar, John hobbled back through the canyon while the children bounded around him. Their survival excursion had been a success. John had pointed out a variety of plants and explained how each herb served as a remedy or as food, and how to tell which plants were which. Paradise Valley was a veritable greenhouse of roots, seeds and bark that the Apache used to treat maladies and to season food.

John had also directed the children's attention to a mesquite tree and informed them that it was referred to as the Apache survival tree because it served so many useful purposes. From it a man could acquire food and medicine. The tree limbs could be burned in winter without drawing unwanted attention because the wood gave off very little smoke. Since the fragrant mesquite flowers attracted bees, the tree was also a reliable source of honey. The pods and beans could be used for flavoring, for eating or fermented for drinks. The leaves, he'd told the youngsters, were used for making tea and poultices. The gum of the tree could be applied to wounds and sores or even boiled to make candy.

All the while that John was pointing out ways to survive off the land, the children were amazingly attentive and treated him as if he were a part of their family circle. He never thought he'd experience that feeling again after he'd sneaked away from the reservation. But here, living in this space out of time, he felt as if he truly belonged somewhere. It was a most gratifying feeling—

Whoa, don't get sentimentally attached, John cautioned himself as he stared at the cabin in the distance. He had a mission to conduct, as soon as he was able. Any emotion these children stirred in him must be restrained.

John didn't lead the kind of life that invited tender feelings. Just look what had happened when he let emotion cloud his judgment during his disastrous confrontation with Raven. John knew damned well and good that a cornered Apache—even a blood brother—was the most dangerous of enemies. Feelings had gotten in John's way and he'd nearly paid for the mistake with his life. He had to erect an emotional barrier between himself and these adorable kids or he'd be reduced to a useless mass of sentimental mush.

Loaded down with wild potatoes, grapes and the rabbits that he and the children had snared without using noisy weapons that attracted unwanted visitors, John halted near the cabin to show the boys how to build a small mesquite campfire to roast the meat, while the girls trooped inside to steam the wild vegetables.

With his leg throbbing in rhythm with his pulse, his ribs burning fiercely, John decided he'd overdone it—and then some. He crawled onto his pallet to catch some shut-eye before the children served up supper.

Feeling amazingly relaxed and refreshed, Tara returned from a leisurely bath at one of the secluded springs on the west end of the canyon. The trickling waterfall that cascaded over a stairway of rocks was like her private corner of heaven. That, coupled with an hour's nap, made her feel like a new woman.

As John had suggested, she'd gone searching for herself, never realizing she was lost because she'd never devoted any time whatsoever to herself. She still might've been sprawled in the shallow stone pool if a tarantula in search of a drink hadn't crawled over her arm.

Tara pulled up short when she spied the boys gathered around a small campfire in front of the cabin. Ah yes, she'd almost forgotten that White Wolf's warriors-in-training were in charge of supper. From the tantalizing aromas drifting toward her, this meal was going to be worth the wait. Her stomach growled in eager anticipation.

"Feeling better?" Samuel asked when he noticed her. She smiled and nodded.

"Good. After your hyena seizure we were worried about you."

"Yes, well, John said something that struck me funny," she hedged. "I wouldn't actually call that a seizure."

"Sure you're okay?" Derek questioned, studying her astutely.

"Peachy perfect," she enthused. "Where are the girls?"

"Cooking the vegetables we gathered in the wilds," Calvin replied. "This is gonna be a humdinger meal."

"No doubt." Tara noticed the sense of confidence and accomplishment the boys exuded after their afternoon with John. His attempt to teach self-reliance was obviously a smashing success. Even young Calvin, who was usually self-conscious about his limp, was practically strutting around the campfire like one of the roosters. Of course, she didn't think Samuel and Derek needed more spring in their cocky strides. The boys—young men; how could she keep forgetting?—had been exhibiting all the signs of rebellious adolescence for the past six months.

Samuel squinted skyward. "According to the location of the sun, it must be about five o'clock," he announced with all the authority of an expert astronomer. "Supper should be ready in an hour."

"It's more like five-thirty, I'd say," Derek argued.

"As if you'd know, squirt," Samuel said, then snorted.

Suddenly, a scuffle erupted, though Tara couldn't say exactly how it happened or why. One minute the boys were chitchatting, and then wham! Fists were flying. One fist caught Derek in the nose. He yelped in pain and outrage, then launched himself forward to tackle Samuel so he could pop him in the eye.

"Stop it!" Tara shouted.

They didn't cease and desist, but rolled in the grass, growling and snarling like panthers in the heat of battle. One clenched fist flew, then another. Muttered curses erupted.

"That's enough!" The booming male voice came from the front porch.

Tara lurched around to see John propped on his improvised crutch, glaring pitchforks at the boys. His raven hair was standing on end.

The scuffle ended immediately. Samuel and Derek bounded up like jackrabbits to wipe their bloody wounds.

"Get cleaned up on the double," John ordered brusquely. "Calvin can tend the cooking while you're gone."

There was no back talk, Tara noticed, just perfectly executed about-faces and forward marches to the water barrel that sat beside the barn.

"I just don't understand those two these days," Tara said with a baffled shake of her head.

"Don't you?" John asked as she stepped up beside him on the porch.

"No, I don't. We can be in the middle of a conversation and suddenly a battle breaks out over little or nothing."

"Intelligent woman that you are, Irish, I'd think you'd be able to figure those two boys out."

She threw up her hands in exasperation. "Well, I can't. I suppose you have the answer, O great and wonderful Apache wizard."

"They're smitten, infatuated," he told her.

"Smitten?" she repeated stupidly.

"With you. It's all part of male posturing and masculine rivalry that causes them to try to impress you and gain your notice and attention."

Tara stared at John as if he were speaking a foreign language she couldn't translate. He chuckled at her bewildered expression.

"The Apaches are wise enough to establish rituals, rules and regulations to follow during this difficult phase of adolescence. The whites, of course, just leave it all to hapless chance. You don't see a respectable warrior walking around with a bloody lip or black eye. Energy and fighting is saved for battling enemies. If a warrior is interested in an Indian maiden, he simply appears beside her wickiup in the dark of night and stakes his horse by the door. If the girl favors the warrior's attention she leads his prize horse to water. Of course, a maiden wouldn't think to tend the horse the first day. That'd make her seem a mite too anxious or desperate. But then, leaving the animal standing for four days is regarded as playing extremely hard to get, and a warrior might wish to rethink the prospect of courtship."

"And what if the young maiden isn't interested in courtship?" Tara asked, a smile twitching her lips.

"If not, the poor horse stands there, neglected, for four days, at which time the jilted suitor knows his affections aren't returned and he'd best hobble his prize horse on somebody else's doorstep. If you see another horse tied in front of your sweetheart's wickiup, then you wait your turn. Simple as that.''

Tara's amused laughter danced on the evening breeze.

"Uh-oh, you aren't gonna have another one of those hyena seizures, are you?" Calvin questioned worriedly.

Samuel and Derek, their recent battle forgotten, came running to check on Tara. Flora and Maureen appeared at the front door.

"I'm fine," Tara hastily assured the children. Her gaze shifted to John, who was doing his best to conceal his grin. "I simply find John amusing. No harm in that, is there?"

"No, but if it turns out you're not so fine, I'll give you herbs to cure you," Flora announced. "Zohn Whoof taught us how to gather all we need to make good medicine bundles that can cure whatever bothers anybody."

"How is dinner coming along?" John asked the girls, without taking his eyes off Tara.

"Thirty minutes," Maureen predicted. "C'mon, Flora, we don't want our part of the meal to burn on the stove."

When the children resumed their tasks, Tara forced herself to glance away from John. Staring too long into those silvery pools surrounded by long thick lashes gave her strange, tingling sensations. If she wasn't careful she might get lost in those hypnotic eyes. They were entirely too magnetic, too entrancing, too overpowering.

"So...what do you suggest I do to alleviate this situation that has developed with Samuel and Derek?" Tara asked.

"Pretend to show interest elsewhere," he replied.

His husky voice drew her gaze. Mistake. *Big* mistake. He was watching her in that unique, soul-searching way that sent all sorts of warm ripples undulating through her body. Mercy, she was exceptionally aware of John Wolfe.

Tara wondered if the Apache had a medicinal herb to cure infatuation. If so, she needed it—desperately.

"You could use me," he murmured. "After all, I owe you a favor."

"I don't think that's a good idea," Tara tweeted, then was startled by the strangled sound of her voice.

"Why not?"

"If you don't know the answer to that then your instincts and your Apache training have failed you."

Tara wheeled around to seek shelter in the house. Behind her she heard a bark of laughter, not unlike the hysterical fit she'd pitched that morning. Also behind her she heard Cal say, "Oh no, now John has turned into a hyena!"

John knew he was being ignored by Tara at supper, which turned out to be an exceptional feast. The rabbit meat was tender and juicy. The vegetables, seasoned with mesquite seeds, had a marvelous flavor. While the children chatted on—and on—about their survival excursion, Tara stared at her plate and ate her meal in silence.

All right, so John knew that crack he'd made about using him to discourage the boys' amorous interests was way out of line—and too dangerous for his own good. And certainly, he'd told himself several times not to become attached to Tara. But hell, he was, damn it! She didn't seem to have a clue about how attractive she was, especially in those trim-fitting breeches and shirts that accentuated every alluring curve and swell. She seemed to think that because she was a woman, with all the necessary body parts, a man would regard her as nothing more than a possession to be used for his lusty purposes. She didn't seem to realize that it was her personality and character, as well as her ravishing good looks, that attracted male interest.

Why get into this? John asked himself as he chewed

on the medley of wild vegetables. He was going to be the perfect gentleman while he shared the same space with Tara. He'd be gone soon and he didn't want to hurt her in any way. She'd be hurt if he did something really stupid like...oh, say, forge a physical liaison.

If he felt the urge to satisfy an itch, then he could get himself into Rambler Springs to find a woman who made her living appeasing men. He'd made a pact to keep his hands off Tara, no matter how tempting she was. Furthermore, she'd find her own way to resolve the male rivalry going on between Samuel and Derek, without breaking their tender young hearts.

And so, being ignored as he was by Tara, he was thunderstruck when she pushed away from the table, came to her feet, strode to the head of the table where he was sitting and planted a kiss on his lips—right in front of five startled children, God and every deity known to the Apache nation. True, it wasn't much of a kiss, as kisses went, yet the feel of her soft lips melting upon his sent his male body into a slow burn—and left him burning long after she withdrew. John struggled to draw a breath that wasn't thick with her fresh, clean, alluring scent.

"Good night, John dear. I have some sewing to do before I go to bed." She glanced surreptitiously at Samuel and Derek, whose eyes were bulging and whose jaws were scraping the table. "Somebody around here ripped their shirts during the Battle of Paradise Valley, and I'm the one who has to stitch the fabric back together."

No one uttered a word. No one moved until Tara exited the room to retrieve her sewing kit, then reversed direction to breeze out the front door. Just as John predicted, all goggle-eyed gazes zeroed in on him.

"How come you kissed Tara when I'm the one who loves you and told you so, huh?" Flora demanded that very second.

"She kissed *me*," John corrected.

"I never saw Tara kiss anybody on the mouth before," Calvin said.

Samuel and Derek slouched down, as if their breath had been knocked clean out of them. Maureen slumped in her chair, staring at him as if he'd just broken her heart in about a million pieces. John had the uneasy feeling he had a silent admirer. Well damn, he was as oblivious as Tara, who hadn't realized Samuel and Derek were infatuated with her.

And Tara, damn her ornery hide, had dropped a live grenade in his lap, then walked off, leaving him to answer awkward questions. He ought to storm outside and shake the living daylights out of her for that.

John sat there, wondering how to extricate himself from this situation, then decided changing the subject was the best strategy he could come up with. "While you children are clearing the table, I'm going to brew a poultice to pack on my wounds."

"Are you sure you aren't going to go outside to kiss Tara again?" Flora asked suspiciously. "Maureen says that's how people make babies."

"Flora! Shut your flapping jaws!" Maureen shrieked, humiliated.

Calvin blinked. "We're gonna have more babies around here?"

Damn, could this situation get any worse? John wondered. Strangling Tara for her mischief was becoming more appealing by the second.

"Babies don't come from kissing," Samuel told Maureen, whose face had turned the color of cooked beets. "Damn, don't you know anything?"

John's eyebrows shot up to his hairline. He stared nonplussed at Samuel, then tried to speak, but his tongue was stuck to the roof of his mouth.

"Tara said not to curse in front of the children," Derek

scolded. "And what do you know about making babies, anyway?"

Flora glanced up at John. "Where do babies come—?"

John flung up both hands to forestall the barrage of questions he didn't want to answer. "Enough! We'll discuss this later." In about a hundred years, if he had his way about it!

"You mean tomorrow while we're on another survival excursion?"

Leave it to little Flora to pin him down, he thought in dismay. "Yeah, sure. That'd be good."

Samuel and Derek perked up immediately. John wanted to swear, but there'd been enough of that already. Apparently, Maureen had recovered from her humiliation, for she was staring curiously at him, as if she had a million questions to ask on the subject of the birds and bees. Hell!

John got up, limped out the door and went looking for Tara. He found her perched on a quilt, taking advantage of the last rays of sunset. Her nimble fingers flew over the rips in Samuel and Derek's grass-stained shirts.

"You, Irish, have a devilish sense of humor," John muttered.

She glanced up, grinning elfishly. "Oh, are you referring to that kiss I bestowed on you at the table?"

"Hell, yes, damn it," he snapped. "Next thing I knew Flora was spouting off that she's the one who loves me, and then she wanted to know if kissing is what makes babies."

He could see Tara battling back a giggle. He wished he was in possession of a chain—one size smaller than the swanlike column of her neck.

"Is it?" she asked, eyes glinting with humor.

John was so exasperated that he found his train of thought derailed. "Is it what?" he asked, befuddled.

"Is kissing what makes babies?"

John rolled his eyes when she cackled and flung herself back on the quilt to bust a gut laughing—at his expense, damn her.

"Hell's bells, Irish, I don't know how to handle these kids," he grumbled, exasperated.

"You were doing a grand job this afternoon," she said between snickers.

"Survival training I can handle. Discussions on sex I *cannot.* You pull another stunt like that and I'll have your scalp, hear me?" He bared his teeth for effect—not that it did a damn bit of good. And that irritated him, too, because he knew for a fact that he could freeze outlaws in their tracks with his steely-eyed glare. It was one of his finest trademarks. Unfortunately, Tara seemed to be immune to it.

She levered herself upright, wiped the tears of laughter from her eyes and retrieved her discarded needle. "Well, you asked for it."

"I most certainly did not!" he all but shouted at her.

Eyes dancing with mischief, she peered up at him. "Did, too. You told me to use you to discourage Samuel and Derek, because according to you, they're suffering bouts of puppy love."

"Well, you didn't have to kiss me at the blasted table," he exclaimed.

"What good would it do to kiss you in private?" she asked reasonably. "That would defeat the whole purpose of letting the boys know my interest lies elsewhere."

"With that piddly peck on the mouth?" he said, then smirked.

"What was wrong with my kiss?" she demanded, offended.

He swooped down and hoisted her to her feet. Then he bent her over backward and gave her a kiss that was part frustration, part hungry need, part revenge…well, whatever. He couldn't calculate fractions when his brain shut down the instant he tasted her deeply, felt her supple body pressed intimately against his masculine contours. His heart slammed against his tender ribs when she responded rather than shoving him away—which was what she should've done if she'd had a lick of sense.

Before some insanely curious kid came bursting through the front door, asking the kind of questions that John didn't want to answer, he hauled Tara upright and stepped away from her. He enjoyed a smidgen of satisfaction when her legs folded up like a tent and she landed in a tangled heap at his feet. Well, good. He was glad to know he wasn't the only one around here who came unwound because of the mind-boggling sensations ignited by that kiss.

"And that, Irish," he said, striving for a steady—and yes, he'd admit it—arrogant tone of voice, "is the kind of kiss that'll work as effectively as leaving your horse tied up for four days in front of a wickiup. But don't even think about giving me another one like that in front of those kids without granting me fair warning. And next time, *if* there's a next time, I'm going to be the one who walks off and leaves you to field their unnerving questions. You got that, Irish?"

John leaned on his crutch and hobbled off. He was going to stir up a sure-cure poultice that would heal his wounds so he could get the hell out of Paradise Valley while the getting was still good. And maybe he'd whip up an antiaphrodisiac while he was at it. He was in dire need of a strong, fast-acting potion to counter the ungovernable cravings that kissing this green-eyed leprechaun aroused in him.

Gawd, thought John. He didn't even want to think what would happen to him if he actually kissed that woman for no other reason than to appease his pure, pulse-pounding desire. He'd kissed her once to counter the maddening pain. She'd kissed him once for show, then he'd kissed her in frustrated anger. Yet the effects were pretty much the same—devastating. There was not going to be a fourth kiss, because, damn it all, he just wasn't sure he could handle that kind of physical and emotional suicide! The woman was so potent that she left his head spinning!

John staggered off, and he couldn't remember where the hell he'd been intent on going when he left her lying there, staring up at him with those kiss-swollen lips and passion-drugged eyes that were more compelling than a siren's spell.

He definitely needed to find someplace to cool off.

Chapter Five

Tara's hands were shaking so badly she couldn't sew a straight stitch. Her mind was whirling like a cyclone and her body was buzzing with white-hot sensations. For goodness sake! Being kissed—*really* kissed—by John Wolfe was like nothing she'd ever experienced. She should've known that when he got serious about kissing he'd be intense....

And why'd he have to go and do that, anyway? The kiss she'd given him at the table was quite enough to heighten her awareness of him and to discourage two smitten teenagers. Tara had seen her opportunity and she'd taken it. How was she to know the children would bombard John with embarrassing questions? Well, she certainly wasn't to blame for that, was she?

It took considerable effort for Tara to get herself under control and concentrate on mending the garments. She drew in another fortifying breath and tried to block that amazing, spellbinding kiss from her mind. Things were getting out of hand between John and her. It was one thing to deal with him while he was flat on his back, helpless and overcome with pain. It was something else entirely to deal with him as a virile, dynamic man. Tara was definitely going to have to establish some ground rules around here. Sort of like how he claimed the Apache culture dealt with tricky situations so everyone knew how to act and react.

When the mending was completed Tara entered the house, to see that the children had washed the dishes and put them away. Flora and Calvin had left the cabin to walk the lambs. Maureen had buried her nose in a book, and Samuel and Derek cast her deflated glances, then focused their rivalry on a checkerboard.

Tara put away her sewing kit, then paced the bedroom from wall to wall, trying to decide how to go about calling a truce with John. They had to reach a working arrangement so she could settle back into her normal routine with the children. Well, except for that smitten business with the boys. Tara wanted them to think of her as an older sister, not a potential sweetheart.

The boys obviously needed to meet girls their own age. A trip to town was in order, she decided.

Tara sighed heavily, then plunked down on the edge of her bed. She supposed this complication with John was mostly her fault. He'd assured her, after their first kiss, that it wouldn't happen again. She'd initiated the second one. And no matter what her reasons, the second kiss had led to that third scorching kiss, which made her burn in places she hadn't been aware she had!

Well, she'd strive to reestablish the camaraderie and friendship they'd enjoyed the past week. They'd be honest and direct with each other. They'd avoid touching, and she'd try very hard not to get lost in the depths of his stunning eyes. Yes, that'd be a good place to start, she decided. *Not* touching. *Not* staring.

Tara came to her feet and squared her shoulders. Things were most definitely going to return to normal around here. For the children's sake, she didn't want tension flowing between John and her. The children needed security, stability and harmony. Her whimsical feminine desires weren't going to interfere with what was best for the children.

The night she'd fled from Texas she'd made a solemn pact with herself that she'd never ask for more than a home to call her own. She'd dedicated her life to providing for these children no one else wanted—except perhaps to overwork or enslave. But Tara *wanted* these children. No matter what their strengths, weaknesses and vulnerabilities, they were her family to keep, and she'd asked the Lord above for nothing more than that. She couldn't change the rules now. She and the Almighty had made a pact and she meant to keep it.

John was relieved to see that the poultice he'd smeared on his ribs and thigh showed immediate results. In fact, he could put limited weight on his leg without burning pain spreading in all directions. The long soakings he'd been taking in the springs also contributed to his recovery. The only thing making him uncomfortable was the anticipation of that dreaded discussion on the facts of life he'd promised the children.

Two days earlier, a thunderstorm that began in the afternoon and lasted all night had provided the perfect excuse to postpone the hike with the children through the canyon. Like a coward—and he'd never considered him to be one before—he'd feigned the need for rest and had closeted himself in the bedroom, hoping Flora and Cal wouldn't intrude to fire all sorts of embarrassing questions he didn't want to answer.

That night, while thunder rolled and lightning crackled, Flora and Maureen had scurried into his room like frightened mice and snuggled up on the bed so they could be near him while he slept on the pallet. It hit him right where he lived that these little girls felt they could come to him for comfort and protection. Damn, how was he supposed to keep his emotional distance when these kids kept boring into his heart like worms into a blasted apple?

Tara had left John pretty much to himself the previous day, and she'd rattled off dozens of chores to keep the children occupied in the house, barn and root cellar. John discovered that she conducted reading and arithmetic classes for the children three days a week, regular as clockwork.

John had heard the boys object, claiming they already had more education than they needed, thank you very much, but Tara would hear none of their grumbling. Clever as she was, she'd requested that the older boys tutor Flora and Calvin, then had presented them with reading material and math problems that challenged their adolescent minds.

John had noticed the previous evening, while he was brushing down his stallion, Pie, that Samuel and Derek had withdrawn from him and had very little to say in his presence. It didn't take a genius to realize Tara's kiss at the table had had the desired effect. Now, however, the boys perceived John as a rival for Tara's affection. It'd take some doing to return to their good graces, he predicted.

Limping along on his quest to gather fresh herbs for a salve and poultice, he heard the hum of a human voice near the bathtub-size spring beside the south canyon wall. Crouching down—well, as close to a crouch as he could manage with his gimpy leg—he peered through the underbrush...and nearly swallowed his tongue. Damn, he'd assumed Tara was at the cabin, supervising the children's chores. Unfortunately, here she was, sprawled naked in the springs. Her back was to him, her head tilted upward. Sun rays danced in her glorious mane of red-gold hair.

John cursed soundly when his male body responded dramatically to the enticing sight of her. The incident reminded him of that day she'd returned from town and slipped from her dress while she presumed he was napping. Only this was a damn sight more erotic because now he wasn't battling extreme pain and his body wasn't numbed by sedatives.

Like some disgusting, perverted Peeping Tom, he crouched there, memorizing the sight of silky arms and satiny legs. He could see just enough of Tara's tantalizing figure in the clear water to make him break out in a cold sweat. The vague memory he had of her standing in the shadows of the bedroom, while the fuzzy haze of pain and medication hampered his vision, was nothing compared to seeing her in the light of day. There wasn't a damn thing wrong with his vision now, and his body was clenched so tightly with unappeased desire that he had to smother a groan.

He should get up and walk away. It was the noble, sensible thing to do. But he didn't move. He studied her as if she were the most magnificent masterpiece of art he'd ever laid eyes on—which she was. John wasn't sure how long he would've been content to sit there and gawk, but the plodding of hooves, the jangle of bridles and bits and the murmur of deep voices jolted him to his senses. He'd been tracking renegades long enough to detect the sound of trouble when he heard it.

He didn't even consider the embarrassment he'd cause Tara when he showed up out of nowhere to alert her to the presence of unwanted intruders. He simply reacted to instinct and training. Limping as quickly and quietly as he could, he approached Tara from her blind side, then hunkered down to clamp his hand over the lower portion of her face. When he'd muffled her reflexive shriek of alarm, he contorted his body so she could see who had silenced her. John noted the absolute terror in her wide green eyes and wondered what caused such an intense reaction. When she tried to stand up—bare naked—to escape, he made a stabbing gesture with his arm toward the south.

"Intruders," he whispered in her ear. "Where the hell are your clothes, Irish?"

She directed his attention to the rock steps of the miniature waterfall. John finally noticed the clothing she was soaking in the springs.

The sound of gravelly laughter and baritone murmurs spurred John into action. He wasn't going to present much of a threat to the intruders if he was squatting beside a naked woman, with only his knife for protection. His Colt, he was sorry to say, was unloaded and lying under his pillow on his pallet—doing him no good whatsoever. Damn, he'd let his guard down so completely during his convalescence in the canyon that he'd forgotten every precautionary rule he normally lived by.

Scrabbling around the stone pool, John snatched up the waterlogged garments and flung them at Tara, who was trying to shield her nakedness with her hands and arms. John refused to glance in her direction for fear of getting sidetracked from his objective of keeping a watchful eye on the four riders picking their way down the narrow path.

"Are you dressed yet, Irish?" he asked without taking his gaze off the intruders.

"Not quite," she whispered back.

"Well, hurry it up…. Where's your rifle?"

"I didn't bring it with me, since I hadn't planned on hunting."

"Great," John said, then scowled. "And here I was counting on you to have a weapon to defend us."

"You're the legendary marshal," she snapped. "Why didn't you bring one with you?"

He would've whipped his head around to glare at her, but he couldn't risk a distraction. Pensively, he studied the terrain that lay between him and the oncoming riders, then motioned for Tara to circle the spring and join him.

"Keep yourself tucked out of sight," he ordered.

"While you do what?" she demanded.

"I'll circle around to confiscate the drag rider's rifle so I can get the drop on the rest of them."

"With injured ribs and a gimpy leg?" she asked incredulously.

He stared her straight in the eye. "This is what I do, Irish."

"Maybe so, but not when you're incapacitated. You can save your customary heroics for when you're well."

Before he could grab her, the idiotic woman rose to her feet and flapped her arms like a duck going airborne. John cursed her bravado inventively.

"Yoo-hoo! Over here!" she yelled.

Swearing in English—since there was no such thing as Apache obscenities, and this situation definitely called for salty oaths—John slunk beneath the small waterfall, then inched along the stairway of rock so he could circle the pack of riders. Tara, damn her courageous hide, stepped into clear view to divert attention. In that wet shirt and breeches, which clung to her like a coat of paint, she got the riders' attention, all right. Catcalls and wolf whistles echoed around the canyon walls.

Sensing no threat whatsoever from a woman, the scruffy riders moseyed down the path toward Tara, who'd pasted on a wide smile, as if welcoming home long-lost friends. John hunkered down on the overhanging ledge and watched four pair of lecherous male eyes zero in on Tara's shapely body—and he swore all over again.

"And here I thought we'd just be lucky enough to find a place to quench our thirst, boys," the lead rider purred in lusty anticipation.

"I get her first," the second rider insisted.

No one's going to get his filthy hands on Tara, John vowed silently. She'd placed absolute faith in his ability to handle this situation while she provided plenty of distraction. He might've disappointed Gray Eagle and the entire Apache nation because he couldn't ease their plight on the reservation, but he wouldn't allow Tara to meet with harm. She had a brood of children depending on her, damn it!

"Well, well, what a pleasant surprise," the lead rider said as he reined his steed to a halt in front of Tara.

She lifted her gaze to the shaggy-haired hombre and said, "You're welcome to drink your fill at my spring before you go on your way."

"Your spring?" One of the men smirked. "Well, ain't that neighborly of you, honey. But we'd be wantin' a bit more than a drink. In fact, we're just decidin' who's gonna take a turn with ya first—" John launched himself off the ledge, knocking the trailing rider off his horse and giving the man a sound whack on the head with the stone he clenched in his fist. By the time the other three riders twisted in their saddles to determine what had happened, John had a Colt in his hand and was biting back the howl of pain that his flying leap had caused him.

Tara, bless her, took advantage of the distraction he created to snatch the lead rider's rifle from its sling on the horse's withers. Two-against-three odds were acceptable, John decided. He'd faced worse before, plenty of times.

He surged to his feet, ignoring the pain shooting up his leg. "Climb down," he commanded gruffly. "The first man who makes a move to grab his hardware bites a bullet. If you want a drink, then take it now. Fill your canteens, friends. If you behave yourselves you can be on your way."

"Look, mister, we don't mean no harm," the lead rider hastened to assure him. "Don't get trigger happy."

John didn't reply, just shifted sideways so he had a clear shot at all three men—in case one of them decided to test his accuracy with a pistol.

It wouldn't be the first time that had happened, he reminded himself.

Tara backed up a step to let the men approach. The strangers dipped their sweaty hats in the spring, slurped water and filled their canteens. John refused to let them water their horses because he expected they'd try to use their mounts as shields. He gathered the trailing reins to lead the horses forward, keeping himself between the men and their mounts.

"In the future," he told the men gruffly, "remember this is private property. Next time you pass through here, make the three-mile ride into Rambler Springs to fill your canteens."

"Who the hell are you, anyway?" one of the men demanded.

He shot them a steely-eyed stare. "John Wolfe."

Three pair of eyes widened apprehensively. John couldn't be sure if the men were reacting to the overblown legends circulating about him or if these hombres were concerned about keeping their identity a secret, for fear he'd haul them to jail. When one of the men darted a glance toward his saddlebags, John's gaze narrowed thoughtfully. Yep, outlaws, he guessed. Folks with something to hide had a habit of darting glances at their hidden stash of cash, just to insure it was safe. That reflexive glance was a dead giveaway.

Well, hell. Some unfortunate rancher, prospector or storekeeper was probably lighter in the pocket, thanks to these scoundrels. John wasn't going to let these ruffians ride out of here the same way they rode in—scot-free.

John caught Tara's movement out of the corner of his eye and nearly groaned aloud when she turned the confiscated rifle on the nearest hombre, then cocked the trigger. "Why don't we just shoot 'em, John?" she suggested. "Nobody around these parts will know the difference. We can bury 'em alongside the other intruders that showed up uninvited last week.''

The men's wary gazes bounced from John to Tara, then back again.

"You aren't gonna listen to her, are you?" the blond-haired renegade asked worriedly.

"Why shouldn't I? I listened to her last week, didn't I? She really gets bent out of shape when folks just ride in here as if they own the place.''

"This canyon is *mine*," Tara said emphatically. "I have a deed with my name on it to prove it, too. I don't want you here. I don't want anyone trespassing on my property!''

Her theatrics were pretty convincing. For a moment, when she swung the rifle barrel from one heaving male chest to the next, John wasn't sure what she was capable of doing.

"Better drop all your hardware nice and easy, boys,'' he recommended, "then lie down so you don't look like you pose the slightest threat to this she-male. The last two travelers got all defensive and she shot one of them before I could stop her. Naturally, I had to shoot the other one so there wouldn't be any witnesses. You can imagine what a mess we made at such close range. Took us two days to clean up the evidence of the killings.''

Three Adam's apples bobbed uneasily.

"You heard him. Drop your pistols and get down!'' Tara screeched.

"Uh-oh, she's getting prickly, fellas,'' John warned, straight-faced. "Her Irish temper's nothing to fool with, believe you me. She shot me before I could tell her I was a lawman. I've got two bullets in me to prove that she prefers to shoot first and ask questions later.''

To verify his claim, John pulled open his shirt to expose the bandage around his ribs, then he limped forward to join Tara. "She nearly killed me dead, then patched me up when she discovered I was wearing a badge."

The men's alarmed gazes leaped from his bandages and gimpy leg to Tara's wild-eyed expression. Damn, the woman had missed her calling as an actress, John decided. She practically had *him* convinced she was loco.

"I'm getting that twitchy feeling again, John," Tara said as she stabbed the rifle barrel against the nearest hombre's chest. "Let me shoot one of 'em at least."

"Hey, lady, take it easy," the man chirped, hands held high. "We're gonna drop our pistols."

"Then do it!" she shrieked, stamping her foot impatiently. "Hurry up!" Although the men hurriedly discarded their weapons and sprawled spread-eagle in the grass, Tara wasn't satisfied. "I still think we should just shoot them," she insisted.

"You can shoot the first one who moves—will that make you happy?" John asked as he limped over to retrieve the coil of rope dangling from one of the saddles.

"Okay, one will be good," she replied, leveling the rifle barrel toward another shaggy head. "How about this one?"

The man flinched. "Nobody move," he ordered his friends.

While Tara held the men at gunpoint, acting just crazy enough to be convincing, John sliced off sections of rope and bound up the men.

"Easy now, Irish, give me the rifle," he cooed. "I'll keep an eye on them while you ride back to the house."

"No, you said I could shoot one of them. You promised!"

"Maybe later, okay? My leg is hurting something fierce. I'm not up to digging more graves right now. Maybe after I have a chance to sit down and rest a bit." When Tara breezed past him to hand over the rifle, John murmured confidentially, "Bring Samuel and Derek back with you."

She nodded, then vaulted onto the nearest mount. She walked the horse right overtop of the downed men before she spurred the animal into a gallop and let loose with a fine impression of a cackling witch.

"Damn, that is one bloodthirsty she-male," one of the hombres muttered into the grass.

"You don't know the half of it," John agreed. "Last week she shot down a man for looking at her the wrong way. When I'm feeling better, I'm gonna have to find a way to haul her to jail. She's a menace to society." He discreetly dipped his hand into the bulging saddlebag and came up with a heavy pouch of gold and several loose banknotes. Just as he'd thought. Some poor robbery victim was missing his hard-earned money.

While John waited for Tara and the boys to return, he hobbled over to tie up the unconscious man he'd hammered on the head. A few minutes later, Tara came thundering through the canyon with Samuel and Derek hot on her heels. The boys stared goggle-eyed at the captives.

"Help me get these hombres on the horses," John instructed the boys.

Samuel and Derek scrambled from the saddle to assist him. All the while, Tara was wielding the rifle and chattering about how she wanted to use the prisoners for target practice. It was more than obvious that the half-crazed, unpredictable female with a rifle struck more fear in the hearts of outlaws than a capable gunslinger. Even Samuel and Derek kept casting apprehensive glances at Tara.

When the four men were draped and tied on the backs of their horses, John strapped the heavy saddlebags on Samuel's mount, then drew the boys aside. Tara was still yammering about blowing heads off, diverting the captives' attention.

"I'm counting on you to take these outlaws into Rambler Springs and deliver them to the town marshal. Don't stop for any reason or listen to any excuse these men might use to catch you off guard. Understand?" When the boys nodded solemnly, he added, "Give the saddlebag to the marshal, tell him I'm in the area and that I'll be in to see him soon."

John noted immediately that he'd returned to the boys' good graces by giving them a man's job. They were eager to prove their capabilities. John just wished it hadn't required drastic circumstances to win the boys over.

When Samuel and Derek rode off, their captives trailing behind them, John pivoted to see Tara smiling triumphantly. He, however, was not the least bit amused by her daring theatrics. "Damn it to hell, Irish!" he roared at her. "The next time I tell you to do something, you do it. Got it?"

Her smile turned upside down. "Well, excuse me for helping apprehend those hooligans," she snapped back. "You needed my help and we both know it. If you think I'm the kind of person who cowers when trouble arises, then you've misjudged me. Furthermore, I won't have you getting yourself killed or aggravating your injuries on my account."

Her chest heaved in indignation. John's gaze dipped to the damp shirt that revealed more than it concealed. Willfully, he raised his wandering gaze to her flashing green eyes and livid expression.

"You think I haven't found myself in dire straits and narrow scrapes since I gathered the children and headed west?" she demanded. "Just because I didn't go into detail about our exodus to Arizona Territory doesn't mean there weren't some tense moments along the way. Believe me, I've handled plenty of stressful situations in my time, Marshal Wolfe."

"Irish—"

"I was trying to save your injured hide, damn it!" she shouted. "If those four men had gotten past us and attacked the kids in the cabin—Maureen especially—I don't even want to imagine the horror they'd endure. No one's going to hurt those kids, not on my watch. Ever!"

He'd seen mother grizzlies less protective of their cubs, John thought. Tara was all teeth and claws. Although she was only five feet nothing tall and couldn't have weighed much over a hundred pounds dripping wet, she had a core of steel and exhibited death-defying courage. Yet in the presence of the children she was cheerful, optimistic and kind. If he hadn't realized it already, he knew beyond all doubt that there was more to this woman than met the eye.

"You can calm down now, Irish. It's over," he said soothingly. "I'm sorry I jumped down your throat, but I'm accustomed to working alone. Fretting that you'd get yourself shot made me twitchy. The Apache custom is that when someone saves your life, then you *owe* that life. If you get yourself shot, or worse, and I can't prevent it, then it's a mark on my soul. Your safety is my responsibility."

By the time he was through apologizing, Tara had managed to calm down—slightly. She knew she was operating on sheer nerves and adrenaline. It'd been easy for her to act half-crazy, because that's exactly how she'd felt. The prospect of John being injured or killed unnerved her. The thought of those men finding the children terrified her. Always before, when a tense moment passed, Tara had gone off alone to compose herself without upsetting the children. Now John was standing five feet away, and she felt the reckless urge to hurl herself into his arms and hold on until she gathered her wits…. Before she realized it, she'd indeed launched herself at him, flung her arms around his neck and buried her head against his chest.

"Good gad," she gasped.

She heard as much as felt laughter vibrate through his chest. "You did fine, Irish. Better than fine, actually," he said approvingly. "I'll admit your daring heroics scared the living daylights out of me, but you were thoroughly convincing. Did you, by chance, spend time on the stage during your pilgrimage to Paradise Valley?"

"No, but I used to act out fairy tales to entertain the children at the orphanage," she said against his shirt.

"Well, you're exceptionally good at it." He patted her on the back.

"How do you do it?" she asked between seesaw breaths.

"Do what?"

She tipped back her head to stare curiously at him. "How do you face down outlaws on a regular basis? Do you have nerves of steel? I'm still shaking like a leaf."

Indeed, she was. John rubbed his hands down her arms in a soothing gesture. "I made peace with dying years ago," he confided. "I was trained to do battle, to outwit the enemy. Sometimes things don't work out the way you plan and all hell breaks loose. Then you just respond instinctively and hope you can dodge oncoming bullets that have your name on them. And Irish?"

"What?" Tara tensed when she noticed the somber look in his eyes, the sober expression on his handsome features.

"What happened to that sadistic Texas rancher who buried his wife, or whatever the woman was to him, in the backyard?"

Tara jerked back. She sensed John knew the answer before he'd asked. She presumed that something about the way she'd gone a little crazy when facing down the intruders who intended to abuse her had come through to him loud and clear.

"I better get back to the cabin and check on the other

children," she murmured evasively. "They'll want to know exactly what happened."

"I'm not here to judge, Irish," he said to her departing back. "What happened?"

Tara stopped in her tracks, pivoted, then offered him the truth she'd never told another soul. "I was forced to kill him. I was so bruised and beaten that I couldn't give him a proper burial, not that he deserved one, because he certainly didn't...." Her voice shattered and tears clouded her eyes. It took a moment before she composed herself. "What happened with those outlaws was nothing compared to my ordeal with Mortimer Lindsey."

"I'm damn glad to hear he's dead and gone. That saves me the trouble of looking up that crazy son of a bitch and killing him myself."

Tara swiped at the tears, noting John was standing rigidly, hands clenched at his sides. She realized he meant what he said about not passing judgment on her, about avenging the torment she'd endured at that perverted rancher's cruel hands. Oddly enough, Tara felt better having bared her soul to John.

There was nothing more to hide, except this growing affection for him that she was helpless to control. John Wolfe easily could become the man she loved for all times. She admired him, respected him, marveled at his skills and abilities. She hadn't meant to, but she'd come to depend on him, to lean on him for comfort and support.

Inhaling a bracing breath, she turned around and headed for the cabin. She had curious children awaiting her return.

John's breath whooshed out like a deflating balloon as he watched Tara walk away. He didn't like the fact that she'd been involved in a near brush with the kind of violent life he led. He regretted that she'd been reminded of the horrors she'd endured at the hands of Mortimer Lindsey, that maniac rancher who'd obviously derived wicked enjoyment from overpowering and tormenting women. John was damn glad to hear that bastard was already frying in hell.

John didn't have the slightest doubt that Tara had acted in self-defense, but he'd check to see if she was wanted for murder in Texas. He'd ensure her name was cleared. He wondered if the name Tara Flannigan was as fictitious as John Wolfe was. He wondered if she, like him, had felt the need to assume a new identity. He recalled her fit of hysterical laughter after he'd announced there was no John Wolfe. He wondered if it had struck her funny because there was no Tara Flannigan, either. That'd certainly explain her peculiar reaction.

Limping noticeably, John walked off to gather herbs for his poultice. Well, one good thing had come from this harrowing incident, he consoled himself. That dreaded discussion on sex would have to be postponed again until another day. He was pretty sure that rounding up outlaws was going to be a snap compared to fielding questions from a brood of curious children.

Chapter Six

John bit back a grin when Samuel and Derek, who'd left the canyon as boys, seemed to think they'd returned as men. As instructed, they'd delivered the prisoners to jail and had given their message to Tom Glasco, the town marshal. It turned out there was a reward for the capture of the gang, who had robbed a trading post up north. The marshal had patted the boys on the back for a job well done, handed them two hundred dollars and sent them home, telling them to keep the spare horses as their own because the prisoners weren't going to be needing them for a good long while.

"What do you plan to do with the money?" John asked while the family sat around the supper table.

"Well, I suppose it really isn't ours to keep," Samuel said. "After all, you and Tara captured the thieves. We just transported the gang to town."

"In that case, I want my share of the reward deposited in the family treasury," John announced.

"Same goes for me," Tara stated, smiling at the children. "But it seems to me that everyone had a hand in the excitement."

"I didn't do nothin'," Flora said sullenly.

"Me neither," Calvin added.

"Yes, you did," Tara insisted. "Calvin, Flora and Maureen held the fort. If those men had gotten past John and me, then attacked Samuel and Derek, it would've been up to you three to defend our home. If the worst had happened I'd rest easier knowing that a small part of me would remain with you because we are a family."

The theory sounded so logical to the younger children that they nodded in agreement—until Maureen had time to give the matter more thought.

"But that would never have happened, because John was on our side. Nobody would ever get past him."

John was uncomfortable with his invincible-hero status and the gaze of slavish devotion Maureen directed at him. "That's not quite true, Maureen. The man who shot me is still on the loose," he pointed out.

"Exactly," Tara said, focusing her unblinking gaze on the three youngest children. "There's always the possibility that you'll be called upon to show courage. Sometimes that means locating a safe hiding place until I can find you."

"That sounds like a coward's way out," Calvin muttered. "I don't want to be a coward."

Tara took his hand in hers, giving it a fond squeeze. "If you're the witness who identifies a criminal, then you can do your part to ensure he's put behind bars. John's been teaching you survival skills to make sure you remain safe. I have his assurance that all of you are quick studies."

The brood of children shifted their attention to John. "Best students I ever had," he confirmed, then found himself repaid a thousand times over. Their proud, radiant smiles could've led him through a blizzard.

"Which brings me back to the point I was about to make," Tara continued. "Considering how the capture and transportation of the outlaws was pretty much a family effort, I think we should take some of the money and make a trip into town tomorrow. Everyone gets to make a special purchase, something you've always wanted and never could afford.''

When excited chatter erupted around the table Tara flung up her hand, requesting silence. ''You can decide what you want while you finish your chores. I'll do the dishes so you can start immediately.''

The passel of children broke and ran for the door. John was left at his end of the table and Tara was still sitting at hers. Not once had she met his gaze directly after offering her grim account of her ordeal with Mortimer Lindsey. John wasn't concerned on that count. Something else was bothering him after the confrontation with the outlaws at the spring.

''Irish, this is only the beginning of unwanted intrusion,'' he told her. ''Although the Apache and Navajo are confined to reservations, there's another imminent threat. People are migrating to this area, especially since rumors of new copper and silver strikes are flying. Outlaws prey on travelers and prospectors. This valley offers protection from inclement weather, and several good water sources. You really need to find a place to live in town.''

Her chin shot up at a stubborn angle. Her spine became ramrod straight. ''This is our home. I told you how important it is for these children not to be uprooted again. They love this secluded valley as much as I do. Flora gets plenty of exercise and fresh air. Calvin's gimpy leg gets stronger with each passing day. His limp isn't half as noticeable as it used to be.''

''There'll be other intruders, Irish. Samuel and Derek don't know how to handle a pistol or rifle effectively yet. I don't know how capable you are. I haven't actually seen you at target practice, just heard you ranting about how you were eager to blow off a few heads for the sport and spite of it.''

''I can usually shoot what I aim at,'' she assured him.

"If you're concerned, then you can teach the boys to shoot properly before you leave."

"It would still be safer for you in town," he contended.

"And you'd be healthier if you found a nice, safe occupation that didn't involve outlaws using *you* for target practice," she sassed him.

"Damn it, I have the future of an entire Apache nation resting on my shoulders, not to mention a load of guilt weighing down my conscience. I took this position in law enforcement so I'd have the legal authority and opportunity to change public opinion and protect the Indians. I have to ensure they aren't swindled out of more land and resources. Furthermore, I'm pretty certain the outlaws I was chasing when I was shot are the ones that disguise themselves as Indians when they hold up stages, freight offices and ranches. Jacob Shore, my supervisor, believes they're a band of renegade Apaches on the loose, but that's not true."

"Only *one* renegade Apache," she mused aloud. "The one who shot you."

He nodded curtly. "And that particular Apache happens to be Gray Eagle's true son."

"I'm sorry," she murmured. "I didn't realize how difficult the encounter was for you."

"Yeah, well, I'm between the devil and the deep. Raven is so desperate for freedom that he hooked up with ruthless cutthroats. Gray Eagle wants me to sneak him back to the reservation before he gets arrested—or worse."

Tara, apparently, had been struck by a delayed reaction. Her luminous eyes widened and she gaped at him. "It was your *adopted brother* who shot you? I know for a fact that you had ample opportunity and just cause to shoot him. But you wouldn't fire at him, would you? He obviously doesn't abide by your code of honor."

John reflexively defended Raven, since he'd been doing

it most of his life. "Raven was left on that hellish reservation while I walked away to freedom. I turned white to save myself. It's understandable that he's bitter and resentful. I can't guarantee I wouldn't have felt the same, done the same thing, if I'd been in his place."

Tara slapped both hands on the table and hoisted herself to her feet. "If you can say that, then you don't know yourself as well as you think you do, John Wolfe. Something tells me you're making excuses for your adopted brother and he isn't half the man you are."

"You don't know Raven," he said, and scowled. "You don't understand what captivity can do to a man who's born to roam without restriction and boundaries."

"Fine, you go round up Raven and sneak him back to San Carlos. In the meantime I'll be here defending my canyon," she said as she scooped up the plates and silverware.

"*Your* canyon?" John bolted to his feet, ignoring the pain in his thigh, focusing instead on the pain in the ass that went by the name of Tara Flannigan. "Pardon me, Irish, but this place was Apache sacred ground before you jumped this claim and set up housekeeping."

The comment must've taken the wind from her sails because her gaze plunged to her booted feet. John should've shut his trap, but deeply embedded frustration had taken hold of his tongue. "You have no idea what it's like to have your food supply slaughtered, your land invaded, your clan massacred for the sake of white man's greed for material possessions. You don't know how it feels to have the truth twisted so that your people constantly look like villains. There's plenty of publicity about violence committed by Indians, but no one's interested in hearing the other side of the story. No one bothers to mention what provoked the acts of retaliation or the injury, thievery and manipulation against them.

"Indians were once inclined to be hospitable to whites,

but that was blotted out by white treachery. Stories of the white man's ingratitude and conniving have been passed down through generations of Indian children. Tribes were reduced to using their own brand of deceit against whites and relying on cunning against overpowering weapons. It's the whites who provoked Indians to retaliate. Whites are now regarded as our natural enemy because of the bloody history between us.''

John sucked in a quick breath and kept ranting. ''Can you even begin to imagine how it feels to be surrounded by soldiers and herded like cattle into a camp sitting on barren land that no one else wants? How'd you like to be told the godforsaken reservation is where you'll live out the rest of your life? Do you know what it's like to be surrounded by armed guards that have orders to shoot to kill if they think you have the slightest inclination of sneaking away?

''Do you have any idea how many Apache have been shot for sport, only to discover that the soldiers involved in the killings lied to their superiors and were *believed*, even when Apache witnesses supplied entirely different versions of the incidents?''

Tara's gaze locked and clashed with his. ''No, but is it anything remotely like being left alone in the world, dropped at an orphanage where you're treated like an extra mouth to feed, another body to clothe? Is it like being herded onto a train, without being told the purpose or destination, then being passed over at one whistle stop after another, until you're delivered into the clutches of a demented man who tries to chain you to his bed and—''

Her voice broke. John stood there helplessly watching Tara battle her living nightmare. Color suffused her face and tears ran in rivulets down her cheeks. She clutched the dirty dishes to prevent herself from dropping them and having them shatter in pieces—like her unsettled emotions.

"I'm sorry, Irish," he murmured apologetically.

"I'm sorry, too, for all that's unfair and unjust in this world. But it doesn't change my determination to stay in this valley until the children are raised. I can't risk living in a town where too many people ask too many questions about how we came to be a family.

"We are *not* your responsibility, John," she reminded him tersely. "You have enough on your plate without fretting about us. Now please go outside and do your ceremonial dance, or whatever it is that you Apache warriors do at dusk. I have a kitchen to clean and I'd like to do it alone!"

John stalked outside, pulled up short on the porch, then dragged in a deep, steadying breath. Why, he wondered, was he the only one who caught the sharp edge of that Irish termagant's tongue? The children thought she stood in line for sainthood, what with all her patience, understanding and reassuring smiles. Clearly, there was more than one side to that woman's personality. Having seen her in action this afternoon, having argued and debated with her on several occasions, John realized he'd met his match when it came to headstrong, willful and stubborn.

Correction, he thought as he stalked off the porch to intercept the two children who were walking sheep. Tara held the world title for stubborn. John had only *thought* he knew the meaning of the word before he met and clashed with Tara Flannigan!

Tara's conscience had been giving her fits after her heated argument with John. She supposed that having her emotions run the gamut during the course of the day had contributed to her testy temper and lousy mood.

Now she lay on her pallet in the barn loft, staring through the window that provided a breeze and a view of twinkling stars, wondering if maybe she should apologize for coming down on John like a ton of rocks. Until today she hadn't realized what torment he'd suffered when he'd confronted his blood brother. Considering John's complicated background, she understood that he'd been forced to take an assignment to track down the one person he never wanted to capture.

Pushing upright, Tara raked her fingers through her wild tangle of hair and stared pensively at the ladder. She couldn't fall asleep knowing John was irritated with her—and with good reason. She couldn't leave for town in the morning knowing there were things she needed to say to him in private.

Resolved to offer a sincere apology and form a truce, she descended the ladder. She walked barefoot from the barn and circled to the bedroom window so she wouldn't disturb the sleeping children. She inched open the window, then eased a hip over the sill—and suddenly found herself yanked sideways so fast her head spun like a carousel. She flinched when she felt a steel blade pressed threateningly against her throat.

"It's only me," she peeped.

"Damnation, Irish," John growled as he set her on her feet. "Next time you decide to sneak in a window after dark, announce yourself first."

She should've known a man with John Wolfe's uncanny instincts slept with one eye open and both ears alert to approaching trouble.

"Why the hell are you here?" he asked as he tossed the dagger aside.

Moonlight filtered through the window, spotlighting the skimpy loincloth he wore for sleeping. Quickly, Tara jerked her gaze back to his face. "I came to apologize," she murmured, trying very hard not to become distracted by the arousing sight of his bare chest and muscular thighs. It wasn't as easy as she hoped. Masculinity radiated from him, heightening her awareness. *That* she did not need!

"You're forgiven. What are you apologizing for?"

He retreated into the shadows. She silently thanked him for that. She couldn't keep her wits about her when she was ogling his magnificent body.

"It hasn't been a particularly good day," she said for starters. "The incident at the springs sort of stirred up memories I prefer not to revisit. Then, when we argued, I got a little snippy and defensive."

"That's putting it mildly. You got a *lot* snippy and defensive."

"Well, so did you...." Tara blew out her breath, raked her fingers through her tousled hair and told herself not to initiate another shouting match that would rouse the children. "Forget I said that."

"Said what?"

"Thank you. The thing is, I don't want to be at odds with you." She began pacing the floorboards and wringing her hands. "Neither do I want the children picking up negative signals between us."

He smirked. "Ah, yes, everything must be perfect here in paradise."

She ignored his sarcasm. "I'm here to call a truce."

"Fine. Truce accepted. Go back to bed, Irish."

She glanced at the shadowed corner where he stood. "Your tone of voice indicates you aren't being very receptive," she pointed out.

"I'm not? Well hell, I thought I was agreeing with everything you've said. I happen to think I'm being exceptionally receptive," he muttered.

Exasperated, Tara threw up her hands. "I don't understand your mood."

"Don't you? Well, let me explain a few things to you."

He stepped forward. Moonlight beamed across his masculine physique. Her gaze dropped and roamed over every exposed inch of his virile body. Willfully, she focused on the air above his left shoulder.

"Look at me, Irish," he commanded sharply.

"I'd rather not, thank you."

"Why not?"

She swallowed audibly. "Because you aren't fully dressed."

"And you've been pacing in the moonlight, wearing a gown that's about as thick and concealing as cobwebs. I've already seen you naked once today, which was once too many for my peace of mind. Next, I watched you tramp around in wet clothes that left so little to the imagination you might as well have been wearing nothing at all. I promised I'd keep my hands off you, damn it. Then here you come, getting me all riled up again."

Indeed, he was riled up and aching with unappeased need he was damn tired of fighting, especially when he was damn tired, period. Seeing that alluring profile of thrusting breasts, concave stomach and long, shapely legs draped in a flimsy gown was enough to make him want to throw back his head and howl like a tormented coyote.

Maybe if Tara realized she was hell on his self-control she'd keep her distance. That was the only way he'd be able to continue his rehabilitation here in the valley. Having the personification of every man's fantasy underfoot was no picnic. He was doing his damnedest to resist temptation. And damn it to hell, his male body was getting mighty annoyed with his noble conscience.

"I rile you up?" she asked, her wide-eyed gaze flying to his.

"Hell yes! Have you looked at yourself in a mirror lately?" he snapped.

She smirked in disbelief. "Next you'll be telling me that a skin-and-bones urchin from the streets of Boston has become a ravishing beauty. Well, I know better. I'm fully aware that I'm conveniently available, because of our close quarters, and that a handsome man like you is undoubtedly accustomed to…well…receiving affection with no more than an interested glance.''

''Hate to blow a hole in your theory, Irish, but I don't bed hop from one end of this territory to the other. For your information, there haven't been all that many women in my life,'' he informed her curtly. ''Believe it or not, I've even been known to turn down women who don't interest me.''

''Then we don't have a problem, do we? I'm getting the distinct impression that you don't like me very much, especially tonight.''

When he barked a laugh, she clamped her hand over his mouth. ''Shh!'' she hissed. ''Don't wake the children.''

John removed her hand from his face before the scent and feel of her crumbled what little resistance he had left. ''I like you, Irish. I'd like to strangle you on occasion, but I do like you.''

She studied him thoughtfully. ''Does that mean you wouldn't mind kissing me again, though we agreed not to?''

''Yes,'' he admitted frankly. ''So I think you understand why it isn't such a hot idea for us to spend time alone together…in the dark.''

''Yes, I do understand,'' she whispered softly.

''Good. Then you also realize that you need to leave this room. Now.''

Yes, she did understand that, but all those sensible arguments just didn't seem so sensible while she was gazing up into eyes that glowed as brilliantly as the moon. Something about this man called to her on such an elemental level that she felt defenseless against the urgings of her feminine body. John was the only man she trusted not to hurt or abuse her. He'd defended her at the risk of his own life this afternoon. Plus, the children absolutely adored him. She was exceptionally partial to him, too, except when he tried to order her around as if she were a soldier under his command.

"John, all you've said is true, and I'm in total agreement, except…"

"Except?" he repeated cautiously, his voice strained.

"Except it's been a lousy day and I really think I'd feel much better if you'd kiss me, hold me."

He stood there so long, so still, that the old familiar feeling of rejection swamped her. When she was one second away from turning around and slinking out the window, he reached over to tilt her face to his.

"Are you sure that's what you really want, what you need, Irish?" he murmured, staring deeply into her eyes.

"I'm sure. There are times when strangling you holds great appeal for me, too. But when I get over being angry, I find that I still like being with you, still like you. A little more than the day before—"

His sensuous lips slanted over hers, shushing her. Tara melted against him, marveling at his tenderness, at this innate sense of right that consumed her. When he drew her body against his, letting her feel his desire for her, she roped her arms around his neck and willingly surrendered to the compelling sensations of warmth and pleasure that streamed through her.

She felt his hands shift, measuring the indentation of her waist and the curve of her hip. She sighed as he nipped gently at her bottom lip, then dipped his tongue into the recesses of her mouth to taste her thoroughly. When she practiced that arousing technique on him, he groaned. When she slid her arms down his back to his hips, he murmured something in the Apache dialect that she couldn't translate.

Tara quivered helplessly when he slid a bare leg between her thighs. She forgot to breathe—couldn't remember one reason why she needed to—when his wandering hand slid over the ultrasensitive flesh of her thigh.

All the while he continued kissing her, turning her mind to mush, her body to molten lava. His fingertips drifted between her legs, stroking her, caressing her. White-hot waves of desire rippled through her when he touched her intimately. When he glided his finger inside her Tara moaned raggedly, clung to him as if he was the only stable force in a careening universe.

John felt the spasm of passion shimmering through her body, echoing into his. She'd come apart in his hands, bathing his fingertips with liquid flames. Every male instinct was raging at him to press her to the bed and bury himself in her softness, to ease this aching need that burned him alive. Yet a small insistent voice kept reminding him that he was taking liberties that weren't his to take.

He'd been very much afraid the kiss she requested wouldn't be enough to satisfy him. It turned out he was right. He wanted more than he knew he deserved from a good and decent woman like Tara. He couldn't trust himself when he was alone with her. Not trusting himself was more than a little unnerving because, in his line of work, he'd learned that he was the only one he *could* trust.

Considering Tara's terrifying ordeal with that maniac rancher in Texas, John didn't want to do anything to trigger a nightmare that might cause her to shriek in alarm and wake the household. Thus he was exceptionally attentive, tender and gentle with her—which left him marveling at each fascinating response he drew from her.

He'd never taken so much time with a woman, and he was amazed that he derived so much pleasure from arousing her. But if he didn't call a halt right now, this very minute, he wasn't sure he had the willpower necessary to stop before things went too far. Neither did he want to risk having one of the children burst in to find them in a compromising position. Heaven forbid that he'd have to explain *that!*

Teeth clenched against raging need, John set Tara away from him. He was aching so badly for her that standing upright turned out to be sheer hell. Damn, he'd never wanted a woman as much as he wanted Tara. She'd quickly become an obsession, an addiction he could scarcely control.

"You'd best go, Irish. *Right now,*" he wheezed, his voice sounding as strained as his body.

She pushed up on tiptoe and kissed him so gently that he wanted to scream in tormented frustration. Somehow he managed to keep his lips clamped together so he wouldn't emit an agonized sound.

"Good night, John," she murmured against his taut lips.

"Yeah, ain't it though," he growled under his breath.

When she was gone, and he was as alone as he ever remembered being in his life, he plunked himself onto his pallet and counted about a thousand woolly sheep. He was definitely going to have to find something exhausting to do during the day so he'd collapse at night and *not* dream about what it'd be like to hold Tara, feel her feminine heat surrounding him, purifying him with the hottest, sweetest fire imaginable.

He'd suspected she could teach him the meaning of exquisite tenderness, sweetness and unparalleled pleasure—all those things that were foreign and unfamiliar in the world where he resided. But years ago John had forced himself to bury his personal wants, needs and every vulnerable emotion in order to survive the constant upheaval that had been his life. He'd refused to acknowledge the need to love and be loved. Furthermore, John had left too much undone in the world beyond this secluded valley to even consider making a life here. He *had* to distance himself from these feelings and maddeningly sweet sensations Tara evoked in him. He could *not* have her, he told himself—repeatedly.

Kissing Tara had been a mistake of gigantic proportions. He'd discovered a foretaste of heaven. He imagined that making love to her would change his entire perspective. That he couldn't afford to do. His life wasn't his own. Finding himself in love with that Irish siren, who didn't even realize the full extent of her own beauty and power over a man, would become the curse of his life. There simply was no room for tender emotions like love in his harsh and often violent world. He'd be better off if he never let himself forget that.

Chapter Seven

The next day, while John remained behind at the ranch, Tara and the children rode into Rambler Springs. The children chattered incessantly during the three-mile ride. Samuel, Derek and Calvin announced they were going to spend their share of the reward money on store-bought shirts. The girls decided to buy dresses. Tara, however, had every intention of saving her share for those rainy days when money was hard to come by.

There had been a lot of rainy days the past two years.

The moment the entourage arrived in town, the children scattered in different directions. Tara granted them three hours to stroll down the streets and enjoy their free time, but she cautioned them to remain in groups and keep a watchful eye out for trouble. She made a beeline for the house situated behind the general store so she could tend her housecleaning duties. Working fast and furiously, she spiffed-up the Pragues' house, then hurried to the Dentons' home located behind the restaurant. She managed to squeeze in time to clean the church sanctuary before the designated time she was to meet the children at the restaurant for their afternoon meal.

While waiting outside the restaurant, Tara eavesdropped on a conversation between two men who were discussing the latest spree of robberies and murders committed by a war party of renegade Indians. According to what she overheard, the gang had rustled cattle and horses from a ranch near Tucson and murdered two cowboys.

Tara was pretty sure the so-called Indian war party was the gang John had been tracking when he was wounded. On one hand, she felt obliged to pass along the information to him. On the other hand, she was hesitant to remind him of the duties awaiting him in the world beyond Paradise Valley. That was selfish of her, but the truth was she craved his companionship. After their late-night encounter she was pretty sure the *liking* she felt toward him was evolving into something deeper, more profound.

Tara had the inescapable feeling she'd fallen in love with John Wolfe. From the moment he'd kissed her the previous night, she'd felt her inhibitions sail off in the wind. Perhaps she'd gotten caught up in the erotic dimension of passion he'd introduced her to, but Tara knew herself well enough to know she'd never have responded to him with such reckless abandon if John hadn't already owned a piece of her heart.

The fact that he could've taken full of advantage of her helpless surrender—and hadn't—increased her respect for him. He'd denied his own needs to offer her pleasure. She hadn't realized any man was capable of that sort of sacrifice and self-restraint, but John Wolfe obviously was.

After Tara and the children treated themselves to a delicious meal at the restaurant—a meal they didn't have to prepare themselves—they set off for home with their new purchases, their spirits soaring. Tara wished she could afford these excursions on a monthly basis, but money was too hard to come by.

The moment the procession descended into the canyon, Samuel, who was leading the way, let out a shout that prompted Tara to reach reflexively for her rifle. "My goodness gracious, John's been busy while we were gone," Samuel hooted. "Look at our barn!"

Tara blinked in surprise when she noticed the sagging door had been repaired and the broken fence rails had been replaced. An extension had been added to the corral to make room for their newly acquired horses. She'd assumed John would spend the day resting. Instead, he'd taken the lumber she'd stacked in the barn and attacked several projects.

"Zohn Whoof!" Flora yelled, flapping her arms. "Where are you?"

John appeared from the shadows of the barn to wave a greeting. The children scrambled from their mounts and rushed toward him to display their purchases. Tara felt a pang of regret for allowing the children to become so attached to him. Already John had made a place for himself here and the children considered him a part of the family. Tara didn't want to deal with the emotional consequences the kids would encounter when John mounted up and rode away.

"Look what I bought!" Flora untied her package and held up the sunny yellow dress for John's inspection.

He squatted down on his haunches to take a closer look. "You picked this out all by yourself, half-pint?" he asked as he brushed his hand over the lace-trimmed fabric.

"I surely did," she said proudly.

"You have exceptionally good taste, young lady," he exclaimed.

Flora's smile was as radiant as the sun. "I do, don't I?"

"Indeed. I'll always be able to see you coming because you'll look like a ray of sunshine in this dress."

Flora flung her spindly arms around his neck and hugged the stuffing out of him. Tara's heart twisted in her chest. The little girl was so emotionally attached to John that it would take months to recover.

"I bought a new dress, too," Maureen murmured as she unwrapped her package.

With feigned concern, John surveyed the dainty blue gown that boasted frothy ruffles and satin ribbon. "It's breathtaking, Maureen, but surely you realize that when you wear this lovely dress to town you'll heap considerable responsibility on your older brothers."

Maureen studied him quizzically. John reached over to touch the tip of her pert nose, then tugged playfully on her strawberry-blond hair. "I'm absolutely certain that the young boys in Rambler Springs will be trailing after you, captivated by your dazzling good looks and this stylish new dress. Samuel and Derek won't want just any ole boy talking to their sister."

"I won't, either," Calvin said loyally.

"I didn't figure you would," John said with great confidence. "A man has to protect his sisters, after all."

The three boys were so anxious to display their new shirts they couldn't wait their turns. They held up their garments simultaneously, waiting for John's approval. He didn't disappoint them, even though the boys had chosen identical navy-blue shirts.

"Nothing I like better than shirts that make a statement," John said, appraising the garments.

Calvin glanced down at his shirt. "You do? What statement do these shirts make?"

"They announce that all three of you have arrived and you're giving everybody fair warning that you're all for one and one for all. If anybody messes with one of you they'll have to answer to all of you. Brothers through thick and thin, that's what these shirts say."

"I wasn't thinking about all that stuff when I picked out this shirt," Calvin said honestly.

John chuckled. "It's not something you have to think

about. It's just the way you feel about your brothers and the bond between you.''

The three boys exchanged looks, then nodded, well satisfied with the meaning John read into their identical purchases.

When John glanced past the children to meet Tara's gaze, she realized abruptly she was sitting atop the mare with her eyes dripping sentimental tears. John had a way with the children that touched her deeply.

''And what did Irish purchase?'' he asked.

''Tara didn't buy nothin','' Flora answered for her. ''She said she couldn't find nothin' as special as having us as her family. But we took up a collection from our reward money to get something for *you,* since you didn't come with us.''

John was taken completely by surprise. Tara doubted that happened very often.

''We wanted you to have a spare shirt that didn't have a bullet hole in it,'' Calvin said as he unwrapped the last package. ''We hope it fits, John, and I reckon it says the same thing our shirts say, only we were too busy buying these new clothes to figure that out.''

''Yeah,'' Derek chimed in. ''Anybody messes with you and they have to answer to us.''

Tara was pretty certain John had been struck speechless. He opened and shut his mouth a couple of times, but no words came out. She had the unmistakable feeling that no one had given John a gift before, at least not in the years since he'd escaped the Apache reservation. She should've realized the children would conspire to do something nice for him. Having received very few gifts themselves in life, they followed the Golden Rule about doing to others as you'd have done to you.

''Thank you,'' John murmured as he accepted the shirt.

''I think we should dress up for Sunday dinner,'' Maureen announced.

"But Tara doesn't have new clothes," Flora reminded her sister. "She doesn't even have a petticoat anymore 'cause she tore it into strips to make bandages for Zohn Whoof."

All eyes shifted to Tara, making her feel extremely conspicuous. She recovered in time to smile brightly as she dismounted. "I'll sew some lace on my dress so it will be sort of like new," she suggested. "Now come along, children. We need to change clothes and tend our evening chores."

She felt John's pensive gaze on her as she scurried toward the cabin. She sincerely hoped he wasn't feeling guilty—or some such nonsense—that she'd used her petticoats as bandages. She didn't like wearing those hampering undergarments, anyway.

Tara breezed into the bedroom, then skidded to a halt. The pallet in the corner was gone. Was John leaving? The thought of losing his companionship and never experiencing those tantalizing sensations he stirred in her sent her heart plunging to her knees.

"I've been wearing your petticoats? I wish I'd known."

Tara started at the unexpected voice so close behind her. "Even injured, you move with the silent tread of a cat. I suppose that's because of your extensive Apache training and the skills necessary for your occupation. Now, what was the lecture you gave last night about announcing oneself?"

John smiled wryly. "That's one of the things I admire about you, Irish. You have the uncanny knack of taking my words, twisting them to your purpose, then throwing them back in my face. And before you try to sidetrack me again, I want to pay for your petticoats."

Tara shrugged carelessly. "Thanks for the offer, but I prefer breeches. Dresses get in the way while doing chores. I guarantee it wasn't a woman who designed those confining garments. It had to have been a man.''

''Be that as it may, I still owe you new undergarments,'' he insisted.

''You already repaid me by making repairs and improvements on the farm that I haven't had time to tend to. Thank you for that, by the way.''

''You're welcome. And by the way, I'm taking up residence in the barn so you can have your room back.''

She stared up at him, wide-eyed. ''Then you aren't leaving?''

''No, do you want me to?'' he asked, watching her intently.

''No,'' she said without a moment's hesitation.

''Good, because I'm not quite ready for rigorous cross-country rides. In the meantime, I plan to earn my keep by making repairs around here.''

''Tara! Come see how John spiffed up our loft!'' Samuel hollered.

Frowning, Tara strode past John, then climbed the steps to the loft where the boys slept. Tara stared in astonishment at the suspended beds that hung from the ceiling rafters by ropes. John had provided more floor space for the boys. Wooden boxes has been cleaned and carted from the barn to provide makeshift shelves and drawers for clothing and boots. An odd looking gadget of twine, beads and feathers hung from the loft window.

''Dream catcher,'' John explained, following her curious gaze. ''Several Indian cultures believe that hanging a dream catcher traps the good spirits and wards off the evil ones.''

''I'm gonna make one for Tara in my spare time,'' Calvin declared. ''She needs one in her window, too. So do my sisters.''

Tara glanced down at Calvin. It was the first time she'd heard him refer to Flora and Maureen as his sisters. ''The girls will appreciate your thoughtfulness,'' she assured him as she sank down to give him a fond hug.

"This is the best room I ever had," Derek insisted, beaming proudly.

"You never had one at the orphanage," Samuel reminded him teasingly. "But even if this is the only room I ever had, it's still the one I'd pick because John fixed it up special. Thank you."

"You're welcome," John replied. "I was hoping I could count on you boys to help me make some changes in the girls' room tomorrow. Don't want to leave them out, do we?"

"We'll be glad to help," Derek said enthusiastically. "We'll get up extra early so we can finish our chores, then help you with the project."

"And speaking of chores," Tara interjected, "we better get a move on. The horses need grain, the sheep—"

"Already taken care of," John interrupted.

She gaped at him. "How on earth did you find time for that?"

He shrugged those impossibly broad shoulders and smiled at her.

"Well, I wish I had your gift of efficiency," she said as she descended the steps. "Maybe then I'd get more accomplished around here."

"Make a wish list," John suggested for her ears only. "Since you refuse to budge from this place, despite trouble that might arise, we may as well make improvements and turn this cabin into a well-protected fortress."

So he'd decided not to nag her about moving into town, had he? She wanted to kiss him for that. But as she'd discovered, kisses led to intimate caresses and there was a houseful of curious children underfoot.

John ran his hand over the brand-spanking-new shirt the children had purchased for him, and then he swallowed down the sentimental lump in his throat. For years now his life had been clearly defined. He'd been an instrument of law and order, the man Jason Shore called in for particularly difficult cases—renegade outlaws who cleverly eluded capture. No one seemed to care about him personally, just that he got the job done. And hell, he'd never stayed in one place long enough to make friends, feel part of a community. Now he was surrounded by a bunch of kids who treated him as if he was special, and they'd generously purchased a gift for him with a portion of reward money they could've spent on themselves. Even more overwhelming, the boys had presented him with a shirt the same color as their own. As if he was one of them and they all belonged together.

John knew he couldn't allow himself to get mushy and sentimental, to start thinking of himself as a permanent member of this family. He couldn't stay here indefinitely because he had obligations hanging over his head. Several of them, in fact.

Scooping up the shirt and clean breeches, John descended the steps of the hayloft and headed to the spring to bathe. He'd get gussied up to attend the Sunday dinner Maureen had planned. He'd sit across the table from Tara, who'd be wearing her only dress, the one he'd watched her peel off in her bedroom. He'd recall other moments when he'd—

John squelched the tantalizing, forbidden memories, but he couldn't outrun the erotic fantasies, even when he worked himself into exhaustion every blasted day. Damn, he'd have to be dead a week—maybe two—before he ceased responding to the sight and memory of that woman. He'd rattled off dozens of sensible reasons to discourage himself from sneaking into her bedroom window to ease this ravenous craving, but the ache of wanting never went away.

Teeth clenched, John ordered his contrary male body

to stop reacting to thoughts of Tara. He needed a cold bath and he needed it *now*. He'd leave Paradise Valley without taking Tara to bed, he vowed—though the looks he intercepted from her indicated she harbored a few fantasies of her own.

"Damn it to hell," John muttered as he made a beeline to the spring. He wanted her, but he told himself it was just a physical attraction to a beautiful, spirited woman. What he needed he could get from any female who offered her wares in Rambler Springs. Unfortunately, he couldn't muster much enthusiasm to ride into town after dark. So what did that mean, exactly? John wasn't sure he wanted to know.

Frustrated, he doffed his clothes and sank into the icy water.

"Okay, now here's the plan Derek and I came up with," Samuel said as he and the other children huddled together in the bedroom loft. "We might be able to keep John permanently if we can get him and Tara together."

"That shouldn't be too hard," Flora said. "We saw her kiss him at the table. That must mean she likes him."

"Of course she likes him," Calvin interjected. "What's not to like about John? He's the smartest, strongest, nicest man I ever met."

"I'm sure he likes Tara, too," Derek concluded. "She's the prettiest woman in the whole territory, maybe in the whole country."

"And there's us," Maureen added confidently. "We know they both like us."

The children were in complete agreement on that point.

"Now here's what we'll do," Samuel announced, then proceeded to explain the scheme he and Derek had dreamed up.

Chapter Eight

Feeling awkward, John sat down to a meal where the girls looked so prim and proper in their new dresses, and the boys sat rigidly upright rather than slouching comfortably the way they usually did. Truth was, John knew nothing about formal affairs. He'd gotten used to dining with this crowd in the past weeks, but this meal drove home the point that he was still more Apache than white.

Oh sure, he'd observed, taken note of and emulated nuances of white behavior when he'd returned to "civilization," but he still felt like a fraud. Now, conversation tended to be overly polite and stilted where it was once relaxed, natural and casual. In addition, the children seemed to be behaving oddly, casting discreet glances at one another at irregular intervals. With the exception of Calvin and Flora, that is, who wouldn't know discreet if it walked up and smacked them on the forehead.

"Don'tcha like the meal we prepared, Zohn Whoof?" Flora asked when he lingered too long in thought.

"It's delicious, half-pint," he assured her.

"Tara cooked it, you know. She's a wonderful cook," Maureen was quick to point out.

"And she takes really good care of us, just like she took good care of you when you were hurt," Calvin chimed in. "She does everything perfect and—ouch!" He glared at Derek. "Why'd you kick me?"

"Accident," Derek muttered, shooting Cal a silencing glower.

Something was going on here, John surmised. He just couldn't figure out what. He darted a quizzical glance to the far end of the table, where Tara sat in her faded green calico gown, which now boasted eyelet ruffles at the neckline and sleeves. She shrugged in response to his silent question.

"You sure look nice in your new blue shirt, John," Maureen said between dainty bites of steamed carrots.

"Thank you, Maureen," John answered politely.

"Don't you think John looks nice, Tara?" Maureen prodded.

"Exceptionally nice," Tara agreed. "All the gentlemen at the table look grand, in fact."

Personally, John thought he and the boys looked like the identically dressed singing quartet he'd seen down Tucson way a couple of months back, but he kept his trap shut. The fact that the children had purchased this bold blue shirt as a gift and color-coordinated it so he'd be one of them still left him with a warm, fuzzy feeling in his chest.

"Don'tcha think Tara looks nice, too?" Flora asked, her dark eyes zeroing in on John. "I helped her fix her hair special for our dinner."

That explained why the coiffure piled atop Tara's head, with a few curlicue strands coiling around her temples, looked a bit lopsided, John decided. He smiled and inclined his head. "Forgive my lack of manners, Miss Flannigan. You look lovely and the meal is, as always, excellent."

Tara bit back a grin. "Thank you kindly, Mr. Wolfe."

"How come you're calling each other miss and mister?'' Calvin demanded. ''We wanted you to be—ow! Blast it, Samuel, that hurt!''

John arched a brow when Calvin glared meat cleavers at Samuel. Yes, something was definitely going on here. Too bad he hadn't dealt with children often enough to figure out what the hell they were doing. He glanced at Tara again, but she seemed as baffled as he was.

The children finally got their chitchat out of the way and settled down to the business of eating. John relaxed and enjoyed the scrumptious meal of wild turkey, potatoes, carrots and fresh bread. He was definitely going to miss these regular meals when he returned to the wilderness and had to survive on tasteless trail rations. He was going to miss Tara and this amusing brood of children, too. Damn it, when had he gotten so attached?

When the table was cleared, he volunteered to wash dishes. ''This is your free time,'' he told Tara. ''I'll keep the children occupied.''

''That isn't necessary,'' she objected.

''Yes it is,'' he insisted. ''While I'm here I want to share the responsibilities. Go do whatever you feel like doing for a couple of hours.''

''You're sure?'' she asked hesitantly.

''Absolutely,'' he confirmed. ''Now skedaddle.''

Tara pivoted toward the bedroom to change clothes. ''I've been thinking of fencing off an area for the extra horses to graze. I'll hike around the canyon and decide which location might be best.''

''Keep your eyes peeled for unexpected visitors, Irish,'' he cautioned.

''I will.'' Tara exited the room, touched by John's concern and his willingness to take the yoke of responsibility for the children off her shoulders. Blast it, she was going to miss that man terribly when he left.

After hanging her gown on the hook near the door, she wriggled into her work clothes. When she reentered the kitchen, she chuckled at the sight of John, an apron tied around his chest so he wouldn't slop water on his new shirt, up to his elbows in dishwater. The children were sitting cross-legged on the floor, listening to him spin another tale from Indian legend. Since their rapt attention was focused on John, Tara slipped quietly out the door.

A sentimental mist clouded her eyes as she strode off. She'd considered the children and herself a complete family until John entered their lives. There was definitely going to be a void when he rode away. His mere presence was reassuring. His ability to combat trouble made her feel secure. Plus the sizzling feelings she experienced when she stared too deeply into his eyes, when he touched her and kissed her, had become a hopeless addiction. She constantly craved more of him, and the wanting intensified with each passing day. But John continued to maintain his distance. She lay awake each night, remembering their midnight encounter in the bedroom. Aching....

Tara sighed audibly, smothered the arousing thought, and quickened her pace. She was wasting her time wishing for something that couldn't be. If she had any sense at all she'd realize that if the bond between them strengthened more she might actually discover what she'd been missing, which would make it all the more difficult for her when he left.

After a mile-long hike, Tara halted in front of the northern stone face of the canyon and surveyed the plush grasses irrigated by a small spring that bubbled between rocks and dribbled into a shallow pool. This was a perfect place for a small pasture, because the towering rock precipices that surrounded three sides of the area provided a natural pen. If she and the children constructed a corral here, she could graze the horses and reduce the amount of grain she fed to them.

Forcing herself to keep her mind on ranch improvements, not on her fanciful daydreams of John, she set off to gather stones to mark the locations where postholes would have to be dug for the fence. She shrieked in alarm when she heaved up a heavy rock and, too late, realized there was a snake curled up beside it. Tara dropped the stone and leaped back out of striking distance. To her relief, she noted the serpent wasn't of the poisonous variety. Its slender head gave it away, but the blasted thing still coiled and hissed threateningly. She made a mental note to caution the children about paying attention to what slithered and crawled around rocks while they were constructing the new fence.

Two hours later, after collecting some wild berries and grapes, Tara headed for the cabin. Before she rounded the corner of the barn she heard yelps of laughter. She stopped short when she saw John and the children, dressed in their work clothes, each equipped with an improvised club made of willow branches, chasing after a reed hoop.

For several minutes she watched Samuel and Derek playfully shoving John aside, and John playfully shoving them right back. Calvin snaked out his arm to grab John around the thigh, and hung on tight. Then suddenly all four males were tumbling around in the grass, tackling each other and cackling in amusement. Not to be left out, Flora and Maureen flung themselves on the pile of squirming bodies and tickled the closest set of ribs.

It did Tara's heart good to see the children playing and roughhousing with John. She usually gave them chores and responsibilities and loving kindness. John provided something every bit as vital and necessary—pure, unadulterated fun and laughter. She'd have to remember to make time for this Apache-style game after John was gone....

Tara jerked herself upright and ordered herself, right then and there, to stop dwelling on John's departure. He was here *now* and she would enjoy his companionship, his contribution to the children's upbringing and the ranch repairs. She'd learned two years ago to take each day as it came, make the best of it and refrain from whining about what she couldn't have. She was not—repeat *not*—going to let impossible whims spoil her good disposition.

"Tara!" Flora called out between giggles.

John and the children stopped in midtickle and squirmed sideways to glance at her. For a moment, the children looked as if they anticipated being upbraided for their foolishness. She refused to let them think she disapproved of their frolicking.

"Is this the Apache version of a wrestling match?" she asked as she rolled up her shirtsleeves.

"Yep, think you can handle an armload of wiggling little warriors, Irish?" John asked, his eyes glinting with challenging amusement.

He looked so adorable with his raven hair standing on end, his faded shirt twisted, his nose bent sideways because Flora had latched onto his face and was tugging at his earlobe.

"Let me at 'em!" Tara dashed forward to tickle the spot above Calvin's knee that never failed to send him into fits of giggles.

Laughing uproariously, they wallowed around like pigs in the mud. Then Samuel and Derek held Tara down—and refused to let her up.

"Tickle her, John," Samuel insisted. "She's got ticklish spots on her ribs."

Smiling devilishly, eyes glinting with amusement, John hunkered down beside her. "Ticklish, are you, Irish?"

When he ran his fingertips along her ribs, Tara wriggled desperately. All three boys joined in to torment her until she was squawking helplessly. "You win," she gasped. "I give up!" Good sports that they were, John and the boys backed off so Tara could catch her breath. "How many more Apache games have you scheduled for the day?" she tweeted.

"One or two," John said as he offered a hand to hoist her to her feet.

"What are we gonna do next?" the children chorused, hopping up and down with barely contained excitement.

"Bow and arrow target practice," he announced. "Every respectable Indian brave should be able to use a bow. Samuel, go find a piece of sandstone to use as chalk. We'll draw a bull's-eye…on Irish's derriere."

"Hey!" she protested. "I've landed in a cactus patch often enough to know that won't be a bit of fun."

He grinned, silver-blue eyes twinkling. "Okay then, we'll draw a target on the barn if you don't want to be our human pincushion. Derek, take the other children to cut some more willow branches. I'll find some twine."

The children shot off like bullets to gather the needed equipment.

"Thank you, John," she murmured as she dusted off her backside.

John reached over to pluck a blade of grass from her tangled hair. "Thanks for what? Not poking your fanny full of arrows?"

"That, too, but most of all for entertaining the children. You gave me time to map out the new pasture fence."

"You can show me where you want it so the kids and I can put up the fence after we finish our latest project."

Tara glanced at his injured ribs, then his thigh. "Are you sure you're up to all these extra tasks? I don't want you to reopen a wound, especially after I went to so much effort stitching you back together." She hesitated a beat, wondering if she should tell John about the outlaw gang that she'd heard mentioned in town. Not now, she decided. John looked totally relaxed and content. She didn't want to spoil the day for him or the children.

"Something wrong, Irish?" he murmured as he smoothed away her pensive frown.

"Just thinking. While you're fashioning bows and arrows, I'll go whip up some cookies. Then I'll be ready for my instruction on bows.''

"Sounds good. As weapons go, bows are exceptionally effective. They don't make a lot of racket when you're trying to even the odds in battle. The kids think all these activities are fun and games, but there may come a time when they'll need to ward off trouble with a few wrestling holds, a big stick or a bow. I won't always be around—''

Tara pressed her fingertips to his lips to silence him. "I'm not looking too far into the future, and I'm not wasting more time wondering what life is going to be like without you around. I'm sure I'll find out all too soon, and so will the children. Teach us what you think we need to know to protect ourselves and I'll be forever indebted to you.''

He nodded. His lips moved sensuously beneath her fingertips. Tara looked into his eyes and felt the intensity of his gaze. She wondered if what had begun as a careless, incidental gesture had the same effect on him as it had on her. She thought she sensed the same forbidden longing in his expression that she knew must surely be reflected in hers. If that were true, why hadn't he sought her out on all those lonely nights she'd spent alone? Couldn't he tell she was starving for another taste of him?

Obviously not. Astute though he was in certain matters, he couldn't tell when a woman was falling hopelessly in love with him. Either that or she'd lost her appeal for him. Oh certainly, he claimed he liked her fine and dandy, but she doubted she was woman enough to hold his interest very long. No, he probably preferred experienced females who knew how to please a man. Tara suspected her untutored kisses and caresses were shamefully lacking. It was only basic lust and close proximity that stirred him on occasion—where she was concerned, at least.

"Irish, go bake the cookies," he ordered gruffly.

Tara snatched her hand from his lips, appalled that

she'd been tracing them with her fingertips while lost in erotic thought. He, she assumed, was tired of her pawing at him the way Flora usually did.

"Right, the cookies. Coming right up, Mr. Wolfe." She wheeled around like a soldier on parade and marched toward the cabin.

John watched her go, tormented by a mixture of forbidden pleasure and gnawing frustration. Her caressing touch drove him to aroused distraction. He wasn't sure he wanted to be held accountable for what he might do while they were alone. Grabbing Tara to his hardening body and kissing her breathless, while children darted around—and might return any second—wasn't a wise notion.

Flora had already hounded him about having that talk about the birds and bees he'd postponed twice. He'd rather not put on an exhibition this afternoon. Damn it to hell, wanting Tara had become as natural as breathing, but he'd vowed not to complicate this situation.

Someday a fine, upstanding man would catch Tara's eye. He'd be kind, decent and deserving of her love. Someone who could love her completely and devote his life to her and the children. John wasn't that man. Each time he let himself consider what it'd be like to love Tara, he could hear Gray Eagle's voice whispering, reminding him that he was the Apache's only hope of survival in a world dominated and controlled by the white population.

It was up to John to protect the Apache from corrupt Indian agents who stole from the tribe for personal gain. He had to change the views of heartless military leaders and law officers who still believed in Indian annihilation—even though the federal government had done the math and decided it was cheaper to let the Apache live on unfit reservation land that no white man wanted rather than outfit, equip and pay a regiment of solders to slaughter them on battlefields.

And Raven, damn his hide, was consorting with the

worst vermin in the country. The price on his head increased by the week. Yet John remained in Paradise Valley, neglecting his obligations in the outside world, enjoying his convalescence. Selfishly, he wanted to ignore the nagging voice of conscience, but it was never silent and demanded to be heard.

Just a couple more weeks to regain his strength and stamina and to absorb and savor the purity and innocence that had gone missing from his life. Two more weeks—was that asking so much?

"We found the sticks, Zohn Whoof!" Flora shouted as she sprinted toward him. "What do we do next, hmm?"

John cast aside his troubled thoughts and flashed Flora, Maureen and Calvin a smile. Maybe he couldn't enjoy the arousing pleasure he sensed awaited him in Tara's arms, but he'd teach these children how to survive in the world outside their secluded canyon. When he finished their training they'd be competent survivalists, one and all. If all Tara had was a brigade of children to defend and protect their paradise, then they'd know how to give themselves a fighting chance when trouble arose—and it would eventually.

John knew from experience that trouble always did.

Tara ignored the feelings of rejection and inadequacy that hounded her when John shooed her off to bake cookies. She paid close attention to his instructions while he showed her and the children the technique of handling a bow. Although the weapons he'd hastily constructed were crude, he promised to make higher quality ones during future sessions.

It amused Tara that the children hung on his every word and followed his instructions implicitly. They tried exceptionally hard to earn his praise and gain his notice. He seemed aware of that and nodded his approval when they performed tasks correctly. The girls received hugs when they hit the target, and the boys were rewarded with pats on the back. John did not, however, touch Tara in any way. He merely voiced his praise from a noticeable distance. She was pretty sure he was subtly reminding her that he didn't want to get close to her again.

To Tara's amazement, the children were the ones who called a halt to the instruction John had begun on handling a bowie knife. Samuel, self-appointed spokesman of the brood, announced they had chores to tend. The children scattered like a covey of quail without complaint, leaving John and Tara alone.

"I wouldn't mind a private lesson," she requested, staring into the distance, hesitant to meet his gaze and see rejection in his eyes.

"If you wish, Irish," he said with exaggerated politeness.

In an impersonal voice, John walked her through the proper method of handling the knife, showed her the technique of flicking her wrist to ensure trajectory and accuracy of aim. Tara missed the target wide to the right on her first three attempts. John reluctantly stepped behind her to move her arm through the proper motions.

Tara could feel his breath stirring against her neck, and she shivered uncontrollably. Determined to ignore her feminine needs, she focused absolute attention on his instruction. But it was impossible not to become distracted while he was standing as close as her own shadow, impossible not to breathe him in and wish for another of those mind-boggling kisses.

"That's enough practice for today," he said, abruptly retreating. "You can practice on your own tomorrow when I take the children on another excursion."

Deflated, Tara nodded. She ambled over to retrieve the knife, which had barely pricked the perimeter of the target. By the time she pivoted to face John she managed to muster up a smile that belied her feelings of rejection.

Blast and be damned, she'd thought she'd overcome those feelings of being unwanted and unaccepted. Unfortunately, John's standoffishness resurrected those wounded emotions that had tormented her since childhood.

"Irish…" He sighed, then raked his fingers through his hair. "Look, I'm trying not to…"

His voice fizzled out when Samuel and Derek exited the barn. Or rather, they *trudged* from the barn, as if their energy had been zapped. That was highly unusual, Tara mused. The boys had more energy than they knew what to do with. Then, just as suddenly, Flora and Calvin appeared, the lambs trailing behind them. Both children drooped noticeably at the shoulders, and Calvin's limp was more pronounced. They heaved audible sighs in unison as they herded the sheep into the pen. Maureen dragged herself from the house, then half collapsed on the porch bench.

John raised a dark brow and glanced at Tara. She shrugged, then frowned at the children. "What's the matter with you?" she asked.

"Don't know," Derek said as he clomped up the front steps. "Must've worn ourselves out—" he yawned "—during that hoop-and-pole game and the wrestling match."

"Yeah," Samuel chimed in. "I'm really—" he gave a huge yawn and a muffled moan "—beat tonight. Think I'll turn in early."

Tara gaped at him. "Without supper? You usually eat like a horse. I've never known you to skip a meal, even when you're ill."

Samuel yawned and stretched out his arms, then let them droop limply at his sides. "I'm not hungry because I stuffed myself at dinner."

"We all did," Maureen said in a voice that implied she was so exhausted she could barely muster the energy to speak. "But I did fix you and John a picnic supper."

"That's a grand idea," Derek murmured as he lounged negligently against the door. "Maybe the two of you should have a picnic in the canyon so you won't disturb us when we head off to bed." He glanced at John. "You wouldn't mind, would you?"

"Uh…no, of course not."

"Thanks," Calvin murmured, following Derek into the house.

Bewildered, Tara watched the children trudge, single file, into the cabin. Then it dawned on her what was going on and she frowned suspiciously. She had the unmistakable feeling the children, who'd become exceptionally attached to John in just a few short weeks, had decided to do some matchmaking so they could keep him. Those little scamps! When had they become so devious?

Flora reappeared in the doorway, holding the picnic basket. "Here, Zohn Whoof. G'night."

"Well," John said, swallowing a smile, "I guess if no one else around here is hungry we'll have an evening picnic by ourselves. I, for one, am starving."

Tara knew he was playing along for the five matchmakers' benefit. So as not to disappoint them, she manufactured a smile and gestured for him to lead the way. "I'm famished myself. After supper I'll show you where I'd like to build the new pasture fence."

She thought she heard a collective groan of disappointment as she walked away from the door where the children had gathered to eavesdrop. Discussing fence post locations, she presumed, wasn't what the children hoped would be on the agenda after their picnic supper. No doubt, they intended Tara and John to occupy their time with hugging and kissing.

Chapter Nine

"Where, I'd like to know, did those kids learn to be so manipulative?" Tara muttered as she hiked alongside John. "I hope you realize I had nothing to do with this scheme."

"I realize," John replied, chuckling.

He understood their matchmaking plot and he was flattered the kids cared enough to want him to remain a part of the family. He figured the children were trying to nurture his interest in Tara. Well, that wasn't necessary. He was definitely interested and attracted. That wasn't the problem, and he supposed he needed to explain his situation to them without going into the details of his true identity.

"So where do you want to have this picnic?" Tara asked.

John gestured toward the triple spires of stone that were an ageless Apache landmark. The natural monument was surrounded by a copse of cottonwood and willow trees well watered by a meandering stream that spilled from one of the springs at a higher elevation.

"We spent many days at the Altar of the Gods during our coming and going to raid in Mexico," he informed

Tara. "We gave thanks for sparing warriors' lives and we offered sacrifices to the Great Spirit."

"Live sacrifices?" Tara questioned dubiously.

John chuckled at her disapproving expression. "No, Irish, spoils of war we obtained from the Mexicans. They were the first to encroach upon the *Apacheria*. They overran our land in search of their Seven Cities of Gold. There's a treasure trove in the small winding cave at the base of the middle rock spire."

Tara's perfectly arched brows shot up like exclamation marks. "There is? I never noticed it."

"You'd have to know where to look to find it," he said, taking the lead through the trees.

Tara followed closely on his heels as he picked his way along the stream, then sidestepped up the sandstone slope. "I still don't see any evidence of a cave."

"You won't until you're practically on top of it," John assured her. He weaved in and out of the underbrush until he spied the bushy cedar tree that concealed the entrance. "Here," he announced.

Tara frowned curiously. "Why are you showing me this?"

"Because there may come a time when you need to use the Apache treasure to provide for the children."

Tara's mouth dropped open, and then she jerked upright and tilted her chin up a notch. "I can take care of the children by myself. I'm not going to rob from the Apache cache, especially not when these supposed treasures could be used to ease the Apache's plight on the reservation."

John admired her independence—in an exasperated kind of way—but she was being more proud than sensible. "There are hidden caves, filled with pouches of gold and silver, scattered all over this territory. Stolen rings and necklaces from Spanish haciendas are stashed among the treasures, as well. None of them will do the Apache nation any good now. If white men discover the existence of these hidden caches they'll be crawling all over the territory, demanding that more Apache land be handed over. Already the chiefs have been forced to sign over a twelve-mile strip of land on the reservation because veins of silver and copper were discovered by miners who were prospecting illegally.''

"Why, that's outright robbery!" Tara squawked in outrage.

He smiled ruefully. "It's the white man's way. For decades they've herded Indian tribes onto worthless land and have taken the fertile, valuable property for themselves. To the Indian cultures land was never meant to be owned. It's considered a gift from the Great Spirit, to be used, protected and replenished, to share with all other living things. You could own horses and other possessions, but never the land. To the Apache, it would make as much sense to claim to own the air we breathe, the rivers that flow into the seas. Indians have an entirely different perception of life than whites, who determine who they are by how much property, how much gold and silver and how many palatial homes they own.''

Tara frowned thoughtfully. "It must've been difficult for you to return to white society after being raised Apache. What you were taught to believe in, to honor and respect, wasn't necessarily so in white culture.''

John chuckled as he eased between the bushy cedar and the sandstone wall. "Definitely a shock, Irish," he admitted. "Although Gray Eagle made certain I never lost the ability to speak English, I had to adjust to the way Indians think, then revert back to the way whites think. But because stealth and cunning in the wilderness, the absolute oneness with nature, was so much a part of Apache training, I have the advantage when it comes to tracking white outlaws. What is legendary skill to the whites is nothing but daily routine to the Apache.''

Tara circled the cedar tree to follow him into the cave. "And that's what you're teaching the children," she murmured. "I appreciate that, John, more than you will ever know…. John? Where'd you go?"

He snickered at the alarm that registered in her voice. "Don't tell me, Irish, let me guess. You're afraid of the dark."

"Of course not." Her proud, independent streak returned to override the fear he accused her of possessing. "I just can't see my hand in front of my face, and this is unfamiliar territory," she explained reasonably.

He thought she sounded a little too breathless and apprehensive, despite her claims to the contrary. "Take my hand, Irish. I'm right here."

He laced his fingers in hers, then decided it was a bad idea. Each time he touched her, forbidden sensations overwhelmed him. Determinedly, he ignored the sensations and inched along the rough stone wall.

"Shuffle your feet," he instructed. "The floor slopes downward before we make a sharp turn to the left. Watch out for the overhanging—"

"Ouch!"

His warning came too late. Tara smacked her forehead against the jutting stone. She staggered, and John hooked his arm around her waist before she tumbled down onto the sloping floor, knocked senseless. When she latched on to him for support, another round of ungovernable, undeniable sensations pelted him—hard. Damn it, this trek in the darkness only heightened his awareness of her rather than diminished it. He was too sensitive to Tara's touch, her unique scent. No matter how incidental or seemingly harmless the contact, his body reacted dramatically.

John sighed in frustration. Entering the cave with Tara was another form of torment. "I'm going to let go of you now."

"Must you? I feel a little disoriented," she said shakily.

John accepted the bittersweet torment of having Tara cling to him like ivy. Her scent invaded his senses; the feel of her supple curves gliding alongside his body was sweet torture. But to protect her from another nasty bump on the head, he withstood the arousing tingles.

"Duck your head," he remembered to say in the nick of time.

He practically groaned aloud when she tucked her head beneath his chin and stuck to him like mortar.

"Are we there yet?" she tweeted.

"Almost." He cursed the breathless sound of his own voice.

John made a sharp right turn, then drew her to her knees beside him. He took her hand and moved it over the aging bead-and-leather pouches and metal boxes stashed in a chiseled-out niche in the wall. "If you ever need to borrow from this stash of treasure to survive, you know where to find it. But to appease the gods you must make your own special sacrifice."

"I've heard eerie stories of curses brought down on those who steal or disturb legendary mines and such," Tara whispered uneasily. "I used to think I was cursed because I lost my family and ended up at the orphanage, but I suspect the curse of the Apache nation might be even worse."

When John laughed softly, the sound echoed through the winding tunnel. "There's a difference between stealing and borrowing. If I considered you and the children greedy types I wouldn't have brought you here. All I'm saying is that if you're ever in need, take some of the treasure, then replace it with a gift of appreciation so the gods will look upon you favorably." He paused a beat. "I trust you with the knowledge, Irish."

"Thank you," she whispered, giving his hand a quick

squeeze. "I'm humbled by your trust in me. It means a great deal to me."

The sensations rocked John again. He wondered what had happened to the armor of indifference that he'd worn these past few years. With Tara, and with the children, he'd developed an entirely different perspective of himself. Nothing was the same as it had been, and he was more than a little concerned about how he'd function in the outside world now that he'd regained touch with tender emotion...and begun to crave it.

"C'mon," he said, appalled that his voice sounded like a croaking frog. "I don't want some varmint to rip into the picnic basket we left beside the cedar tree."

John placed Tara's hands on the wall, letting her feel the etched line in stone that led through the twisting cave. Their shuffling footsteps echoed in the darkness as they moved toward the tiny pinpoint of light.

When they emerged like subterranean creatures, Tara blinked and squinted in the twilight. As a child, she'd spent too many nights in pitch-black alleys, hearing the scurrying of rats and two-legged predators. She remembered the cold fear of being discovered and facing disaster. She hated this weakness that compelled her to cling to John as if he were her lifeline. But old torments died hard, she discovered.

Once outside in the fresh air, she breathed deeply, then stepped away from John to retrieve the picnic basket. "Ah, turkey and butter sandwiches," she reported. "A few grapes thrown in for good measure. Maureen was obviously busy in the kitchen this afternoon."

John accepted a sandwich, then sank down in the grass. Tara noted he barely grimaced when he put pressure on his mending thigh. Before long he'd be physically capable of resuming his life outside the canyon.

"I'm not sure how to handle this new problem of

matchmaking,'' he said thoughtfully, in between bites of their picnic supper.

Tara understood what he was being kind enough not to blurt out—that there couldn't be anything permanent between them, and therefore he wasn't interested in temporary complications, either. Although her feminine pride smarted, she told herself that, since John found her *resistible,* she should be grateful he wasn't the kind of man who used a woman to satisfy his physical urges, whether she meant something special to him or not. But blast and be damned, it was frustrating to care so deeply for a man who couldn't return her affection.

''I think it's best that we appear to be good friends,'' Tara recommended as she eased down beside him. ''Although the children will be disappointed that their matchmaking scheme failed, and they can't keep you permanently, they'll come to understand that friendship and respect for one another are important.''

''You're a wise and decent woman, Irish. The children are the focal point of every decision you make. You've no idea what a rarity you are in the world. I've encountered too many greedy, heartless, selfish outlaws who have no regard for anyone except themselves.''

Despite her vow to keep her distance, she reached out to touch his hand, then quickly withdrew. ''I can't fathom what your life must be like.''

''You had a meager taste of it last week,'' he muttered. ''That's as close to violence as I hope you ever have to come again. In fact, I want to show you a few maneuvers so you can ward off assaults.''

''I learned a thing or two in the streets,'' she reminded him.

''Not enough to satisfy me,'' he insisted. ''Humor me. I want no man taking advantage of you.''

''Not even you?'' she murmured under her breath—or so she thought.

John jerked up his raven head and stared at her with those intense silver-blue eyes that always played hell with her pulse. "What did you say?"

"Nothing important." She smiled brightly. "Grapes?"

John curled his fingers beneath her chin to turn her face toward his, because she wouldn't do him the courtesy of looking at him. "I think you've gotten a mistaken impression here, Irish."

Helplessly, her gaze dropped to his sensuous lips. Damn, she really had developed an obsession about kissing him, she realized. "What mistaken impression is that?" she asked in a wobbly voice.

"You have somehow convinced yourself that I don't really want you," he said gruffly. "Fact is, I'd have to be blind in both eyes not to find you attractive. And even if I were blind I'd still have to battle your alluring scent, which befuddles my brain when I venture too close. Then there's the endearing fact that your heart is pure gold. I'm wearing myself out trying not to act upon my need for you. I have nothing to offer, damn it. You know that as well as I do. This has nothing to do with convenient accessibility, either," he added before she could contradict him. "So don't even think about spouting off that crazed theory of yours again."

She peered into those fathomless eyes surrounded by that fan of thick, sooty lashes and heard herself ask, "Then why do you shy away, as if touching me repels you?"

John barked a laugh, but there was no amusement in the sound. He dropped his hand and shook his head. "I swear you whites have an amazing way of complicating what's simple. I don't touch and I don't take advantage because I have nothing to offer in return. There could be no more than stolen moments out of time." He looked her squarely in the eye and said, "You're a very dangerous woman, Irish, because you make me want more than

I can have. I'm committed to the life Gray Eagle assigned to me. What *I* want will always be overshadowed by my vow to do all within my power to ease the Apache's plight. But no matter how hard I try to call attention to injustice and corruption, I am only one voice falling on deaf ears.''

He sounded so tormented and frustrated that her heart went out to him. She also understood what he was saying, because for years she'd wanted to save and provide for every lost orphan, not just the five children in her care. She'd learned to be content to do what she could in her corner of the world, and she prayed there were others who'd do their part to shelter and love the lost, lonely and rejected children who wandered the streets.

John's adopted father had given him a difficult, unending mission. Every day John was reminded that he came and went freely, while his adopted people were held captive, living under military surveillance on godforsaken reservations.

At present, he was recovering from the vicious betrayal of his own adopted brother—and likely feeling guilty as hell about the encounter. He knew he had to track down Raven, who was giving the Apache nation a bad name, though white publicity and propaganda had already been doing that for years. Tara could only begin to imagine what frustration and torment hounded John every waking hour of every day of his life.

She reached out to trace his ruggedly handsome features, compelled to touch and console him. ''I understand that you've been chosen for a greater calling, but I'm not asking for forever,'' she whispered, her heart in her eyes.

He grabbed her hands in his. ''Don't, Irish. Don't tempt me. If there's one person on this planet I don't want to hurt it's you. It will be easier if we part as confidants and friends, for I have so few of them in my isolated world. I'd like to know there's one place on earth I can come, every now and then, where I can be accepted for myself. Here I know I'm not judged by my skills of tracking and handling an assortment of weapons, nor by my hopeless crusade to save a vanquished nation that sees me as the savior I can never be, no matter how hard I try. I need this haven more than you know.''

It was at that exact moment—while she was staring at him, feeling his torment as if it were her own, hearing the intensity of his voice, discovering his remarkable code of honor—that Tara knew without a doubt she was hopelessly, deeply in love with this man. She also knew that he desired her, even while he felt honor bound to protect her from himself and from any unintentional pain he might cause her. In return, she felt as fiercely protective of him as she did of the children.

Tara admired his integrity, his abilities. She respected what he believed in, fought for. She was attracted to his dashing good looks, his powerful physique, but something in his heart and soul called out to her as well. She loved him for the kind of man he was, because being with him filled an empty space she hadn't realized existed until she met and fell in love with him. She wanted to communicate her affection but didn't know how. All she could do was fling her arms around his neck and hug him for as long as he would allow it, savoring the enticing feel of him.

''Ah, Irish, you make this so damned hard,'' he murmured against her neck as he crushed her to him in a fierce embrace.

''You aren't making this easy on me, either, blast you,'' she replied as she nuzzled against him, absorbing his scent, drawing from his strength.

John slid his hand over the curve of her hip, chuckled softly, then shook his head. ''And here I thought Paradise Valley was as close to heaven as a man like me could ever get. Turns out this place is pure heaven and hell in one. Irish, if you don't back off, and be quick about it,

I'll end up doing something I'll regret later. Then I'll be suffering every torment of the eternal damned for caving in to temptation.''

At his request, she retreated, but her arms felt empty without him. She glanced up when she heard a rumble of thunder and saw dark clouds piling up on the western horizon. There was a scent of rain in the night air, a cool wind rushing down from the stone precipices around the canyon.

John grabbed her hand and hauled her to her feet. ''Better show me where you want the pasture fence before the sky opens. One good thing will come of the rain,'' he said as he hustled her alongside him, forcing her to take two steps to his one. ''Digging postholes will be easier.''

Tara gestured toward the towering rock walls that surrounded an area of plush grass. ''This spot won't require much fencing to contain the horses. The small spring trickling from the ledge will provide water. A small sheep pen can be built adjacent to this pasture, too.''

He nodded approvingly. ''Wise choice, Irish. That's exactly where I'd graze the livestock.''

Lightning flickered in the gathering night, then thunder crashed overhead. Tara broke into a run, doubting they'd reach the cabin before the storm descended to drench them. She noted there was still a slight hitch in John's gait as he sprinted beside her, but it barely slowed him down.

Tara thought they were going to make it to shelter in the nick of time, after all. But when they were fifty yards from the house, raindrops hammered down like drumming fingers. Tara was soaked in the time it took to draw a breath. So was John, she noticed as her gaze drifted over the garments that now clung to his muscular body like a second skin.

Odd, she mused, how even cold rain couldn't chill the arousing warmth of hopeless fascination that channeled through her body and her heart. Nothing could prevent her from wanting John Wolfe with every part of her being.

Well, she amended as she leaped headlong onto the porch, she supposed dying could get it done—but not much else.

In the upstairs loft, the children were stacked up on the bed in front of the window like a human pyramid—larger bodies on the bottom and smaller ones on top. They had been keeping watch for a good half hour, awaiting Tara and John's return.

"Confound it," Maureen muttered in disappointment. "They aren't even holding hands."

"Maybe they wanted to hold hands but the downpour forced them to make a mad dash home," Derek said encouragingly. "They could've been kissing before the storm hit."

"Blast this weather," Samuel grumbled, then shifted beneath the weight pressing him down. "We'll have to come up with a better scheme."

"I can't think of nothin' else that might work," Flora mumbled as her bony elbow gouged Calvin's shoulder blades.

"Hold still, runt," Derek ordered. "You're about to squash us and everybody is shifting on top of me. I can barely breathe."

"I don't like storms," Flora complained. "They make me all jittery."

"Me, too," Maureen muttered quietly.

"Don't either of you go running into Tara's room tonight, like you usually do when the wind wails," Samuel cautioned.

"We don't," Flora insisted all too quickly.

"Yeah, you do," Derek contradicted. "We heard you scurrying off the last time it stormed, while John was using Tara's room. But don't you dare go running scared tonight. We gave the impression that we were tired enough to sleep through a cyclone. Don't make liars out of us, okay?''

"Okay," Flora murmured as she rolled off the pyramid. "So, can I sleep with you, Samuel?"

When Derek snickered, Samuel nudged him in the ribs. "You clam up. If the runt is scared, she can sleep with us. And Maureen? If you're feeling jittery, too, you can tuck in with Calvin."

Derek peered curiously at Maureen. "Say, how come you're thirteen and you're still scared of storms?"

She looked the other way. "Just am."

"Leave her alone, Derek. She doesn't badger you because you have a powerful fear of snakes, does she?" Samuel asked.

While the rain beat down in torrents, the children settled into bed.

"If anybody has trouble sleeping, just lie there and figure out how we're going to get John to ask Tara to marry him," Samuel said quietly. "We'll compare ideas during morning chores."

While the children were formulating and discarding various schemes, Tara was sitting cross-legged on her bed, toweling her hair, listening to the crackle of lightning and claps of thunder.

John's words kept tumbling around in her mind, filling her with a sense of relief and satisfaction. Knowing he did care about her and that he was fighting the attraction because he didn't foresee a long-term future for them warred with her philosophy of taking each day as it came. She had learned to live in the moment, one day at a time.

Only recently, after settling in the valley, had she held enough hope to look into the future. She'd accepted responsibility for the children and she wanted to provide the security of a home and the close-knit affection of a family. She'd made personal sacrifices more times than she could count. Was it selfish of her to want to explore the intimate bond between a man and a woman? Was it wrong to long for the pleasure she'd experienced that night in John's arms? Should she tell him that she didn't expect more than he could give, that she wasn't asking for promises or commitment?

Tara rose from her bed to pace restlessly, serenaded by the storm which had passed overhead and then rumbled on off to the east. Lifting the window, she inhaled the purifying scent of rain, felt the damp breeze skim her skin like an invisible caress.

She ached for something she didn't fully understand, ached with a compelling desire that longed to be explored and fulfilled. She was lonely for John's companionship, especially when she knew their days were numbered. She wanted to experience that heady feeling of heightened awareness that consumed her when she was with him. He made her feel alive, feminine. The responsibility she'd undertaken didn't seem so overwhelming, the chores so tedious when he was around. She simply felt differently, looked at life differently when he was here.

What was her life going to be like when he left? Would she regret that she'd never expressed her love for him? Would she regret that she'd bypassed a few stolen moments of being held in his arms? Which would be worse? she asked herself as she stared into the night. To forever wonder what she'd missed, or to actually know the intimate pleasures and be tormented by what would never be again, once John rode out of her life?

Tara smiled sadly as she stared heavenward, watching the clouds part and the stars wink down at her. She'd been wishing upon stars since she was a child, wanting more from life than she'd received, wanting to matter to someone, to be loved and needed. Now she had all those things, yet something was still missing, and the man who held the key to her secret fantasy lay asleep in the barn. He was a good, noble and honorable man, despite the world of violence and turmoil where he resided.

Her lonely soul called out to him across the distance that separated them. Tara wondered if he could feel this nearly unbearable wanting that consumed her, wondered if he could hear her calling silently to him in the night.

John flounced restlessly on his pallet in the hayloft. He should be sleeping, because he'd mentally listed a dozen tasks he wanted to undertake the following day. But thoughts and visions of that green-eyed elf kept dancing in his head. This mental tug-of-war was frustrating the living hell out of him. He told himself to stay put, not to yield to the reckless urgings of his body, not to enjoy the pleasures he and Tara could offer each other. Resolutely, he reminded himself that he'd held out this long without succumbing to this constant need for Tara. He reassured himself that he could endure.

One more week of strenuous chores would be all the rehabilitation he needed before he resumed his search for Raven and the ruthless renegades that terrorized the territory. When he returned to his life outside the canyon… John grimaced, then rolled to his side and stared out the open loft window. When he left Tara, the simple joys and pleasures he'd discovered would be beyond his reach. Maybe he'd reward himself for his hellish job by stopping by every now and then to check on Tara and the children. He'd surprise them with gifts, make repairs and improvements, give Tara some time to herself—and feast his hungry eyes on his forbidden fantasy.

John rolled to his left side to stare at the wall. One week of heaven in Paradise Valley left, he reminded himself. Yet it wasn't exactly heaven when he wanted Tara like hell blazing. Just the prospect of holding her in his arms was enough to make his body clench and harden.

"Damn it," he muttered in frustration. He needed another cold bath in the spring, because that dousing of rain just wasn't cutting it tonight.

John climbed from his pallet, then swore ripely when he konked his head on the rafter. Well, maybe that was a good thing. Maybe a smack on the head would knock some sense into him, because after tonight, all the reasons he had listed why he *shouldn't* take advantage of a beautiful woman who mattered to him as no other female ever had didn't seem to amount to a hill of mesquite beans.

Tara wasn't as skilled at hiding her emotions as John was. He'd had years of practice *not* reacting, and his instincts were sharp enough to sense the answering need in her when she stared too long at him. So why was he being so damned noble? Because, damn it, he *felt* noble where she was concerned. She brought out the best in him, while setting fire to every masculine need he possessed, plus some he'd never encountered before she'd come along and turned his body into a raging inferno.

Frustrated as hell, John snatched up his breeches and stabbed one leg, then the other into the garment. He desperately needed a cold bath, or at the very least, a long walk in the cool night air. He descended the ladder and headed for the barn door, feeling his way along the stalls.

He'd swing by the back of the cabin, just to make sure Tara was asleep. He'd stare at her for a few minutes and imagine what it could be like between them if he wasn't who he was and didn't have the plight of the Apache riding on his shoulders—not to mention the problem of chasing down his bitter adopted brother, who was on the rampage.

Lost in thought, John veered around the corner of the barn and slammed headlong into another body. Self-preservation prompted him to thrust out an arm to ward off the anticipated attack. He realized a second too late that it was Tara. His flying elbow caught her in the solar plexus. She moaned, dragged air into her lungs and staggered clumsily. His hand shot out to steady her before she plunked into a mud puddle.

"What the hell are you doing out here, Irish?" he demanded.

She couldn't reply. She was still having trouble breathing. John whacked her between the shoulder blades.

"Is something wrong with one of the kids?" he asked in concern.

She shook her head. Tangled red-gold strands cascaded over her shoulders and back. She wheezed some more, then tried to clear her throat.

"Something wrong with *you* then?" he quizzed her. When she bobbed her head, he frowned worriedly. "What's wrong, Irish?"

When she could finally speak she lifted her face to his quizzical stare and said, "I'm tired of wanting you and doing nothing about it. The ache just gets progressively worse. I've thought it over and decided I'd prefer to love you and watch you ride away than never know the pleasure of desire at all."

Despite the darkness, broken only by a sliver of moon and a smattering of stars, he could see her eyes flickering with unmistakable need. It was like staring at his own tormented reflection. And suddenly, it was John who for the life of him could not seem to draw breath.

Chapter Ten

"Irish—"

Whatever halfhearted protest John tried to formulate died the moment her dewy, soft lips skimmed over his. The impact of her lush body gliding against his had the same potent effect being shot had. Quite simply, her kiss blew him away.

Instincts as old as time immemorial swamped him. Before he realized it he was dragging her tightly to him, holding on to her for dear life. His answering kiss wasn't chaste or the least bit gentle. It was like a blazing fire that consumed all in its path. He plundered her mouth, wondering if he'd alarm her with his hungry need, but she seemed as greedy and impatient as he was. The voice of reason tried to intrude, but when her roaming hands glided down the taut muscles of his back to settle on his hips, desire became so powerfully intense that reason got burned to a crisp.

"John, I want you. Teach me to please you," she whispered when he finally let her come up for air.

He stared down into her enchanting face, searching the depths of her gaze. "You're sure? You know I—"

Her fingertips grazed his lips; her gaze locked with his. "Tonight is separate from our lives, from responsibilities and obligations," she murmured. "It's separate from our past and future. All I ask is for you to make love to me now, in our private space out of time. I ask nothing more."

John, who was a damn sight more worldly-wise than she, couldn't come up with even one sensible reason to deny her, to deny himself this moment out of time in Paradise Valley. When she reached up on tiptoe and kissed him again, the world spun away and there was nothing left in his universe except Tara and his smoldering need for her.

His knees threatened to buckle beneath him. His heart slammed into his tender ribs—and stuck there. "Ah, Irish," he whispered unevenly. "I can deny you no more than I can halt the sunrise, and I'm damned tired of denying how much I want you."

When she smiled up at him, his legs wobbled again. Determined to make it into the barn loft before he collapsed, John clutched her hand and led the way to the ladder. As they ascended into the loft, he kept telling himself he was being visited by a lifelike dream, that Tara hadn't really come to him, asking for nothing more than a night of passion.

He wished he could make love to her on a feather bed rather than a straw pallet. He wanted this night to be everything she could possibly imagine it could be. Determined to fulfill her every expectation and fantasy, John vowed that he'd touch her with all that was tender and gentle.

His thoughts scattered like buckshot when she stood uncertainly in front of him, wearing that flimsy gown, her hair drifting over her shoulders like a silky golden cape. He suspected her only experience with lust had come at the hands of that lecherous Texas rancher and the drunken prospectors who accosted her in town. Yet she had the courage to seek him out, unsure what to expect from him.

John was humbled by her unwavering faith in him, by her unfaltering belief that he wouldn't hurt her as she'd been hurt before.

He moved closer, vowing to teach her passion tempered with exquisite tenderness. It'd likely kill him to proceed at an unhurried pace, since he was accustomed to nothing more than quick physical release in the arms of an experienced woman. Certainly, there'd never been emotional attachments before.

There definitely was *now,* much as he'd battled to prevent it.

Suddenly John felt ill-prepared for this unprecedented encounter. Violence he understood all too well. Gentleness was unfamiliar. He was stunned to realize he had almost as much to learn about lovemaking as Tara did.

Well, damn. If that didn't beat all!

"John, are you laughing at me?" she asked when he smiled in ironic amusement.

"No, Irish, I was just thinking that you probably should've waited until a better tutor came along. I'm not what you'd call a ladies' man."

"No?" She grinned impishly.

"Not even close." He grinned back at her, and the apprehensive tension streaming through him began to subside.

When her gaze drifted to his lips, and she looked as if she was starving for another taste of him, John lost all interest in conversation. He took her by the hand and drew her down to the pallet. She snuggled trustingly against him, and the innocent movement of her body gliding against his was like an erotic caress. Sweet mercy, this woman was more sensuous than she imagined herself to be. She'd be a devastating seductress if she discovered how much power she wielded over him.

John tipped Tara's head back and found himself tumbling into the depths of her cedar-green eyes. What he'd previously predicted would require conscious effort suddenly became amazingly simple. He didn't have to caution himself to be gentle with her; it just came naturally when he reached out to touch her. He slipped his hand beneath her gown, marveling at the silky softness of her skin beneath his questing fingertips. Her sudden intake of breath, her ragged sigh of pleasure and the sensual promise in her gaze were all the encouragement he needed. He angled his head to take her mouth beneath his, and traced her parted lips with the tip of his tongue. He nipped at her bottom lip, tugging at it in the same way the erotic sensations were tugging at his male body.

He lifted his hand to graze her beaded nipple, and then he rolled the delicate bud between thumb and forefinger. Her body arched upward, testifying to the pleasure he was bestowing on her. Intrigued by her responses to him, he drew the skimpy gown upward, then lowered his head to suckle her breast.

"John...?" she gasped, then melted in his arms.

"Yes?" He smiled against her scented skin, then took the dusky crown into his mouth, flicking it with his tongue, kneading her plump breast with a gentle hand. She writhed and squirmed and made such unbelievably sweet sounds that he smiled all over again.

"What are you doing to me?" she asked dazedly, then moaned when he turned the same dedicated attention on her other breast.

"Whatever pleases me," he murmured. "And everything that pleases you, Irish. You are pleased, aren't you?"

Her response was another breathless moan that inspired him to summon more fascinating sounds of pleasure from her. He wanted her pliant in his arms before the inevitable moment when he hurt her unintentionally. Determinedly, he vowed to bring her to the epitome of mindless desire before he glided over her luscious body to take intimate possession.

While he focused his kisses on the creamy mounds of her breasts, his hand swirled over her flat stomach. When his hand splayed over her inner thigh, he could feel the heat of her desire beckoning him closer. Yet he only stroked her sensitive flesh, again and again. From breast to knee he caressed her, teased her, aroused her until she arched helplessly toward his hand, all but begging him to touch her as intimately as he had that night he'd allowed ardent desire to carry him away for a few mindless, incredible moments.

He tested her with his fingertip and felt the liquid fire of her response burning him like a brand. But it wasn't enough to appease this greedy need that roiled through him. He wanted to taste her need for him, to taste every satiny inch of her, to know her by touch, by heart, by the very essence of what she was and what she'd come to mean to him.

He shifted beside her, still holding his palm against her, then nudged her legs apart with gentle pressure from his elbow. His lips drifted over her thigh as he teased the hidden secrets of her body with deliberate, unhurried strokes of his thumb and fingertip. He explored her, aroused her until she was chanting his name with every gasp of breath.

When his tongue glided over her velvety heat, daring to touch her more intimately than he'd touched any other woman, he felt the sweet pressure of her feminine body contracting around his lips and fingertips. The wonderment of her uninhibited response, the taste of her passion for him, unleashed the ravenous desire he was trying so hard to hold in check. His body tightened with a pulsating pleasure that strung every nerve and muscle as taut as barbed wire. He was burning with her, vibrating with need, aching to become the white-hot flame that blazed inside her.

"John...please!" she gasped, clutching at him in frantic desperation. "I want you...now!"

He knew that as well as she did, but the realization that he could touch her so intimately with lips and fingertips and bring her to lofty heights of passion beguiled him. He loved looking at her exquisitely formed body, loved watching her writhe and coil when waves of ecstasy crested over her. He felt empowered when she reached for him in urgent need.

When she half collapsed, breathing heavily, struggling to recover from the wild crescendo of desire, he began his amorous assault on her body all over again. With each flick of his tongue, the gliding motions of his lips and the penetrating strokes of his fingertips, he could feel her body convulsing, bathing him with her hot, sultry responses. John steeled himself against the nearly overwhelming need to take possession of her quivering body.

"You're killing me," she rasped, clawing urgently at his shoulder. "John, do something to make the empty ache go away!"

He came to his knees, cursing the fact that he'd been so utterly fascinated by the pleasure he received from arousing her that he hadn't doffed his breeches. Tara was staring at him as if she wanted to gobble him alive, and he couldn't wrest himself free of these blasted breeches fast enough to satisfy either of them. When she reached down to help him shed his clothes, he swore he was about to explode prematurely. He surged above her and he buried himself inside her with one frantic thrust. Her hiss of pain, the tension suddenly holding her rigid, made him curse his hungry impatience.

"I'm sorry, Irish. I intended to tell you this might hurt a bit, but I'm afraid I got sidetracked," he whispered huskily.

He held himself perfectly still, letting her adjust to the unfamiliar pressure, knowing for certain that the lecherous Texas rancher hadn't ravaged her completely—thank goodness. And for every terror she'd suffered at that bastard's cruel hands, he'd replace that memory with one of exquisite rapture and devoted tenderness. Slowly, he withdrew, denying his male body the satisfaction it craved. Ever so gently, he glided forward again, filling her, teaching her the cadence of passion.

She moved with him, matching his desire with each penetrating thrust, until need, intense and demanding, overtook them and they moved together in perfect rhythm. The gentleness John had vowed to maintain for Tara's sake abandoned him. He plunged into her, retreated, then drove hard and fast and deep again. His hands clamped around her hips, rocking her against him as the breathtaking throes of passion consumed him. Her breathing hitched. Her nails scored his shoulders, marking him as hers for life everlasting.

And then a tidal wave of pleasure plummeted him into the dizzying depths of desire. He gathered her in his crushing embrace when unmatched pleasure vibrated through him, leaving no part of his body, mind and soul untouched or uneffected by their tempestuous union.

Suddenly, John found himself wondering just what the hell he'd been doing all his life, in the arms of nameless, faceless women from his past. Whatever it was, it was nothing compared to making wild, sweet love to Tara. She unchained emotions inside him that he hadn't been aware existed. Indescribable sensations tumbled forth like a wellspring, leaving him at utter peace with himself for the first time in his memory. It was as if he'd been reborn, reinvented, recreated, and he was absolutely certain he was never going to be the same again. Making love to Tara was a milestone, a reckoning, an epiphany.

His breath ragged, his body spent, John held Tara close

to his heart. Even when she squirmed beneath his heavy weight, and he realized he was probably squashing her, he was hesitant to let go and risk losing the incredible closeness and intimacy of this moment that joined his soul to hers.

Ah, walking away would be a thousand times more difficult now than before he'd made love to her. He wondered, having known her purity and sweetness, if he'd lose that razor-sharp edge that kept him alive in his dangerous profession. If so, he'd be a dead man walking.

"John?" Tara whispered as she trailed her index finger over the muscled curve of his shoulder and the contours of his back.

"Mmm." It was the best he could do at the moment, for speaking demanded an astonishing amount of effort.

"I was wondering…" Her voice trailed off.

"What, Irish?" he managed to murmur—just barely.

"If we only have this one night together, would you mind terribly if we did that again?"

He wanted to laugh—or scream; he wasn't sure which. He was still drifting on a sea of pleasure and contentment, and he wasn't certain he had the strength to move, much less repeat such an incredible performance.

She must've taken his silence for rejection, because she went very still, her self-confidence wavering. There wasn't a chance in hell that he'd allow her to think she hadn't satisfied him in every way imaginable, but he needed a moment to recover from the most heart-shattering, mind-boggling, devastating interlude of passion he'd ever experienced in his life.

"Men, er, need a little time to recover," he told her awkwardly.

"They do? How much time?"

Her hand glided lightly up and down his rib cage. When her adventurous caress circled around to the small of his back, then swept over his buttocks, desire, like a phoenix rising from its ashes, burgeoned inside him. Amazing! Her tender touch worked magic on his spent body.

John levered onto his elbows to stare into her pixielike face. She must've felt him grow hard inside her because a purely feminine look of triumph blossomed there. Grinning devilishly, he ground his hips into hers. Her eyes shot open wide, then she broke into an elfish grin that turned his overworked heart wrong side out.

"Know something, Irish?" he growled huskily.

"What's that, Marshal?"

"I don't think a team of wild horses could drag me away and prevent me from having you again."

"*Having* me?" she repeated, arching a golden brow.

Uh-oh, he thought. Careless phrasing on his part. Before he could formulate an apology, her hand shifted to graze and stroke his thigh.

"I was thinking of *having you* this time. You were going to teach me to please you, remember? We haven't gotten to that part yet."

John wasn't sure he could survive having those deft little fingers roaming all over him. Plus, it'd be impossible for a man to offer instruction when he wasn't even breathing. He knew Tara could take his breath away, because he'd narrowly escaped a couple of heart seizures while *having her*.

She eased sideways, forcing him to settle beside her. When she curled beside him, her tangled mane of flaming gold hair teased his shoulder, his cheek. She reached over to draw figure eights on his chest with her fingertips, then skimmed her lips over his hair-roughened flesh.

"Does that arouse you?" she asked.

Her hand skimmed across the sensitive flesh of his belly. Muscles leaped, then contracted. Desire coiled tightly inside him. "Definitely." Was that his voice? He sounded like a bleating lamb.

"And this?" Her fingertips skied over his hip, then traced the muscular column of his thigh. She avoided touching that place where he was most a man, but she ventured close enough to double his heartbeat, alter his breath and arouse him by tormentingly tender degrees.

"Irish, I—" His voice dried up when her hand curled around his rigid flesh. Erotic sensations rippled through him and a groan rattled in his chest.

He'd never allowed a woman such intimate liberties, and he was eternally thankful for that. Together he and Tara had explored unfamiliar, uncharted dimensions of passion. It was as if he'd known instinctively when the right moment was upon him, when the right woman, capable of touching every emotion he possessed, had arrived in his life. They were making unforgettable, unrivaled memories together...and if she didn't stop what she was doing to him, John wasn't sure if he could restrain the maelstrom of sensations that engulfed him and left him shaking with desperation.

"Irish, no!" he muttered between clenched teeth.

"One mustn't stifle a student who is willing and eager to learn," she murmured.

Over and over again she tested his willpower, stroked him, fondled him and came dangerously close to driving him over the brink into mindless oblivion.

"No more..." he groaned as he roped his arm around her waist, rolled sideways and imprisoned her beneath him. "I swear, Irish," he wheezed. "You're going to pay dearly for driving me absolutely crazy with pleasure."

When she smiled impishly, his heart stuttered and stalled. She moved provocatively beneath him. "I wanted you to want me as much as I want you."

"I've wanted you too much since I first laid eyes on you. That's been my problem, woman. Now, knowing what I've denied myself, I can't seem to get enough of you to compensate for these weeks of maddening need."

He lifted her to him, opened her to his gentle invasion, then filled her with his masculine essence and felt himself become her helpless possession. Her body caressed him intimately, welcomed him, and he lost himself in her for another splendorous moment out of time. They became one living, breathing entity—all of what she was and the best of what he could be when he was with her.

Consumed by the fiery heat of passion, they burned alive in one another's arms. He clung to her as she clung to him, shaken to the very core by the shattering force of their combined needs. He heard her cry out his name, felt her spasms of pleasure caressing him deeply. Suddenly, he was catapulting into a world of incredible ecstasy with Tara in his arms. He held her to him as shuddering release hammered at him, again and again.

This time, John couldn't navigate his way back from dreamlike contentment to consciousness. He drifted off to sleep with Tara tucked possessively in his embrace. In one night he'd compensated for all those years he'd slept lightly, constantly on guard against approaching danger. He was tired of the incessant watchfulness, of the continual alertness, tired of facing constant battle, suffering the effects of excessive heat and bitter-cold temperatures.

Here was the quiet, serene life that had eluded him. Now that he'd discovered tranquility in its purest, sweetest form, he slept like a child in the cradle of Tara's body, oblivious to the sounds of the horses shifting in their stalls in the barn below. For once, he knew the meaning of absolute peace, and he floated contentedly on his very own cloud in paradise.

Tara awoke to the warble of birds and streams of sunlight slanting through the loft window. When she shifted slightly, she felt an unfamiliar twinge between her legs. Without opening her eyes, she smiled, recalling the reason for her discomfort. Well, it hadn't been discomfort at the

time, she recollected. It had been the wildest, sweetest
kind of pleasure she'd ever known. She couldn't believe
her total abandon when John had touched her so familiarly, or her brazen eagerness to know him just as intimately. The thought of what he'd done to her, what she'd
done to him, what they'd done together, made her face
flame with heat.

"You must be awake, or lost in vivid dreams, for your
cheeks to be such a fascinating shade of pink, Irish."

At the sound of his husky voice, Tara snapped her eyes
open to see John's handsome face hovering above hers.
A grin quirked his lips as he raised a thick brow, then let
his gaze roam boldly over her naked body. She felt positively decadent for allowing him to look his fill. Though
she blushed profusely, she made no attempt to cover herself. After all, what would be the point of modesty when
he'd had those skillful hands and sensuous lips all over
her and she'd savored every delirious moment of it?

"Morning," she murmured as she reached up to trace
his tanned features. "Morning!" Tara bolted upright
when she realized she was still lying naked in the hayloft
with John. The children would be up and about very
soon—if they weren't already. If she didn't hightail it to
the cabin and crawl through her bedroom window, she'd
be discovered!

John chuckled as she frantically cast about to locate
her gown and slippers. "Looking for this, Irish?" He held
the gown on his crooked finger.

Tara blushed again. "Give me that, you scoundrel. I
have to return to the cabin before the children see me!"

"Oh hell!" John's teasing smile evaporated in a heartbeat. Hurriedly he tossed her the gown, then groped to
find her slippers. "I still haven't had that chat with the
kids about the birds and bees. If—"

"Zohn Whoof? Are you up there?" Flora shouted from
below.

"Are you ready to build the fence?" Derek called out.

Tara's wild-eyed gaze flew to John, who stared at her in horror. His expression would've been comical, if not for the threat of being discovered by the passel of children milling around at the bottom of the ladder.

"Have you seen Tara?" Maureen hollered.

"Can we come up?" Calvin asked.

John hitched his thumb toward the small mound of straw in the corner, indicating that Tara, still stark naked, should grab her gown and hide. He snatched up his breeches, thrust out his leg, then scowled when he ended up putting the garment on backward and had to begin again.

"Give me a minute," John requested. "I'm not fully dressed."

Tara, clutching the gown to her bare breasts, darted toward the corner. She barely had time to hide before she heard feet clomping on the ladder. The children hadn't waited a full minute before they invaded the loft.

John was still buttoning his shirt when the troop of children assembled in front of him. He didn't dare glance toward the mound of hay, for fear he'd draw the children's attention to Tara's hiding place. Damn, that was close!

"You're up early," he said lamely.

"We went to bed early," Samuel reminded him. "We wanted you to know we're ready to work on the new fence, soon as we feed the livestock."

Good, maybe they'd go away and let him sneak Tara from the loft. "Sounds fine. I'll meet you in the cabin for breakfast."

"We ate already," Flora informed him. "But we can't find Tara."

Although the children looked concerned, John shrugged nonchalantly. "Maybe she walked down to one of the springs for a morning bath."

The children accepted his explanation and then closed ranks around him. John sat down to pull on his boots, baffled by the serious expressions on all five faces.

"We want to talk about the bees," Flora said as she plunked down on his lap. "You said you'd tell us, Zohn Whoof, but you haven't yet."

John felt heat rising in his cheeks. He gave Flora a fond hug, then set her on her feet. "I remember."

No way was he going to get into *that* while Tara was cowering in the corner! The longer the children remained in the loft, the more likely she would be discovered. And damn it, he'd hoped that by postponing that embarrassing discussion the children would forget about it. Fat chance of that. These little scamps had minds like steel traps.

"We'll have that talk while we're working on the fence," he promised.

"You're sure?" Calvin demanded, intent on pinning him down.

"Yeah, uh, for sure," he said, dreading the most awkward conversation of his life.

Outlaws he could handle unafraid, because he'd spent most of his life training for the necessary skills of battle. But this! John vowed he'd get his thoughts together while gathering supplies and tools. This discussion was going to require plenty of forethought and tact.

Satisfied that they wouldn't be put off again, the children wheeled around and descended the ladder to tend to their chores. When they were out of sight, Tara rose from her hiding place, smiling wickedly.

"Well, shoot, and here I was, ready to hear your detailed lecture on lovemaking, Professor Wolfe."

John glared storm clouds at her sunny smile. "This isn't the least bit funny, damn it."

She patted his arm. "There, there, Professor, I'm sure you'll find the right words. I only wish I could be there for your speech. But then, I'm having a quiet bath at the springs, aren't I?''

John playfully swatted her backside as she sauntered past him. "You're no help, woman, and you should be thanking me for saving you from embarrassment."

Tara pivoted, a bewitching smile on her face, then flung her arms around his neck. "Consider yourself properly thanked."

When she commenced kissing him, John momentarily forgot everything but the tantalizing scent of her, the addictive taste of her and the arousing feel of her body molded familiarly against his. He'd thought—sincerely hoped, actually—that after the splendorous night of passion they'd shared he would be content.

Apparently not. At the first touch of her lips, his body reacted instantaneously, intensely. He wondered if he'd ever get enough of this woman—and seriously doubted it because he felt as if he'd suddenly acquired an obsession that could only be appeased by constantly making love to her. That was a dangerous distraction he could ill afford when he left this canyon, John reminded himself. Furthermore, with five children underfoot, there was always the potential risk of an interrupted tryst.

This morning's sudden intrusion was evidence of that.

Tara withdrew, looking as disoriented by their kiss as he felt. She glanced this way and that, and then peered up at him with those luminous eyes that always made him go weak in the knees.

"How am I going to get out of here without being seen?"

Good question. He wished he had a sensible answer to go with it. Unfortunately, it was going to take a moment for his rioting body to calm down so he could think straight. He glanced thoughtfully toward the loft window, then focused on the ladder.

"I'll help the children with their chores to hurry them

along, then we'll hike off to the new pasture," he told her. "You can keep a lookout at the loft window. When we're gone, you can hotfoot it to the house. But I would advise you to show up to help in a half hour so the children don't get concerned or suspicious."

"Brilliant plan, Professor." She flounced down on the pallet, grinned elfishly, then struck a seductive pose that did not escape his notice.

John forced himself to walk away without looking back, because seeing her lying there evoked vivid memories of the passion they'd shared—

He missed a step on the ladder and nearly tumbled from the loft. Damn, he needed to pull himself together—in a hurry.

When John strode off, he had the unshakable feeling that spending future nights on his pallet would be sheer hell, because he'd envision Tara lying beside him. He was doomed to getting no sleep whatsoever. Not that he'd gotten much anyway, he reminded himself. Before, he'd lain awake, wondering what he was missing.

Now he knew. Oh, how he knew!

Chapter Eleven

John wasted no time in spouting orders and instructions for fence building. He set the older boys to work on digging postholes, and then helped the girls roll out barbed wire. All the while, John marveled at the children's work ethic. Tara had taught them responsibility, and not even the younger children hesitated to do whatever they could to help.

This was indeed a family, even if they weren't blood related. But then, John reminded himself, children were adaptable. He'd been a little older than Calvin when he'd entered the Apache camp. Once there, he'd been given the purification ritual of a bath. His white man's clothes had been burned, and then he was dressed as one of the tribe.

True, he'd been ridiculed by the other children, Raven included, but he'd worked hard, learned the Indian way and been accepted. His height, his muscular build and athleticism were praised and put to use. His ability to speak, read and write English made him an asset when dealing with whites. John had come to consider himself Apache, to think like an Apache, to speak the Apache dialect like a native.

And then the old ways changed. The decreasing population of Apache and increasing number of white invaders forced the tribe to subject themselves to the demands of the conquering hordes.

John had escaped to become white again, while Geronimo, Raven and others like them resisted and continued to battle the odds, just to enjoy a small sense of freedom and to express their resentment. It tormented John no end that he couldn't do more to ease the plight of the people who'd raised and trained him. Every time he remembered the manipulative treachery whites used to cheat and steal from the Indians, he was incensed.

"Zohn Whoof, when are we gonna hear about those bees?" Flora asked as she worked diligently at his side.

John sighed audibly. The embarrassing moment was upon him. He could only hope the speech he'd rehearsed earlier would appease the children's curiosity and limit their questions, but he held little hope of that. These children lived to ask questions. Especially little Flora, whose method of conversation was incessant questions.

Apparently he'd lingered too long in thought because Flora nearly burst as she exclaimed, "Maureen said babies come from kissing. Samuel says they come from sleeping in the same bed for a long time. Which is it?"

John inwardly groaned when five pair of inquisitive eyes targeted him. Hell! This had to be worse than facing a firing squad. "Neither one is true," he answered, rolling out the wire with fiendish haste. "Kissing and hugging and sleeping in the same bed are grown-up ways of expressing affection for each other with something besides words." He glanced swiftly at Flora. "I gave you a hug this morning in the loft, half-pint. That hug was my way of saying I like you, without coming out and saying it."

So far so good, even if Flora's blunt question had shot his rehearsed lecture all to hell. He was stumbling through the explanation now and managing to dodge embarrassing pitfalls. For how long he didn't know. He prayed none of the kids would ask him to get too specific. Otherwise, he was headed for disaster.

"Kissing is pretty much the same thing," he continued, then gestured for Samuel to drop the bois d'arc post into the hole.

"So...that kiss Tara gave you that day at the table was her way of saying she likes you." Calvin spoke up as he kicked dirt around the post, then stamped it with his boot heel.

"Exactly," John replied.

"But you didn't kiss her back," Derek remarked. "Does that mean you don't like her? How can you *not?* She's the nicest, prettiest woman I know."

"Of course I like her. She's also the nicest, prettiest woman *I* know."

"Then how come you don't haul off and kiss her every once in a while?" Samuel demanded.

"Yeah, how come?" the other children chorused.

"I don't know, maybe I was afraid the lot of you would be protective of her and you wouldn't approve of my liking her."

"Not approve?" Derek hooted. "We were trying to—" He snapped his jaw shut. "We like you, too, John."

"Glad to hear it." He grinned wryly, knowing Derek had caught himself before he exposed the fact that the children had been matchmaking. "But there will be no kissing among us men, you understand. A hug occasionally, a handshake, but I draw the line at that."

The children giggled, and John enjoyed a moment's reprieve from the barrage of awkward and embarrassing questions.

"So...what do bees have to do with making babies?"

John winced. Flora—the child with the one-track mind—refused to allow him to get sidetracked. He should've known.

"Learning about birds and bees is just an expression," John replied, feeling the heat rise to his neck. "It's a tactful way of mentioning making babies or, er, making love without being blunt about saying it." He could feel his cheeks grow hotter beneath his tan.

He noticed work had screeched to a halt. Five upturned faces honed in on him. Ah, jeez, he couldn't remember a single word of his speech. Frantically, he scrambled to gather his wits.

"A man and woman who care deeply for each other, who intend to build a life together, communicate their love in a physical way."

"Like with kisses?" Maureen asked.

"Er...yes. Lots of kisses, lots of hugs," John said, willing his voice not to falter. "A man and woman prove their love by giving themselves to each other, um, physically and emotionally and spiritually."

"How does that work?" Calvin asked.

John felt the crimson blush working its way up to stain his hairline. "You know a man and woman are made differently."

Five heads bobbed.

John struggled to draw breath. Damn, facing down a gang of outlaws was easier than facing five inquisitive gazes. "Men and women are made to fit together as one in order to share their love and create another life that's an expression of the lifelong bond between them."

Derek stared straight at him. "Maybe some folks feel that way, but not *my* folks. They didn't want me."

Oh damn, thought John. He was facing five children who couldn't relate to the concept he'd explained because they'd been discarded, rejected and abandoned. "Sometimes things don't work out the proper way," he murmured as he set another post in place. "Sometimes people get caught up in the pleasure of loving and ignore the responsibility of a child. They are too selfish to accept the baby they create. In that case, we are better off somewhere else, with someone who truly cares about us.''

"Like Tara does," Flora stated.

"Like Tara," he confirmed. "She doesn't care how you came to be, doesn't care what circumstances made it impossible for you to remain with the parents who created you. She wants you for what you mean to her, because each of you is special to her. Someday you'll go out into the world and find someone you care deeply about. In turn, you'll create a child you'll be prepared to sacrifice for, provide for and commit to building a good life for. You'll know all those things that make a child happy by remembering how Tara treated and cared for you.''

"I'm told my parents had no choice in the matter," Calvin said quietly. "They died."

"I expect they're smiling down on you right now," John assured him. "I bet they're awfully glad Tara is here to love you as they wish they could."

"I wish you could marry Tara and be our papa," Flora declared.

John hunkered down, then drew Flora onto his knee. "I know you do, half-pint. But I left a job undone. I have a duty to fulfill. Nothing would make me happier than staying here with all of you, but I made a solemn promise I must keep. That's what honor and integrity are all about.''

Flora flung her arms around his neck and held on tight. "But I love you, Zohn Whoof! I want you to stay here and be my papa!"

John's heart twisted in his chest and a lump the size of Arizona Territory clogged his throat. He held little Flora to him and silently wished he could be two places at once. Actually, three would be even better. "I love you, too, squirt. Always will. So will your brothers and sisters."

"Will you come back to visit?" Samuel asked, willfully blinking back the tears swimming in his gray eyes.

"That's a promise," John told the children. "You're my family now."

They were, too. That was a fact. He had every intention of swinging by Paradise Valley to see the children...and Tara. He'd come bearing gifts. For certain, he wasn't doing anything with the stockpile of cash he kept in the bank at Prescott. The salary and rewards he collected from apprehending criminals wasn't of any use to him while he was on the trail. In fact, he could provide a nest egg for each child when he or she was ready to venture out into the world. That sudden inspiration gave him a feeling of satisfaction, of purpose.

"Yoo-hoo. Anybody around here want some lunch?"

John and the children wheeled around to see Tara, smiling brightly, carrying a basket in each hand.

"Where have you been all morning?' Maureen asked.

Tara shrugged lackadaisically. "Doing a little of this and that. I took a bath at one of the springs, then whipped up a hearty meal. Anyone hungry?"

The children dropped their tools and dashed toward her. Her curious gaze darted over their heads to focus on John. She smiled impishly at him and he grinned stupidly. He wondered if the children realized he'd been thoroughly appeased last night. It was probably written all over his face.

"John told us about the bees and birds," Calvin remarked as he dug into one of the reed baskets.

"Did he?" Tara managed to keep a straight face, but her eyes twinkled with wicked amusement.

John scowled at her. He never wanted to go through that again.

"Yeah, we know how it works," Flora added with all the worldly sophistication of a confident five-year-old. "Do you know?"

Tara darted John a conspiratorial glance. "I've learned a thing or two about it, yes."

John's face again bloomed with color. He lurched around to drop the remaining fence posts in the holes. Tara, as it turned out, had taught *him* a thing—or three— about the art of passion. For a while there, John wasn't sure who'd been the student and who'd been the instructor. If this inventive, passionate female learned much more, John wasn't sure he could survive it. She'd nearly been the death of him a couple of times last night.

Tara joined them after lunch to erect the fence for the horses. When the task was completed, Derek and Samuel dug postholes for the adjacent corral that would contain the sheep. With synchronized precision the children strung and secured the wire, then turned to John to inquire what they were going to do next.

"Time to practice survival tactics," he announced as he gathered up the tools and stacked them by the large mound of stones Tara had used previously to mark off the perimeter of the fence. "You're going to learn how to disappear into thin air."

Maureen frowned, bemused. "You're going to make us invisible? How do you do that?"

John winked playfully at her. "Old Apache trick. You rely on cunning and deception, especially when you're outnumbered. It's called going to ground."

Tara stared in astonishment as John dropped down on all fours in the tall grass. He wiggled one foot and then the other backward. He contorted his upper body into a ball, ducked his head, then wormed beneath the blades of grass so that he was lying *in* the grass, not on top of it. Likewise, he speared his arms outward and buried them under the thick clumps. Sure enough, he became invisible, especially since he was wearing brown clothing that matched the dirt beneath him.

The children were properly impressed, as was Tara. If ever trouble rode toward her, while going to and from town, she would know what to do to conceal herself. The same went for the children.

"Now it's your turn to try," John's disembodied voice announced. "Legs first, then head, shoulders and arms. Do it in slow motion to get the hang of it."

The children scattered to find thick grass clumps. John rose to his feet, keeping his back turned while the children made themselves invisible. Then he spun Tara around with him.

"We're going to try to find you when you're hidden," he called to them. "Most folks have a tendency to take a path through shorter grasses, which is why you bury yourself in the tall stuff. Even if Tara or I walk within inches of you, don't make a sound. Don't move, except to retract an arm or leg if we come too close to your hiding place."

Tara and John spun around, seeing nothing but pasture grass waving gently in the breeze. It was difficult to find five children sprawled somewhere ahead of them. She and John hiked forward, but the children didn't make a peep that called attention to their hiding places. When John praised their efforts, five heads and beaming faces appeared above the grass.

"Excellent job," he congratulated them. "Now we come to the tricky part. Let's say, for instance, that someone ventures so close to your hiding place that you're about to be stepped on or you want to take advantage of the element of surprise. You grab the nearest leg to trip a man up, then go directly for his weapon. He'll be too busy trying to catch his balance to react to your attack. But this," he said earnestly, "is a last-resort technique. It's best simply to let your enemy give up and go away."

Tara had to admit that when John instructed the children to hide a second time, she couldn't react quickly enough to keep her balance when she ventured too close to one of the warriors-in-training. The ground came up at her with alarming speed. Her nose was smashed in the dirt when Calvin jerked her foot out from under her and tossed her off balance.

She listened intently when John explained how to use the technique to attract wild game by tying a colorful strip of cloth to a nearby bush.

"Deer and antelope are attracted to the cloth flapping in the breeze," he told them. "At first the animals are wary, then curiosity gets the better of them. When they approach, the grass conceals your scent. You thrust your dagger upward to drop your game in its tracks without making a sound that might attract trouble."

Fascinated, Tara listened to John explain the clever skills of signaling with stones, which he claimed was better than smoke signals when you couldn't be certain if unwanted intruders were nearby. He showed the children how wind, rain and erosion smoothed off the top of rocks. By turning them upside down, leaving the rough, discolored side showing, he marked a discreet path that an untrained eye might overlook.

"Now then," he said, motioning the children toward a grove of cottonwood trees, "hide your eyes and count to one hundred."

"I can't count that far," Flora grumbled.

"Let Maureen count with you."

"Okay, but I won't be left out of this new game, will I?" Flora asked.

"Absolutely not, squirt. You'll probably be the best player of all because you're closer to the ground than the others and you can spot the stone signals easily. The others will be depending on you."

Tara smiled, impressed that John always seemed to know the right thing to say to make the children bream with pride and delight.

"Irish and I are going to leave you a trail so you can find us. Now go!"

The children dashed toward the trees, lickety-split.

"Don't be too obvious or turn stones that lie close together," he instructed Tara. "I'm hoping for a good quarter of an hour of privacy."

She elevated a brow. "What are we going to do with our spare time?"

He grinned rakishly and her heart thudded in response. She couldn't wait to get her hands on this remarkable man.

Leaving a trail of overturned stones, John led the way to one of the springs nestled beside a clump of willows. He abruptly swept Tara off her feet and devoured her with a kiss that made her toes curl.

After more than two weeks of restraint she reveled in her chance to express her affection freely, knowing it was well received. And she was not, she vowed fiercely, going to waste one moment of privacy with John, because she knew how precious their stolen moments were. Every second was a jewel in a golden crown of incomparable memories she'd savor in the lonely weeks and months to come. She loved him, and there was nothing she wanted more than to keep him as her own forever. But she wouldn't ask him to stay when she knew he had obligations elsewhere. She wouldn't ask him to take responsibility for her family. She'd ask for nothing more than the chance to live each glorious moment they had together to the fullest.

And so Tara offered her love in a steaming kiss and arousing caress, treasuring the feel of him, the scent of him, the taste of him. She noticed John was feeling the effects of desire as much as she was, because he thrust his hips hungrily against her, letting her feel the evidence of his passion.

"Damn, Irish," he breathed heavily against her ear, "if we get caught crawling all over each other by those overly inquisitive kids, I'll let *you* explain this time."

She gazed up at him in feigned innocence. "I thought you said the whole purpose of this rock hunt was to grant us privacy."

"Well, forget what I said. It was a bad idea. We don't have time for all the things I want to do to you. Besides, I just gave the children a lecture on being responsible when it comes to making babies. Now I'm turning into a damn hypocrite."

Suddenly, he set her away from him and pivoted on his heels. "Go sit down...way over there." His arm shot out to indicate that he wanted her out of reach. "I plan to ride into town at the end of the week to notify my supervisor that I'm alive and well. By then I should have most of the repairs and improvements made, and I'll have taught the children enough survival techniques to practice until I return."

Tara knew the time had come to relay the information she'd overheard in Rambler Springs. "Raven and the other bandits robbed a ranch near Tucson last week and stole cattle and horses. Two cowboys died in the raid. According to the report in town, the general consensus is that renegade Indians have struck again. But since there was a war party of five, I suspect it's the same gang you're tracking."

He glanced up sharply and frowned. "Damn Raven. I don't know what he's trying to prove by letting those *bandidos* disguise themselves as Indians. He's only making things difficult for the Apache, giving the military another excuse to cheat and steal and tighten security at the reservation. Those corrupt soldiers don't need another excuse, damn it!"

Tara frowned curiously. "How are the Apache being cheated?"

He laughed harshly. "First off, agents tamper with the weights used to measure rations of flour, meat and beans so the weight appears to be twice what it actually is. Then they take half the food and sell it to settlers and miners and pocket the profit. Drunken soldiers use the power of their position to forcefully deflower Indian maidens. When a chief dares to complain, no charges are filed, no soldiers face court-martial."

Tara clenched her fists, knowing all too well the torment of encountering drunken men intent upon appeasing their lust. In addition, the thought of starving the Indians for financial gain outraged her.

"Lately, outlaws have taken to invading the reservation camps, killing unarmed Indians, stealing horse herds and whatever else they can carry off. The soldiers turn a blind eye to the incidents, because they think the fewer Indians left on the reservation, the less guard duty that will be required of them."

"Even annihilation is practiced on the reservation," John added bitterly. "In fact, I suspect some of the soldiers are in cahoots with the outlaws and tell them when and where to murder and raid, in exchange for a cut of the profit." He sighed heavily. "Not a day goes by that I don't wake up wishing I could make more headway with the Bureau of Indian Affairs."

John cited example after example of atrocities against the Indians. Tara understood why he felt compelled to use his position as marshal to report these outrageous crimes, understood why he felt so frustrated that he was only one of too few advocates fighting to protect the Indians.

All the more reason Tara couldn't selfishly ask John to turn his back on the Apache and remain here in Paradise Valley. She and the children might not have much in the way of material possessions, but they weren't being preyed upon, cheated or injured by vicious marauders.

It was sad but true that, no matter how bad you thought you had it, someone else likely had it worse. Plus Tara was feeling more than a little guilty that she owned the deed to this ranch that had once been sacred Apache ground. She profited from the Apache's misery. The thought tormented her, and she wasn't sure how to make amends. The odds against the Indians seemed so insurmountable that she wondered how John dealt with his frustration.

"We found you!" Calvin shouted as he limped through the trees.

The other children filed along behind him, smiling in triumph.

"Of course you did," John said approvingly. "You are scouts of the first order, after all. Well done, troops." He gestured to the rippling pool. "Help yourself to a drink, then we'll gather our tools and head back to the cabin. It's time for your school lessons."

Five faces scrunched up with displeasure.

"I'd rather learn Apache tricks," Derek groused.

"There'll be more tomorrow," John promised. "In the meantime, I'm going to take some measurements to build Irish and the girls some shelves to store their belongings and some additional kitchen cabinets."

"That's not necess—" Tara tried to object.

"I want to do it," John interrupted. "I'll use the lumber left over from the pasture gates for shelving. It won't be fancy, but it will be practical."

Tara trailed along behind the pied piper and his bewitched children, knowing without the slightest doubt that not having John around was going to put a damper on everyone's spirits. Blast it, he wasn't even gone and she missed him already.

He wasn't coming.

Tara stared out her bedroom window, willing John to materialize from the darkness. He meant to keep the vow he'd made that afternoon, she realized. He didn't want to risk being discovered in her room—as she'd nearly been discovered naked with him in the hayloft.

She muttered in exasperation, then squirmed in her bed—her *empty, lonely* bed. John was trying to protect her from consequences that might arise after he left. He wanted her, she knew that, but he was denying himself, and her, pleasures so potent and overpowering that the mere thought of the passion that blazed between them left her body aching with need. He was being honorable and conscientious, and she wanted to curse him for it.

Sighing deeply, she flounced onto her back and stared at the ceiling. When his handsome face materialized above her in her mind, she squeezed her eyes shut and muttered another unladylike curse. She wouldn't go to him. She'd initiated their first—and obviously only—tryst. She had to accept the limitations he'd set for himself. She had to remember that his priorities had been handed down to him by a nation crying out for help. Was she so selfish and possessive that she'd ask the man she loved to turn his back on his people when his sense of honor and devotion were part of the reason she loved him? No, she couldn't live with herself if she did that.

Tara tried to relax, to sleep. She knew from experience that greater hurts existed in this world than loving a man she couldn't have forever. But that didn't make wanting him, and not having him, any easier to bear.

She wasn't coming.

John told himself that he was relieved, but that was empty consolation. His male body had been in a permanent state of arousal since he'd lain down in the straw. He'd just have to endure the ache, damn it.

He hadn't fully realized—until he'd given the children that speech this afternoon about responsibility and consequences—that he hadn't practiced what he preached. He'd been guilty of seeking physical release when the urge struck. The experienced women from his past had means of protecting themselves, emotionally and physically. But Tara didn't, and there was a marked difference between scratching an itch and making wild, heart-shattering love with her.

Last night shouldn't have happened. It couldn't happen again. John repeated that mantra for what must've been a solid hour—for all the good it did, which was no good at all. He still ached for her touch, the erotic taste of her, the tantalizing feel of her supple body shimmering around him, caressing him in the most satisfying, sensual ways imaginable.

Groaning in discomfort, John rolled to his side and stared out the loft window. He couldn't go to her, not even to sleep beside her, to hold her, absorb her scent or to revisit the first true feelings of contentment he'd ever known. He simply couldn't trust himself, because she was his weakness. John didn't think he had too many, but Tara definitely topped the list.

No, he had to keep his distance, use the children as a buffer. In a few days he'd be gone, back to his solitary life of constant watchfulness, continuous danger. When he built up enough resistance to withstand seeing Tara again—without touching her, possessing her—he'd return.

He'd give himself six months, he decided. That would be something to look forward to. Six months wasn't so long, was it? No, he guessed not. Not if you were one of those gigantic turtles he'd heard about that lived on some faraway island and survived for a couple of hundred years. But for a man who was very much afraid he was on the verge of falling in love—and didn't dare admit it to himself because he knew he couldn't act upon his feelings because of prior obligations—six months was an eternity.

Chapter Twelve

John was up at dawn—might as well have been, considering his inability to sleep. He attacked his carpentry projects with fiendish haste because he wanted the shelving nailed together and put in place by noon. He planned to take the older boys with him to a nearby canyon where he knew a herd of mustangs came to breed during the fall season. As a warrior, he'd captured several mares from the herd, despite that coal-black devil stallion that kept a protective watch over his harem.

Training and selling extra horses would bring this family good money during the winter months. John could rest easier knowing Tara and the children wouldn't go hungry like the Apache. He also knew he'd wasted his time showing Tara the hidden treasure beneath the Altar of the Gods.

She wouldn't touch it.

Although the other children were disappointed at not being allowed to join the expedition, John promised an after-supper excursion to pacify them. It was difficult knowing the others felt left out, but what was infinitely worse was meeting Tara's searching gaze across the table, across the room. He was acutely aware that she would've welcomed him with open arms at midnight. His body was still objecting to his denial each time he came within five feet of its obsession. John would be thankful to have that Irish elf out from underfoot for a few hours. With any luck, he'd only think about her every hour or so.

"Where are we going?" Samuel asked as they ascended the winding trail to the south canyon rim.

"Diablo Canyon."

Derek and Samuel glanced uneasily at each other, then at John.

"Doesn't Diablo mean devil?" Derek asked warily.

"Yes, but it's not what you think," he replied as he reined his piebald stallion southeastward. He patted Pie affectionately on the neck. It had been a while since the two of them had ridden off together. "The Apache named the canyon because of the disposition of the stallion that lords over the mustangs. If we're fortunate, that old devil has long since passed on and his successor won't be so protective of his herd."

While they rode abreast, John explained his plan to bottle up the horses in a narrow gully where they could be lassoed and staked out with ropes. When the threesome reached the rugged, rock-strewn chasm, John found the familiar Indian trail that led to the grassy pasture below. He fished his field glasses from his saddlebag to scan the area, spotting the herd grazing at a distance. He motioned for the boys to follow him around the cap rock so they could remain downwind.

Sure enough, that stallion was grazing with the herd. Damn the rotten luck, thought John as he circled the ravine. That cantankerous old devil wasn't going to make it easy for John and the boys to capture the mustangs.

Raven held up the spyglass and scanned the depths of the canyon from his lookout point. He focused on the site where he'd encountered White Wolf, or rather John

Wolfe, as he was known after he'd slithered off like a coward to rejoin his people. Raven's glittering black eyes zeroed in, searching the area for any signs of life in the Canyon of the Sun.

So White Wolf was dead, he presumed. There was no sign of that piebald stallion Gray Eagle had given him. That prize stallion should've been his, Raven mused, gnashing his teeth against the bitter memories that assailed him. White Wolf had been the favored son, and he wasn't even blood Apache! But now White Wolf was gone for good, at long last.

When Raven noticed the large mound of rocks that lay to the north, his presumption that White Wolf had died from gunshot wounds was confirmed. Someone had buried his carcass so animals wouldn't make a feast of him. Personally, Raven didn't care what became of White Wolf's remains. He'd been standing in White Wolf's shadow for years, listening to Gray Eagle's high praise, watching his blood brother assume a position of authority among the tribe—a position that should've been Raven's. But White Wolf had always been taller, stronger, swifter of foot and exceptionally cunning and wise.

Not cunning enough to survive his confrontation with Raven. In the end, White Wolf had come to think like a white man, taking for granted that Raven would submit to captivity. Raven would *never* return to the hated reservation, *never* be penned up like a stray dog, eating half rations, watching soldiers cheat and steal while he could do nothing about it.

Anger and resentment roiled inside him as he circled the perimeter of the canyon to reaffirm his belief, beyond question, that White Wolf had died from the gunshot wounds. With him out of the way, Raven's freedom was secure. He could loot and raid and take out his frustration on the foolish whites that invaded the *Apacheria*. No white man was competent enough to stop him. The whites were fools, every last one of them!

The three white men and the Mexican who rode with Raven depended on his intelligence and cunning. They relied on him to scout and plan upcoming robberies. The fools were short on patience and self-discipline. If not for his influence they'd ride helter-skelter from one robbery to the next. It was always Raven who cautioned them to hide out for a week at a time before scouting the next area of attack. Without his knowledge and forethought, the lawmen scouring the territory would've overtaken the *bandidos* a year ago. But Raven knew how and where to hide, when to raid. He was never predictable.

The stupid whites he'd aligned himself with thought the reason he insisted they disguise themselves as Indians was to conceal their identity. But that wasn't the reason at all. It was to assure the white government that not all Apache would meekly surrender and live on the reservation. Raven was using the ignorant outlaws to make his point.

He smiled arrogantly, recalling how easy it was to manipulate the outlaw gang. They were slaves to their greed, eager to prey on horses, cattle and white captives. Women and children were easy targets, and the white man's government could be counted on to pay a ransom for their return. In addition, the Mexicans paid handsomely for white slaves, because they still harbored resentment over losing territory to the horde of greedy whites that claimed land from Texas to California.

Satisfied that White Wolf—the only man Raven *didn't* want on his trail—was no longer a threat, he rose to his feet to retrace his steps to his horse. Raven stopped dead when he caught sight of movement in the center of the canyon. Reflexively, he dropped to the ground, then retrieved his spyglass. He focused on the monolithic stone spires that formed the Altar of the Gods, then he shifted his attention to the south. A sinister smile quirked his lips when a woman and three children came into view. He appraised the crippled boy child, the two girls and then the woman, whose mane of hair caught fire and burned in the sunlight.

Raven scrambled to his feet, then scurried along the cap rock in a half crouch, darting from boulder to boulder to prevent detection. A clever Apache never attacked until he had counted his enemies' numbers and knew their exact locations. Glancing southeast, he spotted the pasture where three horses grazed. More booty to tempt the greedy desperadoes.

A few minutes later Raven spotted the cabin tucked in a copse of cottonwoods and the barn built against the north wall of the canyon. Sheep milled in a nearby corral and chickens pecked at the grass. But there wasn't a man in sight to protect the woman and children.

Sitting back on his haunches, Raven smiled in sinister satisfaction. Raiding this ranch would serve him well. He could steal livestock, capture the woman and children as slaves or hold them for ransom. More importantly, he'd reclaim the Canyon of the Sun as sacred Apache ground.

He knew the ruffians that rode with him would approve of the booty, and the raid would be easily accomplished. As soon as the four bandits recovered from their drunken spree, Raven would break camp and descend into the Canyon of the Sun. Once again this Apache haunt would be wiped clean of white invaders. And once again the white-eyes would know where Raven had been, but they'd be unable to predict where he'd strike next.

He slithered off, making his way back to his paint pony. Very soon this canyon would be vacated, preserved and returned to the Apache and their gods—as it should be, would be, forever.

Tara paced the grass, then reversed direction to pace some more. It had been hours since John and the boys had ridden off to hunt mustangs. Had something happened? Where the blazes were they?

These past few hours were a vivid reminder of what her life would be like when John left. She felt lost and restless when he wasn't somewhere on the premises. This was definitely a foretaste of what she could expect in the weeks to come, and she didn't like it one blasted bit!

Sweet mercy, how had she gotten so attached to him so quickly? It just wasn't fair, she mused sourly. But then, no one promised life would be fair. She and the children were living proof of that.

Tara caught her breath when she spotted the piebald stallion and rider on the canyon rim. Immeasurable pleasure and relief replaced the lonely, empty feelings plaguing her moments before. Captivated, she watched horse and rider move with the grace of a centaur as they descended into the valley, leading a string of horses. Derek and Samuel brought up the rear, assuring her that they had returned uninjured.

As the single-file procession approached, Tara noticed the mustangs had been lashed together with rope, head to rump, in a clever fashion that made it impossible for them to rear up or kick. Tara shook her head in amazement. Was there nothing this remarkable man didn't know how to do? Except maybe love her with the depth of affection she felt for him.

Young Flora appeared at Tara's side as the procession halted near the barn. "How'd you know how to round up those horses?" she asked John.

Before he could reply, Samuel and Derek grinned and said in unison, "Old Apache trick."

Flora's delicate features puckered in a frown as she peered up at John. "Those Apaches sure do know lots of tricks, don't they?"

"Sure do, sugar," John replied as he swung effortlessly

from the saddle. "Your brothers did a fine job of restraining the mustangs for their march home."

Samuel and Derek beamed proudly. It occurred to Tara that, as much as the boys wanted to think of themselves as men, they wouldn't have made much progress without John's instruction and guidance. He'd taught them more about ranching and survival in three weeks than she could've taught them in ten years, for she relied on trial and error herself.

"Wait till you hear how we bottled up the horses and lassoed the ones we picked out," Samuel said excitedly.

"And man, I wish you could've seen that old dragon stallion rearing up and screaming at us," Derek added.

While Maureen and Flora gathered around to hear the details, John led the horses into the corral without unlashing them. Tara figured he intended to give the spooked animals time to adjust to their confined space before freeing them. Considering their lack of domestication, Tara wasn't in favor of turning them loose for fear they'd tear up the new fences.

"Where's Calvin?" John questioned, glancing hither and yon.

Tara scanned the area. "He was here a minute ago." Her attention shifted to the other children, and then returned to the space Calvin had vacated suddenly. Her concerned gaze flew to John. She could tell by his solemn expression that he was thinking the same thing she was. Calvin felt left out because he hadn't been allowed to join the hunt, and he didn't feel a part of their triumphant return.

"I'll find him," John said as he wheeled and walked away.

John's instinct proved correct. In less than five minutes he located Calvin perched on a boulder beside the nearest spring. He was chucking pebbles into the water that rippled over the stone streambed.

"Cal?"

The dejected boy glanced up momentarily, then focused his attention on pitching rocks. John squatted down to sip the cool water. "Thanks for keeping watch over Tara and your sisters while I was gone."

Calvin shrugged carelessly. "I didn't do nothin'."

"Providing protection sometimes requires no more than keeping your eyes peeled for trouble, but it's still necessary and important."

Calvin snorted. "Didn't see a snake or tarantula or nothin'. I'm just a cripple—"

"Whoa, hold it right there, young man," John interrupted in a stern voice. "You are *not* a cripple and no one around here considers you as such, especially not me. The problem is that you're seven years old, which isn't a disgrace. All of us were seven at one time in our lives, you know."

"Yeah, but when you were seven years old you could probably run like the wind and had the strength to do all sorts of things I can't do."

John propped himself against the boulder where Calvin sat. He crossed his arms and feet in front of him and said very deliberately, "When I was seven years old I was taking beatings from my drunken father. He never gave me the time of day unless he wanted me to fetch whiskey or felt the need to pound me, for no particular reason except that he was a bully."

Calvin's hazel eyes bulged and his jaw scraped his chest. John nodded in confirmation. "The son of a gun broke my left arm when I was five, and it took a while to regain good use of it. I spent years being forced to work like a man three times my size, making repairs on our farm, while dear old daddy got liquored up at night and slept half the day away."

"Did your mama have anything to say about it?" Calvin asked.

"My mama didn't hang around very long, Son. According to my pa, she decided to take off to find a better life when I was three or four years old. She didn't think she'd have much of a chance if she dragged me along behind her. Of course, that was my pa's version of the story. But since my mama never bothered to write or visit, I guess his version is the only one I'll ever hear, especially since my pa decided to take up prospecting and we wandered the frontier."

John laid his arm over Calvin's drooping shoulders. "The point is that I didn't want to do to you what was done to me, Cal. I wasn't old enough or strong enough to do what was demanded of me. I had to grow up before my time and didn't have much of a childhood. I don't want that for you.

"What Samuel and Derek did today took a good deal of strength. Restraining wild horses isn't easy work, but what I need you to do tomorrow is every bit as important. We're going to gentle the horses to ride. Samuel and Derek may be the *caballeros* who rounded up the mustangs and will train them, but you will be the horse whisperer."

"Horse whisperer?" he echoed, perking up immediately.

John nodded his dark head. "Another old Apache trick that you'll be exceptionally good at. In fact, I was hoping to go over the procedure after supper. That is, if you want to learn."

Calvin hopped off the boulder, squared his thin-bladed shoulders and nodded enthusiastically. "Just show me what to do and I'll do it."

John could barely detect the boy's limp as they strode, side by side, to the cabin. But then, it was difficult for a kid to limp when he was practically walking on air, John reminded himself wryly.

"It appears that you worked your magic on Cal," Tara murmured as John helped her clear the supper table.

John made it a point not to venture too close while they shared kitchen duty. He didn't trust himself with Tara any more than he trusted an outlaw to tell the truth. In his experience, twisting a man's arm a dozen different ways or making him think death was imminent was the only way of getting at the truth. *His* truth was that he'd learned to function reasonably well if he didn't venture closer than five feet from Tara.

That was his limit.

John had accepted and acknowledged his limitations. In his line of work overconfidence and reckless daring could get him killed real quick.

"Just what did you say to bolster Cal's self-esteem?" Tara asked.

John set the bowls on the new counter he'd installed early that morning in order to give Tara more working space. "I told him that I had special training lined up so he'd be doing his part in gentling the mustangs. This winter, when money is short, you'll have horses to sell to miners or travelers, and the animals will be well adapted to this rugged terrain and climate."

Tara refused to meet his gaze. She busied herself with scraping the dishes. "Thank you, John. We appreciate all you've done for us."

Damn it, it was hard to behave as if he and Tara were mere acquaintances who shared the same living space. They'd been as close as two people could get, had learned each other's bodies by touch, by taste…by heart. The emotional indifference he'd perfected the past five years wasn't worth a whit when he was with Tara. He *felt;* he *cared.* If time and distance didn't alleviate his fierce and constant wanting, didn't quell this compelling need to share an intimate closeness with one person—namely her—he'd probably go stark raving crazy. He had the unshakable feeling that loneliness was going to top the list of things he disliked about his solitary life.

For the umpteenth time, John restrained himself from reaching out to pull Tara into his arms. He couldn't allow her to hold any hope of anything permanent between them, couldn't let himself hold one ounce of optimism. Even from here he could hear the incessant cries of the Apache, could feel their misery seeping into his soul. And Raven, damn his hide, kept making matters worse by raiding and plundering and murdering and refusing to heed Gray Eagle's command to give up the useless fight.

"Why don't you go outside and give Calvin another dose of self-confidence?" Tara suggested. "I can finish up in here."

Like him, she was careful to maintain distance, John noted. She avoided meeting his gaze directly. John hated this awkward tension between them, but it was the only way to ensure they didn't touch. He remembered with vivid clarity what happened when they ignored self-restraint. Their explosive need for each other was worse than setting fire to blasting powder.

John breathed a deep, cleansing breath the moment he strode outside. He needed to clear his head and his senses of Tara. He smiled faintly, recalling the purification ritual the Apache used on occasion. He'd have to revert to the ritual to rid himself of all the feelings and sensations he couldn't take with him when he left Paradise Valley. He knew a part-time lawman and part-time bounty hunter who carried around emotional baggage had one foot planted in his own grave.

Resolutely, John focused his thoughts on the mustangs. He located Calvin to give instructions, then rounded up the other children. Since the horses were restrained, it didn't take much effort for Samuel and Derek to lasso the steeds' feet and pull the animals to the ground. Even Calvin managed to toss a loop on the dirt for one of the mustangs to step into. Of course, Calvin went flying off the fence where he was perched when the horse battled futilely, then flopped onto its side and snorted in disgust.

Apparently Calvin hadn't landed on his pride because he quickly scrambled to his feet and scuttled toward the downed horse to secure his loop. The boy smiled victoriously when he had the mustang's legs bound tightly with rope.

"Good work, Cal," John said approvingly. "You, too, Derek and Samuel. Now we begin the taming sessions." He gestured for Calvin to retrieve the strips torn from gunnysacks he'd gathered.

John watched Calvin place his booted foot on the horse's neck to hold it steady so he could tie the blindfold in place. After each horse was blindfolded with a strip of gunnysack, Calvin squatted down to blow his breath on the animal's flaring nostrils. He spoke soothingly and calmly, allowing the steed to adjust and accept his scent, to become familiar with the sound of his voice. After several minutes Calvin laid his hand lightly on the horse's neck, stroking from jaw to muzzle, then back again.

The other children hung over the fence rails, watching in fascination while Calvin worked with the horses. At first the mustangs objected to Calvin's touch and flinched at the sound of his voice, but he cooed softly and never lifted his hand while he bent down to breathe on each horse's face.

"How come he's kissing the horses?" Flora questioned—as only Flora could.

"He isn't kissing them. He's whispering to them so they'll become familiar with his scent, his voice and his touch," John explained. "Blindfolded and restrained, the horses have nothing else to do but focus on Calvin. Eventually they'll learn that he means them no harm, that they can trust him to be kind to them."

After a few more minutes passed, Calvin settled down

beside one of the steeds, his hand draped over its withers. The mustang's muscular body twitched, its ears pricked up and its nostrils flared. But Calvin continued to lie beside the animal, to stroke it gently. The children watched in amazement as Calvin scooted closer to drape an arm and leg over the downed horse.

"He's letting the horse adjust to the idea of having someone on his back," Samuel declared. "Well, I'll be da—er—darn. The horse has stopped flinching! They're cuddled up like two bugs in a rug!"

John glanced over his shoulder when he heard the front door creak. From the look on Tara's face, he was sure she was about to have a seizure when she saw Calvin lying in the corral with five wild horses. The boy was sprawled across one of them. Her frantic gaze swung to John, but after a moment she visibly relaxed.

The faith and trust she placed in him was altogether humbling. He felt a funny little flitter in the vicinity of his heart, and he had to glance away to compose himself. Damn it, the very last thing he needed was to get more sentimental than he already was when it came to this captivating woman and these adorable kids.

"Wow, Calvin! You're doing a dandy job," Tara praised as she approached the corral. "You'll have those mustangs eating out of your hand in no time at all."

Calvin, of course, glowed with pride, but he didn't allow himself to become distracted from his task. He was, after all, the leading authority on horse whispering.

"I'm getting hungry again," Flora declared. "Are there any cookies left?"

Tara nodded. The waning sunlight glistened in her hair. John resisted the urge to reach out and run his fingers through the silky gold strands. Damn, his sap was rising again, and all he was doing was staring at her, wanting her, aching for her like hell blazing.

"How can you be hungry so soon after supper?" Tara

questioned, bewildered. "It hasn't been an hour since we ate. Come to think of it, you've been eating like a horse lately, Flora."

"That's 'cause Zohn Whoof gave me a special herb to chew on." She fished a leafy stem from her pocket to display to the other children. "Zohn Whoof says it will increase my *aphatype* so I can get bigger and stronger."

Tara gave the little girl an affectionate hug. "I do believe it's working, because it seems to me that you've been gaining weight and it looks exceptionally good on you, Flora."

"Yeah," the other kids chimed in, "you look mighty good."

Flora, her dark eyes sparkling, hoisted herself up a little straighter on the fence rail. "Someday I'll be a horse whisperer, too, just like Calvin." Her arm shot toward the downed horse. "Can I have that strawberry colored horse for my own? Can I, Zohn Whoof? Please?"

"Sorry, dumplin', these horses are being trained to sell. Fast as you're growing, Irish will need extra money to buy new clothes, come winter."

Obviously the anticipation of new clothes was as appealing as having a horse of her very own because Flora nodded agreeably, then skipped off to the cabin in search of cookies.

"How long does Calvin have to work with the horses?" Samuel questioned. "Can we help him?"

John nodded. "If you like. Just make sure you follow Calvin's lead and don't overwhelm the horses by trying to get acquainted with them too quickly. They've been wild their entire lives. Tomorrow morning, we'll let them stand up. They'll be easier to manage, and less coordinated after being tied down all night. When we halter-break them, then climb on their backs, it will be more difficult for them to buck and kick."

The children scrambled over the fence to practice Calvin's procedure, leaving John and Tara alone. He shuffled sideways, then propped his elbows on the top rail to watch the children gentling the mustangs.

"When are you leaving?" Tara questioned without glancing in his direction.

"Three days. I'll ride into town to telegraph the office in Prescott. Then I'll take to the outlaws' trail again."

John would not mention, now or ever, that he knew Raven by name. As far as the officials at headquarters were concerned, John had no connection to any of the gang members. And that's the way it had to stay if he had any hope of returning Raven to San Carlos. Sneaking Raven onto the reservation and giving him the identity of a deceased tribe member would be mere child's play compared to tracking him and his ruthless cohorts down.

In addition to notifying headquarters, John intended to wire for money so he could leave Tara with a small nest egg to see her through the next few months until the horses were trained and ready to sell.

His attention shifted back to the children, who were crawling slowly and carefully over the downed horses, murmuring softly, imprinting the animals with their scent and touch. Damn, he was going to miss these kids like crazy. And Tara most of all, he mused. They had filled up all the empty places in his heart and soul and drove home the point that there had been something important missing from his life, something he'd ignored for years. But those deeply buried feelings of need, of companionship, of belonging were mushrooming inside him, and he wondered if he could ever stem this tide of feelings again.

Ironic, John thought. He had remained here to recover from injury, but the gaping wound of caring *too much* about this unique family might never heal.

He wasn't coming—again. Tara hadn't really expected John to appear in her room at the stroke of midnight. Fool that she was, she kept hoping.

Three days… The depressing thought made her coil into a tight ball on her bed. But nothing eased the feeling of emptiness and longing that nearly overwhelmed her. Once again Tara reminded herself that she hadn't asked for more in life than to reunite the children and make a home in Arizona Territory. Now she was selfishly wishing she could keep John forever. She'd known since the day she settled in this canyon that she'd never find her soul mate and that no man would be interested in providing and caring for her ready-made family. Yet here she was, wishing John could be her impossible dream come true.

"Go to sleep," she ordered herself.

A few hours later she finally managed to stop tossing and turning, and dozed off into forbidden dreams.

She wasn't coming—again.

John stared at the loft window, watching moonbeams stream across the grass. Nothing moved, except the sheep the children had staked on ropes so the flock could graze. He breathed in the fresh night air that whispered past him, and told himself to go lie down on his pallet. He needed to rest so he'd be alert when it came time to work with the mustangs. Pacing the loft, hoping to catch sight of Tara—when he knew all the sensible reasons why she shouldn't come to him—was futile.

Damn this continuous conflict between his mind and body. If he didn't focus on his duties of finding Raven, rather than lollygagging around, wishing for things that couldn't be, he'd be useless to himself and everyone else.

Scowling, John plunked down on his pallet, squeezed his eyes shut and told himself that even if he couldn't sleep because of this tormenting need, then he could at the very least let his body—most parts of it, anyway— get some rest.

Chapter Thirteen

The creak of splintering lumber, a bloodcurdling scream and the wild whinny of a horse brought John straight up on his pallet. Bleary-eyed, he groped for his breeches and boots. Another terrified shriek sent John scrambling down the ladder posthaste. He took off at a dead run, then skidded to a halt when he saw Derek clutching his ribs and huddling beside the broken fence rail. One of the mustangs had been untied and was staggering around the corral.

"Oh, my God!"

John glanced back to see Tara, dressed in her clinging nightgown, racing toward Derek. "What are you doing out here at the crack of dawn? Blast it, Derek, are you all right?"

John bounded over the fence to kneel beside the boy. Derek's agonized expression testified to his tremendous pain. Tears spilled down his dirty cheeks like muddy rivers as he peered up at John.

"I'm sorry," he bleated, lips quivering. "I wanted to surprise you."

Surprise was not what John was experiencing. Alarm, concern and frustration topped the hierarchy of feelings that bubbled inside him.

"Can you stand up?" he questioned.

Derek shook his sandy-blond head. "I d-don't think s-so. My r-ribs are hurting something f-fierce." He tried to inhale a deep breath, grimaced, then said, "I think I twisted my knee when I bounced off the fence and hit the ground."

John could've kicked himself all the way to Rambler Springs and back for not cautioning the children to await further instruction before they began the second phase of breaking the horses. Obviously, Derek had intended to have one of the mustangs broken to ride before John roused this morning. Unfortunately, the boy wasn't aware that the horse needed to become accustomed to a halter and bit before he climbed on board.

Carefully, John scooped Derek into his arms and pivoted toward the cabin.

"We'll put him in my bed," Tara insisted as she opened the corral gate for John.

Four sleepy-eyed children waited in the kitchen. Alarm registered on their faces when they saw Derek's pained expression.

"Irish, why don't you go down to the spring and bring us a pail of cool water while I get Derek out of his clothes and check his injuries?" John suggested.

Nodding mutely, Tara snatched up her breeches and boots, then darted outside to do his bidding.

Carefully, John settled Derek on the bed, listening to the boy hiss and grimace in an effort to find a comfortable position.

There didn't seem to be one. John knew the feeling all too well.

He unbuttoned the soiled shirt, noting the scraped and bruised skin on Derek's left side. If the kid hadn't broken a couple of ribs, he'd at least have jarred the hell out of himself when he went airborne and crashed to the ground.

"Ow!" Derek gasped, then squeezed his eyes shut

when John eased his arm from the torn shirt. "I think I'm gonna be sick."

"Sorry, kid, just stay with me for another minute and we'll get these breeches off so I can check your knee."

As gently as possible, John peeled down the tattered breeches to inspect Derek's knee. Sure enough, he'd made a bad landing. The joint was discolored and swelling rapidly.

Damn, this was his fault, John berated himself. He should've anticipated something like this. Hell, he was surprised Samuel wasn't in the same shape. These boys were so anxious to prove themselves as men and to impress him and Tara that they acted without thinking first.

Like Calvin, Derek had obviously wanted to prove himself capable. The only difference was that Derek had gotten two steps ahead of himself while handling the mustang.

If John had any secret aspirations of being good father material, they were dashed when he stared down at adolescent blue eyes gushing tears of pain and embarrassment.

"I—I made a m-mess of things with that h-horse," Derek said brokenly.

John covered the boy to ensure his modesty. "I'll take care of the horse." He gently laid his hand on Derek's side. The boy inhaled sharply, then groaned in pain. "I don't think anything's broken. Badly bruised and strained, yes. The knee is another matter. You'll need to borrow my crutch for a few days. And don't even think about climbing on a horse for a couple of weeks, kid."

Derek nodded bleakly, deflated by the diagnosis.

"I'm going to give you some peyote buttons to help you relax. They'll make you feel a mite peculiar, but they'll ease the pain. Just don't try to crawl from bed while you're sedated," John cautioned.

"Yes, sir," Derek mumbled, head downcast.

Tara barreled through the door. Panting for breath, she rushed forward with the bucket. John figured she had slopped out half the water in her haste to return, because her clothes were wet and the fabric clung to her legs and belly.

"What's the diagnosis?" she demanded.

"Sprained ribs, abrasions and a twisted knee that will keep him from dancing a few jigs," John reported. "I'll have the children gather herbs for a salve while I fetch peyote buttons to ease his pain. We'll need to swab him down with cold water, then wrap his ribs for support so he can move without coming apart at the seams."

Without batting an eyelash, Tara strode across the room, grabbed her one and only dress off the hook and proceeded to tear it into strips.

"Oh, no!" Derek wailed in dismay. "No, Tara, don't!"

"It's just a tattered old dress that means nothing to me, especially when compared to you, young man," she told him while she made short shrift of tearing her dress asunder. "Besides, you know perfectly well that I prefer to wear breeches."

John made a mental note to add a new dress to his list of items to purchase in Rambler Springs. "Tie the bandage firmly but not too tightly," he instructed. "I'll be back in a few minutes."

Hastily, he strode off to fetch his medicine pouch from his saddlebag.

"I couldn't do even one blasted thing right," Derek muttered, then flinched when Tara propped him up to draw the bandage behind his back. "Calvin got all the glory when he learned to gentle the mustangs. And Samuel and John did most of the work when we tied up the mustangs in the canyon. I just wanted John to realize I was a good horse trainer, too."

Tara smiled gently as she wrapped the bandage around Derek's midsection. "Just goes to show you that trying to impress folks is more trouble than it's worth. And painful, too. There was no need to impress John in the first place. He knows you're capable and responsible. Otherwise he wouldn't have taken you with him on roundup."

"Well, I want to be just like him," Derek said raggedly. "There's nothing he doesn't know how to do well. You should've seen him working with those horses. He had them lashed together so fast that Samuel and I couldn't figure out how he did it."

"Surely you realize John has years of experience on you," Tara said. "He doesn't expect you to become an expert horseman overnight. You know you should have waited for John's instructions, instead of sneaking out to tackle the task by yourself."

Derek nodded, then grimaced. "I just hope I didn't ruin that horse so he'll be impossible to train. I'll never forgive myself if I did."

Tara raked her hand through her tousled hair and smiled encouragingly. "I suspect John can undo any damage you might've done unintentionally. In the meantime, I want you to rest and let your injuries heal properly."

Derek muttered under his breath. "Yeah, I'll do that, since I've got no other choice. Now somebody else will have to do my chores for me."

Tara took his face in her hands, then pressed a kiss to his puckered brow. "That's what families are supposed to do, Derek. We work together, we share our burdens and we help each other through difficult times. Do you expect Flora and Calvin to pull equal weight around here?"

"No," he mumbled.

"That's because you know we each do what we can, in whatever capacity we can help. Limited or not, it makes no difference. John understands that, too. That's why he took Calvin aside to teach him to be a horse whisperer. Calvin was feeling left out because you and Samuel got to go on the roundup. John gave Cal a task that required patience, not strength. Gentleness, not quick agility.''

''Yeah, but because I botched everything up, I can't do my part now.'' Derek scowled, disheartened.

''I'm sorry, Derek, I truly am. But hopefully, you'll feel up to watching the procedure and you'll know what to do the next time we have horses to train.''

Despite her attempt to console him Derek brooded and sulked while Tara wrapped his knee with cold packs. She wasn't about to fuss at his reaction when she was privately brooding and sulking over the fact that John was leaving and she couldn't ask him to stay.

''This will take the edge off.''

Tara started at the sound of John's baritone voice so close behind her. Never in her life had she known a man who could move with such a silent tread. Derek eyed the peyote buttons dubiously. ''Do they taste bad?''

John's mouth quirked. ''Do your ribs hurt?''

''I was afraid of that,'' Derek grumbled as he accepted the medication.

''This will reduce the swelling in your knee and ease the throbbing from your ribs,'' John told him. ''Since peyote is partly a sedative, you'll probably be dozing by the time the other children return from fetching herbs. Just lie still and let the medication serve its purpose.''

Derek munched on the peyote buttons, made an awful face, then said, ''I'm really sorry about trying to break that horse before you got there. I just wanted to prove I was a good hand.''

''I know,'' John said as he ruffled Derek's straight blond hair. ''Sometimes good intentions go awry.''

John considered himself living proof of that. He supposed Derek felt as disappointed in himself as John felt when it came to protecting this boy from harm, protecting the Apache from corrupt whites...and protecting Raven from himself.

"Now, let's take care of that knee," John insisted as he sank down on the edge of the bed. "Irish, let's leave these cold packs in place while I mix the salve. We'll keep the swelling down as best we can."

Tara eased down on the opposite of the bed to replace the cold packs with fresh ones. She didn't glance at John, just focused her attention on the boy, whose eyelids drooped noticeably.

"I'm not gonna be any help with the horses," Derek grumbled drowsily.

"Of course you are," John assured him. "You're going to be the presence the mustangs feel when we return them to the corral after their training sessions. You can talk to them, make yourself familiar to them. They'll know your scent, your voice, and they'll become accustomed to having you around."

A goofy smile dangled on Derek's face, and his azure-blue eyes took on a glassy look. John knew the sedative was beginning to take effect. It hadn't been that long since he'd dealt with the groggy sensations himself.

"Know somethin'?" Derek asked in a slurred voice.

"What's that?" John grinned at his dopey expression.

"You really oughta marry Tara, 'cause Samuel and me can't do it. We love her, ya know. We even fought over her a few times, but we're just boys, not a man like you. I don't think she'll ever see us as anything but kids."

John shifted awkwardly, refusing to glance in Tara's direction, for fear he'd get lost in her cedar-green eyes and be forced to deal with the tormenting emotions that could tangle up his thoughts in no time flat.

"Just relax," he murmured. "Everything is going to be fine."

"Naw, it's not," the boy said sluggishly. "We tried

our hand at mathmatching...." He frowned comically. "Wha'th-a-mather with my tongue? It won't work right."

"Just sleep," John urged. Unfortunately, the medication was working like a truth serum, and Derek kept yammering.

"We wanted you to be our papa or big brudder, whithever you wanted to be, John. We don't wantcha to leave...ever...."

The kid was killing him, inch by inch. Wasn't it enough that John felt responsible for the boy's injury? That he'd failed to notice the young man's eagerness to prove himself when he constantly stood in the shadow of Samuel, who was a little older, a little bigger and a little stronger? Wasn't it enough that John spent his waking hours lusting after Tara and that he'd taken her innocence, knowing he couldn't offer promises or commitments?

And damn it to hell, there was little Flora, so warm, trusting and demonstrative with her love. The kid was slow to rise, but she could conjure up a thousand excuses not to crawl into bed at night.

And Calvin, who battled daily to overcome his disability and carry his share of the family responsibility. He wanted to grow up quickly so he could consider himself equal to Samuel and Derek.

And Maureen, who had a girlish crush on John and battled some inner demon from childhood that he had yet to figure out. She wanted to be a useful part of this family so she focused her time and efforts on learning to prepare meals and keep the cabin in order.

And Samuel, who had a natural way with animals, but was trapped somewhere between adolescence and adulthood and needed a man to show him the way. A man who would be here constantly.

It tormented John to no end that he couldn't be the man the children needed, the man Tara needed.

Blessedly, Derek's voice trailed off into unintelligible

mumbling. Finally he slept, his arms outflung, his head tilted sideways, his jaw slack.

John stood up. He never took his eyes off the kid, for fear they'd settle on Tara. And damnation, never in all his life had he exerted so much effort *not* to glance at the one and only woman he wanted to stare at constantly! It was making him crazy because he wanted to memorize every smile and expression, and learn to interpret what each and every one meant.

"The children should be back shortly. I'll have them mix and brew the poultice while I work with the loose mustang," John whispered.

Tara nodded, then peered up at him until he could no longer resist drinking in the sight of her. The impact was as it had always been—undeniably intense, potent, all-consuming.

"Don't feel guilty about these children's whims," she murmured. "It's only natural for them to wish for a father, since they've never had one of their own. I know you can't stay. I never expected you to assume responsibility for us. You have enough to worry about without adding us to the mix. We'll be fine, John, really."

"Irish—"

"Go tend your chores," she interrupted. "I'll stay with Derek for a while to ensure he's resting comfortably."

John walked away, leaving Derek in Tara's capable hands, but he was sorry to say he'd just left another part of his heart behind.

By the time he left Paradise Valley, he didn't figure he'd have enough left of his own heart to bother mentioning.

John exited the bedroom to find the other children huddled around the table. The herbs, seeds and bark they'd collected lay beside a mixing bowl.

"Is Derek gonna die?" Flora asked, looking up at him

with wide, haunted eyes that made John's heart flip-flop in his chest.

"No, pumpkin, he'll be fine in a few days. But he'll need some salves to reduce the pain and swelling in his ribs and knee. Can I count on you to brew the medicine while I tend the horses?"

"I'll do anything you ask," Flora said loyally.

John carefully explained how to prepare each of the ingredients, then left Maureen in charge of the two younger children. With Samuel following at his heels, John strode to the corral to stare pensively at the buckskin mustang, which paced restlessly. The animal would need to have one foreleg tied up to prevent it from rearing while he and Samuel broke it to a halter, and then to a bridle and bit.

John lassoed the mustang, tied a loop around its foreleg and stretched the rope over its back. Speaking softly, he approached the animal. Because the children had worked with the horse, it didn't object strenuously when he stroked its neck, muzzle and withers.

"Bring me a halter, then place your hands on her and offer her a few soft words," John instructed Samuel.

While John eased the halter onto the horse's head, Samuel stroked the mustang. "I should've known Derek was up to something when he turned in early last night," Samuel murmured. "I guess he wanted to surprise you by breaking one of the horses, huh?"

"Derek's intentions were good, but he skipped a couple of steps in the procedure. These horses have to adjust to a halter, and then a saddle, before someone climbs on their back. Derek learned his lesson the hard way."

John led the mustang around the perimeter of the corral. The mustang tried to rear up, but the rope tied to its foreleg made that impossible. After a few minutes, the horse settled into the awkward gait and responded to the tug of the rope attached to the harness.

John handed the rope to Samuel, letting the boy practice leading it for several minutes before they placed the bit in the mustang's mouth. All the while, John and Samuel cooed at the horse and praised its progress.

When John was satisfied with that phase of the training, he secured the lead rope to a post, then moved on to one of the horses that had been lying on its side during the night. Blindfolded, the horse wobbled tentatively around the corral without objecting to the harness. Handing the lead rope of the second mustang to Samuel, John released the third horse to start the process again.

While he and Samuel worked with the horses, John explained why it was important for a horse to learn to trust its rider, and warned the boy that sudden movements would continue to alarm a horse until it learned to trust its trainer.

Samuel absorbed every instruction like a sponge, John noted. Like each child in this unique family, Samuel wanted to prove his worth, his capabilities. John was reminded of his own childhood and those first years with the Apache. He'd wanted to be accepted, respected, valued and needed.

"Excellent job, Samuel," he exclaimed. "I'm going to hand the roan's lead rope to you so you can walk the horses while I put the finishing touches on the poultice for Derek's injuries. Don't change your direction until both mustangs are following obediently. And don't stop talking to them in a quiet, calming voice."

"Yes, sir," Samuel murmured as he accepted the lead rope without breaking his stride. "I'll do my best."

"I know you will, Son," John said confidently.

Leaving Samuel in the corral, John returned to the kitchen to oversee the preparation of the herbs the younger children were brewing on the stove.

Two days left, he mused as he ground the herbs once more for good measure, then dumped the brewed ingredients in the bowl. The inevitability of leaving Paradise Valley hadn't hit him quite so hard until now. He could think of a dozen more repairs he wanted to make, ten dozen more hours he wanted to spend teaching the children to be self-reliant. But duty awaited him. Duty would *always* await him, he reminded himself.

When it came to Tara, he knew his resistance was all but depleted. The only way to ensure that he kept his hands off her was to get out while the getting was good. He *had* to leave, he told himself resolutely, but knowing that didn't make the leaving a damn bit easier!

Tara mounted her horse for her weekly jaunt into town. Assured that Derek was resting more comfortably today, she left John in charge of the children. Although she'd made a habit of wearing a dress when she appeared in Rambler Springs, she decided it was high time the townsfolk got accustomed to seeing her tramping around in breeches.

It was easier to tidy up a house without hampering skirts to trip her up, anyway. Perhaps she'd acquire a reputation of being a bit of a misfit, but Tara didn't care. Her present concern was getting from one day to the next with her emotions in a constant uproar.

Blast it, the possibility of never seeing John again, of knowing that he'd be taking her heart and soul with him when he left, was tearing her apart. He had assured the children that he'd return to check on them occasionally, but Tara knew it would never be the same, because he would be a visitor, no longer an integral part of their family.

Things were never going to be quite the same again, and she was going to have to accept that—like it or not, which she damn sure didn't!

Resigned, Tara reined away from the corral. She'd work off her frustration by throwing herself into her housecleaning chores. She'd be exhausted by the time she collapsed in bed tonight. Perhaps she could catch up on the sleep that had been eluding her, and overcome her exhaustion.

"Irish?"

She glanced over her shoulder to see John standing in the shadows of the barn. Just the sight of him caused her heart to cartwheel around in her chest. "Yes?"

"Take care of yourself," he said, staring intently at her.

She tilted her chin to a proud angle. "I always have."

He walked into the sunlight, and Tara's heart missed several vital beats. Such a magnificent specimen of a man, she thought as her longing gaze roved over his swarthy physique. She memorized each bronzed feature, each hard, muscled plane and sleek masculine contour.

Come to think of it, she should be relieved when John left Paradise Valley. At least she wouldn't have to endure the endless torment of seeing him without being able to touch him, without making love with him as she longed to do.

"If anyone gives you trouble in town, practice the self-defense skills I showed you and the kids," John insisted.

"I'll be fine." Head held high, she nudged the mare toward the winding path. In her present mood, she dared anyone to give her trouble. She was spoiling for a good fight, in hopes of relieving her pent-up frustration.

Without a backward glance, Tara trotted off, knowing that, come tomorrow, it would be John who rode off...taking her heart with him.

"How come you look so sad, Zohn Whoof?"

John glanced down to see Flora sidling up beside him. He'd been so lost in thought, while watching Tara disappear in the distance, that he hadn't heard the child approach. Damnation, his self-preservation instincts were getting rusty. He'd let his guard down too often during his hiatus in Paradise Valley. If he didn't pay attention to what was going on around him he might just as well pitch his badge in the nearest creek and find another occupation.

Ah, if only that was possible.

Forcing a smile, John scooped up Flora and gave her an impulsive hug. "I was thinking how much I'm going to miss you and the other kids when I leave tomorrow."

Flora flung her arms around his neck and clung to him as if she never meant to let him go. "I don't want you to leave," she whispered against his shoulder. "I love you, Zohn Whoof."

"I love you, too, squirt. I always will. But one day, when you grow up, you'll leave Paradise Valley, too. All the children will."

"I won't," Flora insisted. "I'm gonna stay here forever and ever."

He patted her shoulder, then set her on her feet. "If that's the case, then we better make some more repairs around here so the place will still be standing forever and ever."

Hand in hand, they strolled into the barn to construct the new stalls to house the mustangs that he and Samuel were training. John and Flora were just getting started when Maureen appeared with a message from Derek, who had developed a severe case of cabin fever.

"Derek said he is ready to come outside and sit by the corral," Maureen reported.

John nailed the lower rail in place, then handed the hammer to Flora. "Make sure all the nails are secure, squirt. I'll be right back."

"Don't worry, I'll hammer the hell out of them."

"Flora, shame on you!" Maureen gasped.

John winced. "Just hammer them flush with the lumber and leave off with the bad language, young lady."

"How come? Samuel and Derek say hell all the time," she said, rat-tat-tatting with the hammer.

"Then I need to have a talk with them," John replied. "You have to be at least eighteen to curse."

Flora stopped hammering and peered up at him. "How come?"

"Because it's the rule," he said lamely.

"There's rules about saying hell and damn?"

John flung up his arms in exasperation. This precocious kid delighted in tossing around the curse words she'd heard. John was definitely going to have a chat with Samuel and Derek about that!

With Maureen trailing alongside him, he headed for the house. "I don't want you to go," she murmured.

John looped his arm around her shoulder, wishing he had more time to get to know this pretty lass who seemed to hold too much inside. "I'd like to stay, Maureen, but I have obligations elsewhere. But I'll be back."

The girl didn't look as if she believed him. He suspected that nothing short of a return visit would convince her that he meant what he said.

"Would you mind fetching a chair for Derek?" he requested. "We can pad it with a quilt to make him more comfortable."

She nodded, then to his complete surprise, she wound her arms around his waist and hugged the stuffing out of him. "I'll miss you, John, so very much. I love you."

As quickly as she'd hugged him, she darted up the steps. Gawd, thought John, these impulsive displays of affection were getting to him. If these kids kept this up, he'd be sentimental mush by dusk. Surely Derek wasn't going to hug him, too. The kid might strain his tender ribs.

Derek was perched gingerly on the edge of the bed when John entered the bedroom. He glanced at the pallet where Tara slept so she would be close at hand to give the boy round-the-clock attention and encouragement.

"I'm going crazy in here," Derek groused, squirming restlessly.

John was going crazy, period. This was his last day at the ranch. Hell! The thought sat in his belly like an indigestible meal.

Since Maureen had already helped Derek don his shirt, John handed the kid his breeches and assisted him into them. Ever mindful of the boy's injured ribs, he hoisted him up and carried him outside.

Maureen had positioned the padded chair beneath a shade tree near the corral. The mustangs pricked their ears and shied away as they approached.

"All of the horses have been broken to halter," John reported as he settled Derek in the chair. "Samuel and I led them around the canyon for more than hour this morning. They behaved reasonably well. I'll fetch some grain for you to feed them by hand so you can gain their confidence."

Derek nodded, but he didn't speak until Maureen ambled back to the house to prepare lunch. "Couldn't you stay a few more days, just till I'm back on my feet?"

Here we go again, thought John. Another arrow straight into his heart. "I wish I could, Derek, but I've already stayed a week longer than I should have. The outlaws' trail is getting cold. Every day I delay puts another innocent life in danger."

"But what's so damn important about *this* particular outlaw gang? It's not like the territory isn't overrun with a half-dozen gangs. Why can't some other marshal do the damn job?" Derek complained.

John didn't want to get into that right now. "And that's another thing," he said, diverting the boy's attention. "You and Samuel have to mind your tongue around the younger children. Flora was tossing hells and damns all over the place in the barn this morning. Believe me, you don't want a little sister who can outcurse you. She looks up to you and tries to be like you. Same goes for Calvin. Let them identify with the best of you, not the worst.''

''Okay,'' Derek agreed. ''But I still don't want you to go because…I look up to *you*. If I could have a father I'd want him to be you.''

Derek's softly uttered words knocked the air clean out of John's lungs. The compliment and the sentiment humbled John.

''Thank you, Derek. That means more to me than you'll ever know,'' John managed to choke out.

The kid blinked rapidly, then stared at the mustangs. ''Well, you mean a lot to me, John. Always will. I hope you return every chance you get.''

While his emotions churned like a volcano on the verge of eruption, John hurried off to retrieve the bucket of grain. Hell and damn, he thought. If this kept up, *he'd* be bawling like a newborn baby by nightfall!

Chapter Fourteen

John's last day with the children was emotionally draining. In between putting the final touches on his repairs and climbing on the backs of the mustangs for jolting rides, he'd had Calvin and Samuel each approach him in turn. John had been prepared for Calvin's tearful request that he stay, but Samuel's attempt to hide his emotions and prevent breaking down really did John in. The boy insisted he would become the man of the family and do his best to fill John's boots.

For several moments, John had experienced flashbacks of his past, seeing in Samuel that same willingness to accept the lion's share of responsibility. For Samuel it was a struggling family. For John it was a vanquished Apache nation and a blood brother who had gone on the warpath and was wanted—dead or alive.

John had promised himself years ago that what was valued and important would be protected. With his braided hair sheared off, and dressed in unfamiliar white man's clothes, he had stood before Gray Eagle and solemnly vowed to be the buffer between the Apache and the whites.

Now here was Samuel, all of fifteen years old, promising to protect and defend Tara and the other children.

So proud, so determined, so eager to prove himself worthy of respect. Well, the kid had certainly earned John's respect and approval.

When Samuel had extended his hand to say his private goodbye, John had forgone the handshake and hugged the kid close to his heart.

Damn, could it be more difficult to leave this family behind after they'd burrowed into his soul and resurrected emotions he'd buried years ago?

Now tormented, John rolled over on his pallet in the loft and stared through the window at the canopy of stars, hoping the serenity of the night would comfort him.

It didn't. It didn't even come close.

The nicker of horses in the stalls brought John upright on his pallet. When Tara ascended into the loft, John inwardly groaned. Considering the kind of day he'd had, he wasn't sure he had enough willpower to say farewell from a safe distance. Those adorable, exasperating kids had already played hell with his emotions.

As for Tara, she'd tested his resistance on a daily basis, until his willpower was worn too damn thin for comfort. And *too thin* aptly described Tara's threadbare nightgown. He could see the lush curves and swells of her feminine body when she passed through the shaft of moonlight.

"Irish—"

"Don't talk, just listen," she requested as she knelt beside him, a solemn expression etching her bewitching face.

John tried not to breathe, for fear of inhaling her alluring scent and losing what little self-restraint he had left. If he didn't know better, he'd swear those kids had purposely left him swinging on an emotional pendulum so he'd be clinging to the frayed strands of resistance by the time Tara showed up to say her own private goodbye.

Resolutely, John ignored the need to tug her into his

arms and forget everything except the feel of her supple body molded intimately to his.

"I came to thank you for all you've done to improve the ranch," she whispered. "I also appreciate all the skills you've taught the children. Because of you, they have developed confidence and pride in themselves. You can leave here knowing your kindness and good deeds are greatly appreciated, John. You know that you will always be welcome here, that the children will eagerly await your return, even if it can only be for a few short hours. They have made a special place for you in their hearts."

John could feel himself getting all choked up. "You know I'm crazy about those kids," he managed to say without his vocal apparatus failing him completely.

She nodded and smiled. His heart twisted and tied itself in a Gordian knot.

"Yes, I know you are, John. They are wonderful children. You can see why I became so attached to them at the orphanage and why I couldn't bear to be separated from them when we reached the end of the rails in Texas. They've come into their own here in Paradise Valley."

Her gaze locked with his and he could feel the impact like a lightning bolt. "I did what I had to do, then, just as I have come to do what I must do now, which is to say goodbye," she whispered brokenly, her green eyes misting with tears.

She reached out to trail her forefinger over his cheek, his jaw, his eyebrows and lips. She knew this wasn't going to be as easy as she'd rehearsed while she lay on her pallet, waiting for Derek to fall asleep on her bed.

Tara wanted to say her farewell to John in private, but when she touched him this one last time, it seemed that the cruelest punishment she could impose on herself was *not* telling him how she felt about him. Honesty and sincerity were simply a part of what she was.

"I love you, John Wolfe," she murmured, holding his

gaze. "I expect nothing except your acceptance of my affection. I will remember you always, because you are the man who holds my heart."

She leaned down to kiss him, to express just a small degree of her affection—and found herself enveloped in his powerful arms. His masculine scent engulfed her and she breathed him in, savoring the moment.

"Don't love me, Irish," he rasped. "Don't make this more difficult than it already is."

Tara lifted her head from his shoulder and smiled ruefully when she noticed his anguished expression. "Don't love you? You might as well ask me not to breathe, because loving you feels just as vital and necessary. These feelings have become part of who I am. I took a new identity, as you did, to protect the children, and myself, but that doesn't change what's in my heart. Ask anything of me, John, but don't ask me not to love you. It's about two weeks too late and two centuries too early to expect me to forget how I feel about you."

John knew defeat when it was staring him in the face— the face of an angel of mercy, a siren from his forbidden dreams. Her words, the sincere tone of her silky voice, the expression in her green eyes were the final blows that shattered what was left of his resistance.

For the life of him, John couldn't recall any of those noble reasons why he shouldn't make love to her one last time, why he shouldn't fill this aching emptiness that left him hollow and incomplete.

Wasn't it enough that he wanted her with every fiber of his being? Did he have to *need* her with that same burning intensity?

"Love me for all the lonely tomorrows I'll spend without you," she whispered as her lips lingered a hairbreadth from his.

John pulled her head to his and kissed her with penetrating thoroughness, savored the sweet nectar of her lips.

Flames of undeniable, incomparable desire spread through him like wildfire. He slid his hand beneath the hem of her gown, then pushed it out of his way to caress her from ankle to hip, marveling at the silky texture of her skin.

Ah, she was pure heaven to touch, so unbelievably responsive. He wanted her naked in his arms—now, this very second. He wanted to touch every inch of her satiny body, taste her thoroughly and absorb every fervent response he summoned from her. He wanted to memorize every little sound of pleasure she made, every provocative movement of her body, so he could revisit those sounds, scents and exquisite sensations in his dreams during all those lonely nights of isolation to come.

Her voice would come to him on a whispering breeze; her scent would drift to him in the rain. The feelings she stirred in him would be imprinted on his mind and body. No matter where he was, she would be only a memory away, a delicious fantasy waiting to accompany him into sleep.

He removed her nightgown and feathered his lips over her shoulder, finding that sensitive point he'd discovered at the base of her neck, delighting in her helpless response. His kisses trailed over her breast, his tongue flicking at the rosy peak. Her arms glided around his neck, cradling his head against her satiny flesh as he suckled her, then tugged ever so gently with his teeth. She moaned softly and her fingertips flexed in his hair, assuring him that he gave her pleasure.

John traced the soft flesh of her inner thigh as he brushed his lips over her taut nipples. He stroked the secret petals of her femininity and felt her shiver, then melt upon his hand.

Sizzling pleasure rippled through him as he probed deeper and felt her contracting around his fingertip. The moist heat of her desire radiated from her body and burned him like a searing flame.

Hungrily, his mouth came back to hers, absorbing her ragged cries of need, his tongue imitating the tender stroking of his fingertip.

He cherished her wild response, marveled at the indescribable pleasure that consumed him when he touched her. Ah, he could kiss and caress her for hours on end and never grow tired of discovering new ways to arouse her.

John's thoughts scattered to the four winds when Tara began to caress him tenderly in return. He clenched his teeth and hissed in tormented pleasure when her adventurous hand trailed along the band of his loincloth, then dipped inside to enfold his hardened flesh.

His breath left his lungs in a shuddering gasp when she unfastened the garment, then touched her probing fingers to his throbbing shaft. She traced him with her thumb, caressed him with her fingertips. He couldn't contain the groan of pleasure that rumbled in his chest, nor could he stem the flow of titillating sensations that flooded through him, engulfing him with immeasurable pleasure.

Lips as soft as silk whispered over the ultrasensitive skin of his chest and neck. When her hands glided over his hips and swirled downward again to stroke his erection, sensual lightning throbbed through him. The tender pressure of her hands folding around his rigid length left him shaking with ardent need, made him gasp in an effort to draw breath. Pulsating pleasure thrummed through him, drawing him closer to the edge of his control—what little was left of it, which wasn't all that much when Tara cast her sensual, magical spell.

A silvery drop of need betrayed him and the last shred of restraint came dangerously close to deserting him. He should stop her, he knew, but the pleasure she aroused in him seemed to have a will all its own.

John kept hearing a voice whispering inside his head, telling him this would be the last time they touched each other, held each other, loved each other. He also knew he'd been deceiving himself all along. Making love to Tara for only one night hadn't been enough to satisfy him. Two nights wouldn't be enough, either, but this was all he had and he wanted it to last until dawn. But he'd never last if she plied him with another round of exquisite torture.

John eased away, pressed her to his pallet and dipped his head to capture the peak of her breast once more. He flicked her nipple with his tongue, then suckled her gently. Her back arched in helpless response, and he cupped his hand around the creamy globe, kneading her, arousing her until she was chanting his name like an incantation.

His free hand trailed deliberately over her stomach. His prowling fingertips coasted ever nearer to the triangle of golden hair between her legs. When he cupped his palm over her again, he found her as hot and wet as before.

His ability to make this woman want him desperately gave him a heady sense of masculine power. He brushed his thumb over the hidden nub of passion, once, twice, and felt her entire body quiver with anticipation. He dipped his finger inside her once more and felt her weep upon his hand. Then he shifted her above him, opening her to his intimate kiss. He circled her softest flesh with his tongue, his lips, traced her with his fingertips and smiled in masculine satisfaction when she cried out his name again and again.

Her hands clenched on his shoulders, as if trying to steady herself against the sensual waves of passion that buffeted her. He felt helpless shudders consume her, and he waited a heartbeat, then aroused her once more. She came undone on his fingertips, his lips. She caressed him secretly, burning him alive with her need for him.

"No more," Tara breathed raggedly as she twisted from his grasp. "I need to touch you again."

"I want—" His voice dried up when she leaned over him. Her silky hair grazed his belly; her fingertips circled him, stroked him until he groaned in unholy torment. A white-hot bolt of desire speared him, robbed him of another precious breath and held him suspended in immeasurable pleasure.

He was amazed that Tara had become such a skillful seductress in two quick lessons. But he remembered thinking that first time that she would be beyond dangerous if she realized the power she wielded over him. Now, she had to know, without question, that she could leave him begging for more. She was touching him everywhere, turning his muscles to pudding beneath her butterfly caresses.

"I need you now, Irish," he whispered breathlessly.

She withdrew slightly, holding him gently in her fingertips. In the moonlight he could see her impish smile, see the challenging tilt of her head.

"Do you indeed?" she asked in an exaggerated Irish brogue. "I think perhaps you need to know just how desperate need can truly be."

Her hand glided down his rigid flesh, and John swore he was going to explode if she didn't stop arousing him. "I know my limits," he said raggedly.

She smiled as she lowered her head, sending that waterfall of silky hair tumbling over his thighs. "And I think you misjudge yourself. Shall we find out for certain, O great and mighty Apache warrior?"

Again she stroked him with her hands. John howled in maddeningly sweet torment. His body was so sensitive to each touch, each kiss, that the pleasure raging through him left him shaking with urgent need. His heart skipped several beats. His breath jammed in his lungs.

If it had been possible to speak—which it wasn't—he would have told her that she had taken him so close to the yawning abyss of rapture that he was going to die—

right here, right now, at this very moment. So there was no need to test his limits further. He'd passed them about a thousand incredible sensations ago.

Helpless, frantic, he surged upward, and she settled over him, welcomed him into her body, rode him into mindless abandon. John clutched at her hips, trying to hold her still so he could regain his control, but the erotic cadence she set drove him right over the edge.

"Not like this," he said, then groaned as the world spun out of control.

"Exactly like this," she assured him as she met and matched each hard, penetrating thrust.

John felt the universe explode, felt the billowing heat of passion burning him to cinders. But most of all, he felt Tara's body secretly caressing him as he shuddered against her. He clutched her to him, knowing he should roll away and spill his seed in the straw. Yet that innate sense of belonging, of rightness was so overwhelming that he couldn't release her from his arms.

John wasn't sure he could have let go even if his life depended on it. He simply shuddered in helpless release, again and again. He struggled mightily to draw breath, and held her to him—body to body, heart to heart, soul to soul.

"When you come to say goodbye, Irish, you don't mince words, do you?" he said a long while later.

She tittered softly as she moved sensuously above him. "Better to be precise and to the point, I always say."

He grinned at the double meaning. This Irish leprechaun had a bit of deviltry in her. He had seen evidence of it during their stolen moments together. She was passionate and playful and altogether irresistible. Some lucky man would come along and win her love....

John winced at the unwelcome thought of Tara spinning her web of Irish magic around another man. *He* was the one who had introduced her to passion. *He* had been her instructor and guide, although, admittedly, she had taught him things he hadn't known about desire.

He was sure she had ruined any future sexual encounters for him, because he was pretty certain that if he ever dared to touch another woman he'd be making comparisons to the mystical pleasures he shared with Tara. Having sex with one woman while mentally making love to another, didn't sound the least bit appealing. He didn't think that nonsense about a man forgetting about one woman by losing himself in the arms of another was going to work effectively for him.

John's thoughts trailed off when the aftereffects of sublime passion, compounded with the physical and emotional rigors of his last day at the ranch, caught up with him. He eased Tara down beside him, then nestled her spoon fashion against him. With his arm lying possessively over her waist, he drifted off to sleep.

Tara felt John's breath stirring against her neck and knew that he was asleep. Carefully, she inched away, although there was nothing she wanted more than to awake in his arms. But she had discovered the first time they made love that she slept too soundly in his embrace. She couldn't chance the children showing up at the crack of dawn to interrupt them.

Quietly, Tara retrieved her gown and made her way down the ladder. Guided by a full moon and a dome of twinkling stars, she ambled across the grass. When she crept in the bedroom window, Derek didn't move a muscle, thank goodness.

Tara lay on her pallet for a few minutes, recounting every sensual pleasure, reveling in the wondrous sense of belonging she experienced each time John held her in his arms. He completed her. He was the other half of her soul. Watching him ride away would be like dying inside while forced to go on living.

Yes, she'd have the children and her home, but the

place she truly belonged would be wherever John Wolfe traveled by day and where he slept at night. But if giving her heart and soul to him would ensure that he remained twice as alert and provided him with the additional strength to counter the dangers that prevailed in his world, then she'd gladly do without her heart and soul. As long as John Wolfe lived, as long as he survived, she could exist for the sake of the children. She'd go on loving John and she'd have these sweet memories to store in that hollow place where her heart had once been.

A faint noise brought Tara's head up. She glanced toward the window to see a shadowed figure looming outside. Her defensive instincts immediately sprang to life as she rolled quickly from her pallet and tiptoed to the window. No one would get past her to hurt the children. If all else failed she'd send up a shout of alarm to alert the other children to the danger.

Tara's good intentions flew out the window when a steely hand clamped over her mouth. She was all set to sink in her teeth—until she recognized the familiar scent of the man who whisked her outside and set her on her feet.

"I thought you were asleep," Tara whispered as John took her by the hand and led her away from the cabin.

"I was asleep, until I realized you were gone," he murmured without breaking his long, graceful stride.

"Where the devil are we going?"

"To the spring."

"Now? In the middle of the night? What for?"

"Blast and be damned, Irish, you ask more questions than Flora."

"You didn't answer my question," she reminded him. "Why are we going to the spring in the middle of the night? If there's another Apache treasure buried out there I do *not* want to know about it."

"No treasure, just a fantasy."

Tara gave him another puzzled look. He smiled enigmatically as he tugged her along at a faster clip.

"A fantasy?" she repeated when he didn't elaborate.

"The one I had when I saw you bathing at the spring and the intruders arrived to spoil the whole day. It's there at the spring that I want to say my farewell."

"But I already said—"

"Exactly," he interrupted. "Now it's *my* turn to say goodbye to *you,* Irish. And since I've overstepped every boundary, broken every rule I established where you are concerned, I've decided I might as well enjoy my forbidden fantasy."

John halted beside the spring that was surrounded by a stone ledge and miniature waterfall. When he peeled off his breeches, Tara angled her head, stared boldly at the evidence of his arousal, then smiled elfishly.

"I could've sworn you said you had certain limits," she teased him.

"You proved me wrong. I stand corrected. Now take off that gown, Irish. My fantasy has everything to do with you being naked."

"I swear, John Wolfe, when you discard all those rules and regulations, which, by the way, no one except you wanted to observe in the first place, you really—"

Before she finished her long-winded sentence, he scooped her up and tossed her smack-dab into the middle of the silvery pool. She resurfaced amid moonlit ripples and spouted like a whale.

"You'll pay dearly for that, Wolfe!"

"With what? Irish vengeance?" he taunted, undaunted.

He stepped into the pool at the same moment she disappeared from sight again. A few seconds later her hand snaked around his ankle and she gave a hard tug. John flailed his arms for balance—not that it did a whit of good. He tumbled into the pool with a great splash and swallowed about a gallon of water.

Tara's unrestrained laughter met him when he resurfaced. John caught his breath when she rose up like a genie to captivate him. Water droplets glistened on her exquisitely formed body like diamonds in the moonlight. John felt the urge to howl at the moon. And so he did.

While he sat there, bedazzled, bewitched, mesmerized, Tara sank beneath the surface once more. She reappeared to climb the stairway of rocks beside the waterfall. The mist surrounded her and rivulets of spray trailed over the peaks of her breasts, drawing John's rapt attention.

"Am I fulfilling your fantasy?" she asked as she struck a seductive pose on the ledge.

"Not quite, but very close," he purred as he waded deliberately toward her. "And very soon…"

There, beneath the canopy of stars and the glowing, silvery moon, John said his last farewell without uttering one word. He gave to this woman—who was unafraid to love him, who asked nothing but his acceptance of her love—all that he had to give, save the two promises he'd made to the man he called Father. Those two promises would take him away from Paradise Valley, but that part of him that he hadn't acknowledged for two decades, those tender emotions he had ignored, he gave freely to Tara for safekeeping.

Again, as before, the phenomenal passion they ignited in each other flared to life, consumed them in its fiery blaze…and burned through the night.

Chapter Fifteen

Tara stood beside the group of solemn children who formed a semicircle around John. He was saddling his piebald stallion. No one uttered a word. She could hear Flora and Maureen crying quietly beside her, but she didn't look down at the girls, for fear the sight of their tears would provoke her own.

Tara had decided last night, while she and John lived out a splendorous fantasy at the spring, that she'd watch him ride away and focus only on those playful moments when he'd let his guard down completely and displayed yet another fascinating facet of his personality.

When the horse was readied, John pivoted to face Tara and the children. He spoke not one word as he shook hands with Samuel, Derek and Calvin. He gave Maureen a quick hug, then lifted Flora off the ground to enfold her in his arms.

It was no surprise that the only one to break the stilted silence was Flora. "I wrote my name on this piece of paper so you could put it in your pocket. I don't want you to forget me."

"No chance of that, half-pint," he said as he set her to her feet and tucked away the folded paper.

Tara lifted her gaze when John halted in front of her. She resisted the overwhelming urge to fly into his arms one last time, and then reminded herself that she had to keep her composure for the sake of the children, who had turned their attention to her. If she'd didn't keep a firm grip on her emotions the whole group would be bawling their heads off.

"Irish, take care of yourself," he murmured for her ears only, then bent to press a chaste kiss on her brow.

Tara blinked rapidly as he swung agilely into the saddle. The clip-clop of Pie's hooves sounded like repetitive claps of thunder in the silence. Tara plastered on a smile she didn't feel as John disappeared behind the boulders and trees that obscured the trail leading up to the canyon rim.

"How about a game of hoop and pole?" she suggested with as much enthusiasm as she could muster.

Five glum-faced children stared back at her.

"I don't feel like playing," Flora mumbled. "I'm going to walk the sheep."

"I'll help you," Calvin volunteered.

"I'll go check on the horses in the new pasture," Maureen insisted.

"I'll go clean out the stalls," Samuel announced.

"I'll go talk to the mustangs," Derek decided.

When the children scattered in all directions, Tara was left standing alone on the grass. She glanced this way and that, wondering what on earth she was going to do to occupy her mind. She'd pick wild berries and grapes, she decided. But she'd definitely avoid the spring where she and John had lived out their secret fantasy in their space out of time. The memory was too fresh, the ache of loss too painful.

Tara ambled off to fetch an empty basket. She wondered how long it was going to take to settle into a routine now that John was gone. Life after John, she predicted, was going to take some getting used to.

Tara wasn't sure she ever would.

Raven crouched in the underbrush on the canyon's west rim and scanned the lush valley below him. He had returned to double-check the head count he'd made a few days earlier. From his vantage point he could see the flame-haired woman picking berries. The two small children were herding sheep toward a spring to drink. Raven frowned, wondering at the whereabouts of the strawberry blond girl he remembered seeing before.

Silently, he circled the cap rock and moved quickly past the stone spires that divided the Canyon of the Sun in half. His dark eyes narrowed when he spotted an adolescent boy sitting in a chair beside the corral, which held five mustangs.

Raven had intended to make a morning raid, but the lazy gang of outlaws was still sleeping off last night's bout with whiskey. In disgust, Raven had gathered the liquor bottles and hurled them against the nearest boulder. Then he'd decided to double-check the canyon to ensure there were no other settlers who had escaped his notice a few days earlier.

Squatting down, he waited a quarter of an hour before he saw the teenage girl emerge from the cabin to join the injured boy sitting by the corral. A moment later another teenage boy appeared from the barn.

Raven smirked at the foolishness of this white family— one defenseless woman and five children who had invaded sacred Apache ground. There was no threat of force here, he decided. This raid would be easier than confiscating the supply wagon he'd stolen, single-handed, the previous day, while his cohorts were drinking themselves blind and senseless. The raid on the wagon had been a simple matter. Raven had disguised himself in a sombrero and serape, planned his surprise attack and made off with a full load of supplies and provisions that would last the gang for weeks.

Another quarter of an hour passed while Raven crouched in the underbrush. He scanned the homestead carefully, but saw no sign of other whites coming and going from the ranch. Only five children and a woman, he concluded. They would be no match for him and the bandits. By midday the family would congregate in one place, he predicted. It was then that he would strike. Six captives would bring a fine price from the *Comancheros* in New Mexico Territory or from the Mexicans.

The horses and sheep could be sold to the miners—if they lived long enough to enjoy their freshly butchered meat, Raven thought wickedly. It was not unusual for him to lure in unsuspecting prospectors, offering to sell them livestock, and then dispose of the trusting fools so he could sell the animals a second time.

Assured that he'd meet with little resistance during this raid, Raven retraced his steps along the canyon rim. There were no sharpshooters to pick off riders that descended into this panoramic valley, only a helpless woman and children. What would have been a natural fortress for the Apache—with posted lookouts on the cap rock—was nothing but a trap for these sitting ducks, who would bring a fine price.

Raven swung onto his pony and reined toward the secluded campsite south of the Canyon of the Sun. He scowled derisively when he arrived and found the four men sprawled on their pallets, just as he'd left them three hours earlier.

Dismounting, he strode over to nudge Hank Burton with his moccasined foot. "Get up," he snapped in stilted English.

The burly man groaned miserably, then rolled to his side. "My head's killin' me. Go 'way, Injun."

Raven gnashed his teeth. He tolerated the disrespectful name only because Hank Burton served a useful purpose. Hank and Gus Traber, both army deserters, often made use of their military uniforms to lure in unsuspecting travelers, ranchers and miners. Although they were drunkards, both men were passable shots with rifles when they were sober.

Pivoting, Raven nudged Gus on the shoulder, jostling the man awake. "Time to get up."

"Go to hell, Injun," Gus grumbled crankily.

"Shudup, all ya," Elliot Cunningham snarled as he crawled unsteadily onto all fours. He shook his bushy head and pried open bloodshot eyes. "What the hell's goin' on, Injun?"

"It is time to raid the farm that lies in the canyon to the northwest," Raven announced.

Thanks to knowing White Wolf—and this was the only benefit Raven appreciated from that association—he could communicate in English with these ruffians who considered themselves his superiors. Typical whites and Mexicans, thought Raven. Without his perfected skills and expertise these fools would've been caught and hanged long ago.

"Wake Juan up," Elliot ordered as he staggered sluggishly to his feet.

Raven strode over to the place where Juan Drego, the Mexican who made arrangements for the trade of captives, was still snoring loudly. Raven was certain the Mexican hadn't moved since he'd pitched forward and fallen facedown in a drunken stupor.

Raven scooped up Juan's sombrero—the one he'd borrowed when he decided to steal the supply wagon—then dipped it into the nearby stream. He poured water over Juan's matted, coal-black hair, listening in wicked satisfaction as the man sputtered and cursed in Spanish.

Since Hank Burton and Gus Traber were still slow to

rise, Raven used the sombrero to give the two army deserters a dash of cold water to bring them to their senses—what little they had.

"Get cleaned up," Raven ordered brusquely. "We'll ride in two hours."

"Damn Injun thinks he's in charge," Elliot muttered as he raked the tangled hair from his eyes.

Raven *was* in charge and always had been, even if these fools refused to acknowledge the fact. The day would come when he no longer needed any of these ruffians, and he'd turn on them as mercilessly as they turned on their own kind to appease their ravenous greed for money.

While the four men hobbled barefoot into the creek, without bothering to doff their clothes, Raven started a small campfire to brew the coffee the men insisted they couldn't start the day without. Although Raven needed little help in capturing the woman and children, he did need these ruffians to be clearheaded enough to round up the livestock. Now that he'd destroyed the whiskey supply, he could keep these hooligans sober until they traded the captives for gold and ammunition.

By midafternoon, the gang would be transporting their captives southeast toward the *Comanchero* encampment. Raven smiled in satisfaction. The Apache haunt in the Canyon of the Sun would be purified, once more untainted by whites. The canyon belonged to the gods, and Raven had made his own sacrifice to them recently. White Wolf was buried there, and Raven rested easier knowing his blood brother would never again stand between him and Gray Eagle.

John wasn't surprised by the attention he received when he rode Pie down the main street of Rambler Springs. The piebald stallion had become his trademark while he traveled through Arizona Territory. People identified his horse with his widespread reputation as a marshal and part-time bounty hunter. Although he was recognized on sight, very few people spoke to him, unless he approached them directly. No one was particularly eager to associate with him; it was as if the renegade bandits he tracked somehow tainted him.

He supposed townsfolk feared that he'd *attract* as much trouble as he was hired to alleviate. Most folks wanted the territory cleared of riffraff, but they wanted it done in the wilds, away from their homes, business establishments and families. In short, John was an outsider who was tolerated because of the necessary service he provided for civilized society.

During the month he'd spent in Paradise Valley, he'd grown accustomed to being accepted and wanted by Tara and the children. Now people were giving him a wide berth again, and those feelings of isolation, even in a crowd, were more pronounced than ever.

Dismounting, John nodded a greeting to two older women who lingered on the boardwalk. They ducked their heads and scurried off as if the devil himself were hot on their heels. Typical, he thought sourly.

Leaving Pie tied to the hitching post, John strode toward the telegraph office. The clerk smiled nervously, jotted down the message, took John's money, then quickly turned away.

John shook his head in dismay as he exited the office. He'd grown so accustomed to being wanted and accepted in Paradise Valley, so accustomed to the children's constant chatter, that it was going to take time to settle back into his old routine, where silence was the rule.

His next stop was the bank. He arranged for the deposit of cash—which his supervisor would be sending, at his request—to be placed in Tara's account. He completed the transaction within a few minutes, and with very little conversation on the bank employee's part.

John returned to the boardwalk, then glanced this way

and that. When he spotted the general store, he strode off to tend to his next task.

"I need traveling provisions and...er, a dress," John told the shopkeeper self-consciously.

The bald-headed proprietor's eyebrows shot up like exclamation marks. "A dress?" he parroted in disbelief.

John had never purchased a dress in his entire life and he suddenly felt inept, especially when the man kept looking at him as if he was loco.

"Er...you're the one they call Wolfe, aren't you?" Henry Prague asked warily.

John nodded. "Yes, but I still need a dress."

Henry Prague gestured toward the rack of gowns in the corner of the store. "Maybe I should call Mama to help you with your selection."

While Henry scuttled off to summon whoever Mama was, John ambled over to the rack. He glanced over his shoulder when he heard approaching footsteps. He appraised the thin, gray-haired woman who scrutinized him through her wire-rim spectacles.

"Henry says you're in need of a dress, Mr. Wolfe. My name is Wilma Prague. May I help you find what you're looking for?"

John could tell the woman was dying of curiosity. He decided, there and then, that it might benefit Tara if folks in town knew she was a friend. If his connection to Tara and the children deterred troublemakers from hassling her, then all the better.

"Irish—that is, Tara Flannigan is a friend of mine. I want to buy her a new dress to return her kindness to me," he explained.

Wilma's pale blue eyes widened in surprise. "You know Tara?"

John nodded. "She treated my injuries and I want to repay her with a gift."

"Such a sweet girl," Wilma replied, quickly warming

to the safe topic. "She's been cleaning house for Henry and me since she arrived in the area a couple of years back. I'm grateful that she's a hard worker. I'm so busy with the store that I don't have much time to tend our house."

John's eyebrows shot up to his hairline. Tara had never mentioned her job. He assumed she made her weekly ride into town to sell eggs and restock supplies. "She cleans house for you?" he repeated stupidly.

"Oh, yes," Wilma replied. "Tara also cleans for Corrine and Thomas Denton, who run the best restaurant in town. Corrine is as busy as I am. And of course, Tara spiffies up the church while she's in town, too."

Good gad, didn't that woman have enough to do without taking more jobs in town? John thought it over for a moment and realized that sounded exactly like Tara, who worked tirelessly to ensure the orphans had food on the table and clothes on their backs.

He turned his attention to the rack of gowns. "I've decided I want two gowns instead of just one. I'll need all the proper feminine paraphernalia to go along with them."

Wilma blushed slightly, but she chattered about colors and styles while she thumbed through the dresses on the rack. John realized there was at least one person in town who wasn't afraid to strike up a conversation with him. Wilma Prague's endless chatter could rival Flora's.

"Here's a dress that should fit Tara nicely," Wilma said as she held up the garment for his approval.

The gown was all that was sensible and practical for a female who spent her time in town working fiendishly to clean houses for extra money and who never said a peep to anyone about her part-time jobs. John decided the blue calico gown was acceptable, but his second purchase wasn't going to be the least bit practical. It was going to be anything but! Something feminine and frilly and dazzling. Something that complemented Tara's stunning beauty.

Pensively, he scanned the rack, then reached over to pluck up a deep green gown that would accentuate the startling color of her eyes. True, the gown dipped daringly at the neckline and tucked in neatly at the waist, but John wanted to give Tara something spectacular. As spectacular, at least, as anything that could be found in this small frontier community.

"I'll take this one, too," he announced.

"You have excellent taste, Mr. Wolfe," Wilma exclaimed. "Tara will look stunning in this gown. The community founders are planning a picnic and street dance next month. I'm sure your friend won't be wanting for dance partners when she arrives in this splendid dress. In fact, there are several young bachelors in town who've asked after her. I'm afraid I don't know too much about her because I'm usually working while she's cleaning, so we don't have much time to chat. I think she has one or two younger brothers or sisters living with her, isn't that right?"

John wasn't about to divulge information Tara didn't want spread around town. If the community had a grapevine, he suspected Wilma never hesitated to send tidbits down the line. Rather than answer the question, he nodded noncommittally.

The prospect of eager suitors following on Tara's heels derailed John's train of thought. Worse, an odd knot coiled tightly in his belly. Was jealousy nipping at him? He couldn't be sure because he'd never experienced the possessive sensation before. Well, whatever the source of the unpleasant feeling, he simply had to get over it, because he knew another man would eventually take his place in Tara's arms. John didn't have to like the idea—which he sure as hell didn't—but he couldn't offer her promises that another man might be able to fulfill. Still...

"I'll wrap up the gowns and necessary undergarments while Henry helps you gather your supplies," Wilma said, jostling him from his disturbing thoughts.

Willfully, John turned his mind to gathering travel provisions, and tried very hard not to visualize Tara whirling beneath the streetlights, dancing in the arms of another man, wearing the seductive gown John had purchased for her.

"When Tara comes to town, please see that she receives the gifts," he called after Wilma.

"Certainly, Mr. Wolfe. It will be my pleasure."

Several minutes later, John exited the store with an armload of supplies. He took time packing his saddlebags, then patted Pie's sleek neck and aimed himself toward the town marshal's office for a briefing on criminal activity in the area.

John nodded a greeting to the leathery-faced marshal sprawled negligently in his chair there, booted feet propped against the edge of the scarred desk.

"Marshal Wolfe, I see you finally made it to town." Tom Glasco hauled himself to his feet, then extended his hand. "What brings you to this part of the country? Not to track the worst desperadoes in the territory, I hope."

"I thought maybe you could answer that," John replied as he shook hands with the stout lawman, who sported a handlebar mustache. John never could figure out why whites bothered with that ridiculous facial hair ornamentation. But then Apaches—who, unlike other tribes, didn't even bother smearing on war paint—had raised him, so what the hell did he know?

"Last I heard, the home office in Prescott had you tailing a bunch of wild Indians that have been playing havoc with ranchers and travelers down Tucson way."

"Actually, they're white outlaws masquerading as Indians," John stated.

Tom's bushy brows jackknifed. "Well, I'll be damned. Hadn't heard that. How'd you figure that out?"

"Footprints."

"Huh?" Tom frowned, bemused.

"Indians have an entirely different way of walking than whites," he elaborated. "Even wearing moccasins, a white man leaves a distinct indentation with his footprint. Indians balance their weight differently."

"Damn, how do you know so much about Indians, Wolfe?" Tom asked curiously.

John shrugged evasively. He wasn't going to get into that. Only one white person knew his carefully guarded secret, and that was Irish. Tom Glasco wasn't going to be privy to that information.

Tom plunked into his creaky chair again and stroked his mustache thoughtfully. "Well, I don't recall hearing any reports about a band of marauding Indians stirring up trouble in these parts. The only problem we've had lately is an incident involving the wagon hauling supplies to the general store. That happened a couple of days ago. The driver and his assistant stopped under a shade tree to rest a bit during the trip. They claimed they dozed off awhile and they were awakened to the sound of their team of horses and wagon thundering down the trail like they'd been spooked."

John frowned curiously and waited for Tom to continue.

"Somebody tied a saddle horse behind the wagon, but instead of climbing onto the seat, the sneaky bastard wedged himself between the team of horses so no one could get a clear shot at him. The driver and shotgun rider saw nothing but a dingy serape flapping in the wind and the top of a sombrero above the horses' withers. Some thieving Mexican, I reckon. Whoever he was, he made off with the horses and wagon, and the two men had to take a ten-mile hike into town."

Prickly sensations skittered across John's skin. The techniques used to take the driver and shotgun rider by surprise and make it difficult to get off a shot had Apache cunning written all over them. John knew perfectly well that Raven was in cahoots with a Mexican who went by the name Juan Drego. Had one of the gang members stolen the wagon? Had Raven disguised himself as a Mexican?

The apprehensive premonition that Raven was involved intensified with each passing second. "Did the driver and his assistant give a description of the horse that was tied behind the wagon?" John asked anxiously.

Tom frowned in thought and stroked his mustache. "Don't recall. Let me get the report and have a look-see." He rummaged through his desk to retrieve the paperwork. "Yep, here it is. Paint pinto with yellow, white and black markings. No saddle, just some kind of blanket strapped around its girth. 'Kinda like you see on an Indian pony,' the driver said."

John felt as if he'd been gut-punched. Raven... Damn it, had he returned to scout out Paradise Canyon, ensure that John had perished after the confrontation? John didn't like the possibility of Raven being anywhere near Tara and the children. But if his gut instincts were correct, it was Raven, disguised as a Mexican, who'd stolen the delivery wagon.

"I gotta go," John muttered, wheeling toward the door.

"Something wrong, Marshal Wolfe?" Tom called after him.

There was definitely something wrong, John mused as he sprinted out the door without bothering to reply. The hair on the back of his neck was standing on end, and his sixth sense was urging him to make a beeline back to Paradise Valley to reassure himself that Tara and the children were all right.

Although John had intended to take time to sort

through the Wanted posters to see if Tara might've been a murder suspect in Texas, he was compelled to leave town in a flaming rush. The possibility of Raven and that gang of cutthroats preying on Tara and the children terrified him.

John rode hell-for-leather, demanding all that the piebald stallion had to give. He was thankful—and not for the first time—that Pie possessed impressive stamina, speed and endurance. There had been many a time that John credited Pie with saving his hide. The reliable steed made the three-mile jaunt from town to the canyon rim with all the haste John demanded of him.

Although the stallion was lathered with sweat and breathing heavily, John knew Pie had reached his second wind. Surefooted, the horse moved quickly down the winding path toward the canyon floor. Even before John had a clear view of the cabin and barn, he felt the eerie silence and emptiness closing in around him, making it impossible to breathe normally. His heart began pounding ninety miles a minute.

"Damn him to eternal hell!" John scowled furiously when he rode into the clearing to confirm his worst fears. There was no sign of life or activity. There were no grazing sheep, no horses penned in the corral, only a few chickens pecking the grass. The family's milk cow was nowhere to be seen.

John bounded from the saddle and ran toward the cabin. He bellowed Tara's name, but was met with agonizing silence.

The tormenting sight that met him at the front door had his heart somersaulting around his chest. A stream of colorful obscenities flew from his lips as he scanned the kitchen and dining area. The place had been ransacked. Chairs were overturned. Plates and food littered the floor like casualties of war. The table—where he'd taken his meals this past month, while listening to the incessant chatter of children and feeling like an integral part of this close-knit family—lay on its side.

Everywhere he looked he noted the signs of unleashed force—and futile resistance. The torturous thought caused another raft of foul curses to fly off his tongue.

Panting for breath, his heart hammering forcefully against his ribs, John battled the onslaught of emotion that left him staggering for balance. He could visualize with vivid clarity the ruffians staging a surprise attack on this unsuspecting family. No doubt the desperadoes had waited until the family gathered for the midday meal before laying siege to the cabin.

John had never allowed his job to become personal in the past, hadn't permitted himself to dwell on the depths of horror and fear the victims of raids endured. But now his imagination ran rampant as he realized what Tara and the children must have felt when the bandits descended on them like a sinister plague.

He could visualize the fear in little Flora's enormous brown eyes, feel the terror Maureen must have experienced. And the boys, he mused, a sick feeling twisting his gut. He knew those boys who were struggling to become men would feel responsible for protecting the family. Even Derek, who was still recovering from injury, would've fought back, despite his pain.

And Tara… John wobbled unsteadily on his feet. He braced his hand against the wall for additional support when a fierce emotion nearly drove him to his knees. He instantly recalled how Tara had faced down the gang of outlaws who'd intruded in the canyon two weeks earlier. She'd been prepared to defend John with her own life because he was still on the mend. He knew that, when it came to those children, Tara was as protective as a mother grizzly. Despite the possibility of personal injury, or even death, Tara would defend the children against the cruel men who rode with Raven.

That unsettling thought sent alarm ricocheting through him. John scanned the area for signs of blood...and nearly collapsed in tormented frustration when he noticed the dried red droplets on the floor. His heart ceased beating for a moment. His imagination ran wild, assuming the worst.

"Damn it to hell," John snarled as he wheeled toward the door.

He had to get a grip on himself or he'd be of no use to anyone. He had to calm down and think! He was a one-man posse. He was Tara and the children's one and only hope of rescue. If he didn't get his head on straight he'd have five more lives weighing down his overburdened conscience. If he failed on this foray, he wouldn't be able to live with himself—wouldn't want to live, period!

Forcing himself to concentrate—and that was practically impossible when emotions kept whirling through him like the devastating winds of a cyclone—John stormed outside. Suddenly he couldn't seem to remember the usual procedures he followed to locate footprints and determine the direction the outlaws had taken to elude capture. He couldn't think past the distracting emotions that he'd never before had to battle during his crusades for justice. His procedures had always been clear-cut, precise and methodical. He'd done his job thoroughly, capably—like a well-oiled machine. Now his feelings for Tara and the children kept clogging his thought processes, leaving him cold and shaking with gut-wrenching fear.

The stallion nickered and tossed his head, demanding John's attention. Seeing Pie had a calming effect on him. The two of them had been to hell and back so many times they could make the trek blindfolded. John knew the stallion sensed his overwhelming torment and frustration. Pie was trying to console his master the only way he knew how. Indeed, the animal walked forward to brush his soft muzzle against John's quaking hand. The soft whinny, the restless stamping of hooves indicated Pie was as anxious to locate the family as he was. No doubt, the stallion had gotten attached, and enjoyed the attention the children paid to him, too.

Like John, Pie had found a place that felt like home, surrounded by other animals and the laughter of children. Now that feeling of belonging, of contentment, had vanished in a puff of smoke. The aching emptiness in John's soul was crying to be refilled. Precious lives depended on him and he *could not* fail.

Resolutely, he dragged in a steadying breath and forced himself to rely on instinct and training, to ignore the jumble of emotions bombarding him from every direction at once.

"All right, Pie, we have a job to do, so let's get at it." John stared grimly at the horse that had been his constant companion—his *only* companion. "We're making a pact, you and I, right here, right now. Whatever it takes, no matter how long it takes, we're going to track down those bastards and exact revenge."

The horse nickered again, as if in total agreement. It wasn't a question of *if* he and Pie would locate the desperadoes who'd abducted Tara and the kids, but *when.* Neither was there a question about whether to bring back the *bandidos* dead or alive, because John had no intention of inconveniencing himself in the least. Those bastards had sealed their fate when they captured this defenseless family. They were *never, ever* going to terrorize another living soul, John promised himself fiercely. Their reign of terror was going to come to an end—forever—with their deaths.

With the exception of Raven, he amended. Raven's obsessive craving for freedom had compelled him to form an alliance with those ruthless cutthroats. John couldn't ignore the vow he'd made to Gray Eagle to bring Raven back alive. That was a solemn promise that must be kept.

Relying on training and years of practice, John walked toward the dirt path to the corrals. He squatted down to survey the footprints and horse tracks. The smeared prints revealed Tara and the children's struggle to prevent being tossed onto the backs of horses. The tale was told in those marks in the dirt. Again John had to remind himself to remain focused and stifle the churning emotions that distracted him. He concentrated on determining where each child had been placed in the procession.

Flora brought up the rear, he noted as he studied the depth of the hoofprints and small shoe prints. He glanced southeast, noticing that the trail led in the same direction he'd taken the older boys to round up mustangs. John scowled when he saw the evidence of another scuffle that had taken place twenty yards down the path. He studied the set of moccasin prints beside boot prints the exact size of Tara's.

A cold chill slithered down his spine. Raven had recaptured Tara and tossed her back on her horse. John could tell by the hoofprints that Raven led the procession and held the reins to Tara's horse, because the tracks indicated the uneven gait of the horse, which wasn't allowed to set its own pace.

John blinked in surprise when he noticed the overturned stone beside Tara's tracks. He smiled for the first time in hours. Tara and the children had kept their wits about them, despite their terrifying ordeal. They were leaving stone signals for him to follow.

"Good girl, Irish," he murmured as he wheeled toward Pie.

John rifled through his saddlebags to retrieve his moccasins. For the first time in five years he was going to track desperadoes as the man he really was and always would be—pure Apache at heart. White Wolf, the Apache warrior who'd hidden behind John Wolfe's fictitious identity, now lived and breathed and thirsted for revenge.

As he shed his breeches and shirt to don his breastplate, leather leggings, breechcloth, headband and moccasins, he could feel the transformation overtaking him. He was dressing as pure Apache, thinking with pure Apache savvy. The renegades who'd captured this family and their livestock were going to confront Apache wrath in its deadliest form.

White Wolf would show no mercy. He was no longer the long arm of frontier justice; he was the personification of unleashed Apache vengeance.

Chapter Sixteen

Despite the aching bruise on her cheek, the throbbing of her swollen lip and her splitting headache, Tara held herself upright in the saddle. She was determined to project a fearless facade to reassure the children who rode single file behind her.

She could hear Flora and Maureen sobbing quietly. Occasionally she heard Derek's muffled moans of discomfort. She knew the boy had to be hurting because it hadn't been long since he'd been injured by being thrown off the mustang and crashed into the fence.

"I gotta pee," Samuel said, his voice gruff with resentment.

Tara knew exactly why the boy wanted to call a halt. Like herself and the other children, he had demanded to stop at irregular intervals so they could leave stone signals. Although Tara presumed John was long gone from the area, the children were determined to leave a trail for him to follow. She could tell by the expressions on their faces that they had every confidence John would rescue them. In their eyes, he could accomplish the impossible. The children also knew John cared enough about them to track these scroungy-looking renegades, who had stopped briefly to change from their Indian garb into white man's clothes—all except for Raven.

Tara glared at the Apache's broad back. Twice she'd battled that black-eyed devil—and lost. She knew how brutal Raven could be, and she had the souvenirs of their skirmishes to prove it. Seeing the cold look in his obsidian eyes triggered flashbacks of her confrontation with the demented Texas rancher. If Raven had a soul, it was buried so deeply beneath his bitter anger that it would require the skills of a surgeon to find it.

It hadn't taken Tara long to realize this vicious Apache was the mastermind of this gang of thieves. While the other scraggly men casually herded the livestock, Raven was on constant alert as he led the way from one concealing ravine to the next. Of course, Tara couldn't imagine who would notice them, seeing as how they were crossing uninhabited country where deep gullies, winding arroyos and rugged buttes were in abundance. Mostly it was just rough terrain, with plentiful rocks, cactus and clumps of native grass.

"I said I gotta pee," Samuel shouted impatiently.

Raven twisted on his pinto to glower at the lad, who met the fierce look with open defiance. Tara knew that expression well, because she'd been feeling the same way since Raven had dragged her—kicking, biting and clawing—from the cabin. She'd left her mark of defiance on his bronzed cheek to prove she wasn't leaving peaceably. In turn, Raven had left his mark on her. But, she consoled herself, she'd drawn blood and that pleased her immensely.

Muttering under his breath, Raven bounded from his pinto and stalked toward Samuel. Swiftly he untied the boy's bound hands from the pommel of the saddle, then roughly jerked him off the horse.

"Be quick about it," the Apache snarled.

Purposely stumbling, Samuel overturned several stones, then trotted toward the underbrush to relieve himself.

Tara cast the other children meaningful glances, silently ordering them not to cause more trouble. There was nowhere to run and hide in this unforgiving terrain. They had to bide their time and choose their battlefield. Now wasn't the time or place for an escape attempt. Furthermore, she'd tested Raven's volatile temper twice, and she wanted to lull him into thinking that she'd accepted her captivity.

"Hurry up!" Raven barked impatiently.

Samuel reappeared and walked briskly toward his mount. He was yanked off the ground, slammed down on the saddle and tied in place with swift efficiency.

Tara studied Raven astutely, noting the resemblance between his and his blood brother's muscular appearance and obvious survival skills. The only difference was that Raven had no sentiment or compassion whatsoever. It tormented Tara to the extreme that John Wolfe made allowances and excuses for Raven's abhorrent behavior. In her opinion, Raven wasn't the man John thought he knew. She suspected John was overly optimistic when it came to searching for noble qualities in his blood brother.

When Raven strode past her, Tara glared at him in disgust. She couldn't find it in her heart to regard him with the slightest sympathy. It wasn't because he was Apache that she disliked him, it was because he was a selfish, awful excuse for a human being. He hadn't exhibited one likable or decent characteristic. In her eyes, he was worse than the *bandidos* riding behind him—and that was saying a lot.

Tara's head snapped backward when Raven yanked abruptly on the lead rope to her horse, forcing the mare to lunge into a gallop. Behind her, she heard Derek groan miserably, jarred by his horse's gait. She glanced back to see tears of pain in his eyes as the procession of children were forced into a thundering lope. The horses were bound together by ropes that linked one to the next. The procession resembled a chain gang of mounted prisoners racing cross-country.

Tara was reminded of the orphan train ride—destination unknown—but she had the unmistakable feeling that the end of *this* journey would be more unpleasant than riding the rails to Texas. Hastily, she sent a prayer winging heavenward, asking for divine intervention, but she knew it was up to her to find a way to save the children— or die trying. Despite impossible odds, she'd go down fighting with her last breath. If she was to become the inspiration for the children not to give up the fight, then so be it.

White Wolf reined Pie to a halt on the rock ridge overlooking Diablo Canyon. Following the children's stone signals, he'd set a swift pace to overtake the procession, which now moved at a slower clip. Herding the livestock slowed the outlaws down, forcing them to ride single file through the winding arroyos that cut gashes in the canyon floor.

White Wolf retrieved his field glasses to scan the chasm. The black stallion had taken his herd of mustangs and thundered off at the first sign of intrusion. John could tell by the five sets of hoofprints that veered to the left that the mustangs he and the boys captured had broken away from the domesticated horses and followed the devil stallion. White Wolf sincerely hoped those horses had given the outlaws fits when they broke and ran.

While picking his way down the narrow trail to the canyon floor, White Wolf appraised his surroundings. He glanced west, watching the sun make its final descent to the horizon. He predicted Raven would camp at the east end of the valley, using the copse of cottonwood and cedar trees for protection. He also predicted, given the direction Raven traveled, that the procession was headed for the *Comanchero* stronghold in New Mexico Territory.

White Wolf had to stage his attack before the outlaws crossed the border. The *Comancheros* kept guards on constant lookout for unwanted intruders. If he didn't overtake Raven and the ruffians before they reached the *Comanchero* headquarters, it could take months to retrieve the children, who would be transported away to become enslaved—or worse.

He refused to dwell on Tara and Maureen's grim fate—which was why his sense of urgency multiplied tenfold. He had to strike tonight.

Tomorrow would be too late.

When an idea hatched in White Wolf's mind, he reversed direction. He needed assistance to provide a distraction. And he knew exactly where to find it. He had to scatter the enemy so he could deal with them one by one.

He patted Pie's muscular neck as he circled the cap rock. "C'mon, boy, we'll form a pact with the devil and bring the wrath of hell into this canyon."

"You cook, paleface." Raven shoved Tara roughly toward the campfire. When Tara called the children to assist her, Raven flung up his hand. "No, only you," he ordered sharply.

Tara pivoted, then nodded toward her bound hands. "If you expect me to prepare the meal alone, then expect a delay. Either untie me or let the children help."

Raven glared daggers at her for a long moment, then nodded reluctantly and motioned for the children to approach the fire.

Tara dug into the knapsack to retrieve the provisions. "There are cans of beans and ingredients for biscuits," she said in a voice that carried to Raven, who'd perched on a boulder to keep watch. "Boys, see if you can manage to open the cans, even if your hands are bound. Girls, we'll try to mix the biscuit dough.''

For Raven's benefit, Tara pretended to give cooking instructions to the girls while they measured ingredients. ''Each of you has done a fine job of forcing delays in the procession,'' she murmured. ''Flora, add more flour, please,'' she said more loudly.

''Are you all right?'' Maureen asked quietly. ''Your face looks awful.''

''I'm fine,'' she assured the girls. ''Maureen, we need more lard.''

''Zohn Whoof will come for us,'' Flora whispered as she sprinkled flour into the tin bowl.

''He might not realize we've been abducted, sweetheart. We have to plan our own escape attempt. Remember when John showed us how to hide in plain sight...? Add a little more lard, Maureen,'' she said clearly. ''This mixture is still too stiff to roll out the biscuits.'' Tara dropped her voice again. ''I expect the bandits will start drinking the whiskey they stole from our cabin after supper. Boys, use the excuse to relieve yourselves again so you can hide in the grass after dark.''

''What about you?'' Flora asked, wide-eyed.

''I'll provide a distraction so you can sneak away.''

''Tara...'' Maureen's voice wobbled with wary apprehension.

The girl's haunted expression left an uneasy feeling in the pit of Tara's stomach. This wasn't the time for Maureen to fall to pieces.

''I'm counting on you. No matter what else happens, I want you to protect Flora, as I have always protected you. Do you understand me?''

The girl's eyes clouded with tears, but she nodded ever so slightly.

''No matter what, Maureen,'' Tara repeated. ''I want your word on it.''

Their eyes met for a long moment. Reluctantly, Maureen nodded again and whispered, "I promise."

"Good job, girls. Now let's roll out the biscuits and put them in the Dutch oven." Hands bound at the wrists, Tara and the children continued to prepare the meal under Raven's watchful eye.

After the outlaws ate their fill, they passed around the bottle of liquor. Tara was disappointed that Raven didn't partake of the drink. He remained on constant alert while his cohorts celebrated their successful raid.

It incensed Tara when Raven refused to let her and the children eat the leftover food. She suspected the heartless bastard intended to keep them faint from hunger. Well, she was having none of that. The children weren't going hungry. They'd suffered near starvation once too often at the orphanage and during their exodus to Arizona.

Determined, she climbed to her feet and approached the campfire.

"Sit down, woman," Raven snapped gruffly. When Tara flagrantly ignored the order, he bolted up to block her path. "I said sit down!"

Tara tilted her chin to a defiant angle. "These children will eat or I won't cook for you again. What you and your men haven't eaten will go to waste, so the children might as well have the leftovers." What she didn't bother to say was that she'd purposely mixed more than enough dough, but she realized, sharp as Raven was, he'd figured that out all by himself.

Their gazes locked and clashed. Boldly, she reached down to scoop up the leftover biscuits. She yelped in pain when Raven kicked her hands, sending the biscuits catapulting through the air to land in the grass.

"Now feed your children, paleface," he said, then smirked sarcastically. "That is how the Apache are treated on the reservation—like stray dogs tossed scraps of food no one else will eat."

Tara stared squarely into those onyx eyes, which glittered with hatred and contempt. "I'm truly sorry that your people haven't been treated fairly or kindly. But you're no better if you impose the same cruelty on defenseless children. No man has the right to cry insult and injustice while he does to others what he does *not* want done to him."

"I think I would like you better, paleface, if I cut out your sharp tongue," he sneered, his eyes flashing with menace.

Tara didn't so much as flinch at the vicious threat; she simply gathered the scattered biscuits, brushed them off as best she could, then distributed them among the children.

Several minutes later, Flora stood up and said, "I need to pee now."

Muttering sourly, Raven nudged Gus Traber in the ribs. "Take the girl to the bushes."

"Take her yerself, Injun," Gus snorted before he guzzled another swig of whiskey.

"I have to go, too," Maureen declared as she rose to her feet.

"Damn kids gotta pee all the damn time," Gus groused.

"Take them," Raven ordered. "Now!"

Gus tried to object, but when Raven's razor-sharp dagger pricked the underside of his jaw, the outlaw swore ripely. "All right, but you make sure those sons-a-bitches don't drink all the whiskey while I'm gone. Hear me, Injun?"

Gus staggered clumsily to his feet, then motioned for Flora and Maureen to trail after him. When they disappeared into the darkness, Tara glanced at Raven. "Have another of your men take the boys to relieve themselves," she suggested. "Then I'll bed the children down for the night."

Raven regarded her suspiciously, but eventually he gouged Elliot Cunningham in the shoulder. "Take the boys to pee," he demanded.

"In a minute," Elliot grumbled. "You're gettin' too damn highfalutin for an Injun. I don't take orders from your kind." He glowered at Raven for a full minute, but when Raven stepped threateningly forward, his hand resting on the hilt of his nasty-looking dagger, Elliot backed down and clambered unsteadily to his feet.

The confrontation assured Tara that the outlaws balked at taking orders from the Apache, but they feared him. It was warranted fear, Tara admitted. Crossing Raven too many times could be suicidal. She suspected she'd already pushed her luck about as far as it would go.

Although greed and lack of concern for human life governed these renegades' actions, Raven was another breed entirely. Hatred, rage and bitterness had poisoned his mind thoroughly, and he was pure evil. Tara made a mental note to tread carefully until they attempted escape.

Sitting quietly, she watched the light from the campfire flicker over Raven's face. She felt a tremor of fear spread through her, but she tamped it down. In a few minutes she'd provide a distraction so the children could go to ground, just as John had taught them. She also knew this might be the last time she saw the children. When she provided a disruption, Raven would show her no more mercy. Grimly, Tara accepted what she had to do to spare the children.

"Damn it, where'd they go?" Gus crowed as he lumbered back to camp. "Did you see them pesky girls?"

Snarling furiously, Raven bolted up from his crouched position. "You fool! You were supposed to watch those brats!"

"Damnation, I lost those cursed boys!" Elliot yelled from a distance. "Come help me round 'em up!"

Raven spun toward Tara, his face twisted in a murderous scowl. He raised his hand to strike her, certain she'd instigated the children's escape. Tara ducked her head and plowed into his belly, forcing him off balance. Then she took off at a dead run—in the opposite direction from the children.

Suddenly, the sound of thundering hooves erupted in the darkness. The eerie howl of a wolf rose in the night and echoed around the canyon.

"White Wolf!" Raven bellowed in frenzied outrage.

Tara felt the earth tremble as the stampeding mustangs plunged toward camp. Men scattered like buckshot to avoid being knocked down and trampled. Vile curses exploded when the wild-eyed mustangs tore through the camp, trampling the plates, cooking utensils and bedrolls.

The howl of a wolf rose again, then a gunshot echoed in the darkness.

From her position beside a tree, Tara lurched around to see Gus Traber clutch his chest, then pitch forward on the ground. She knew without question that the unseen sniper was relying on the light from the campfire to pinpoint his target, and was striking with deadly accuracy.

"What the hell's happening?" Elliot roared as he dived for cover. "What are these damn mustangs doing back here after we ran them out?"

Tara circled behind the stampeding mustangs and headed toward the boulders that covered the steep slope. She saw Juan Drego attempt to dash for cover, then heard the wild scream of a horse. Wide-eyed, she watched a powerfully built stallion—which was as black as the devil's soul—rear up and paw the air. Orange campfire light reflected off the whites of its eyes, giving it a diabolical appearance. The steed seemed to have a personal vendetta against the drunken Mexican. Hooves struck out viciously, hammering relentlessly at Juan's shoulder. The Mexican howled in pain and spun away from another oncoming blow. Tara watched Juan run for his life, swearing foully, cradling his injured arm against his ribs.

The report of an unseen rifle overrode the clatter of hooves pounding the earth as the mustangs raced toward the east end of the canyon. Tara glanced down from her hiding place between two boulders to see Hank Burton stagger backward, then collapse lifelessly on the ground. Two men down and one injured, she counted silently. John Wolfe, wherever he was, was picking off his enemies one at a time.

Hope rose inside Tara as she inched toward higher ground. John had arrived on the scene like hell's avenging fury. He'd keep the children safe—

Tara shrieked when an unseen hand grabbed a fistful of her hair and yanked her backward. She felt Raven's rigid body slam into her. The cold steel of his blade pricked her throat as he clamped his muscular arm around her.

"White Wolf lives," he snarled against her neck, clutching her to him like a protective shield of armor. "You knew, didn't you? Did White Wolf erect that sepulcher of stones in the Canyon of the Sun to deceive me?"

It took a moment for Tara to figure out what the enraged Apache was raving about. Then she remembered the children had stacked up the stones she'd placed at the locations of the postholes for the new pasture fence. Raven had obviously returned to scout the canyon to ensure John had died during the showdown. The Apache assumed she'd buried John beneath the pile of stones.

"You are White Wolf's woman," he snarled furiously. "He is after *you!*"

"No, he's after *you* and your cohorts," Tara contradicted. "He's willing to be lenient with you if you agree to return to the reservation."

"White Wolf would delight in humiliating me by dragging me back to my father. I have stood in his shadow since childhood, listening to my father praise his skills, his instincts and his cunning. I will *never* go back to the reservation. Even if I did, I would not let White Wolf escort me,'' Raven growled as he dragged Tara along with him toward the pinto that was tethered near a cedar tree.

Tara had the sinking feeling that Raven had never considered White Wolf his adopted brother, but rather a hated rival for Gray Eagle's affection and respect. Sweet mercy, all these years White Wolf had been riddled with guilt, believing he'd somehow betrayed and disappointed Raven. But from the sound of things, White Wolf's sense of loyalty and brotherly concern were wasted on this renegade Apache, who was envious of his adopted brother's prestige and influence on the clan.

When Tara tried to brace herself, refusing to be tossed on the horse, Raven grabbed her roughly and hoisted her onto his mount without releasing his painful grasp on her hair. Before she could slide to the ground on the other side, Raven bounded up behind her.

"You will be my bait when White Wolf comes for me," he snarled as he gouged the paint pony in the flanks.

Tara squirmed on the horse, making it difficult for Raven to control both her and the flighty steed, which was scrabbling up the steep incline. Despite her struggles, Raven shoved her face against the horse's neck and practically sprawled on top of her to hold her in place.

Tara muttered a curse as Raven reined his pony between boulders and scrub cedars, never once allowing himself to become an open target. Tara didn't know where John was, but she knew it was impossible for him to get off a clean shot when Raven relied on Apache cunning, clinging to cover and taking her with him for insurance.

In desperation, she squirmed sideways, trying to force

Raven off balance and send him tumbling to the ground. He growled fiercely when she shifted beneath him, very nearly catapulting him into a cactus patch. In retaliation, he grabbed his pistol by the barrel and thumped her soundly on the skull. Tara struggled to remain conscious, but the second blow to the back of her head caused her to slump limply over the pinto's neck.

Exploding pain turned her world pitch-black.

White Wolf cursed thunderously when he saw Raven's pinto winding along the steep incline to reach the cap rock. Hurriedly, he grabbed his field glasses and focused on the escaping rider. Despite the darkness, he quickly determined that Raven was riding double, that another body was draped over the horse.

"Irish," he whispered in torment when he saw moonlight glint off her red-gold hair. Everything inside him rebelled against staying put to dispose of the outlaws while Raven was riding off with Tara as his captive.

But White Wolf knew without question that Tara would want him to erase every last threat to the children—wherever the devil those kids were. As of yet, he hadn't spotted a single one of them.

Resolutely, he went in search of the surviving desperadoes. There would be no mercy here in Diablo Canyon, and White Wolf would give no quarter when he confronted the renegades, who had left a trail of death and destruction behind them these past two years.

After gathering up five saddle horses, White Wolf reined Pie beside the campfire. "Samuel, Derek, Calvin, Maureen, Flora!" he called out. "Come back to camp."

"Zohn Whoof! I knew you'd come to save us!"

White Wolf slumped in relief when he saw five silhouettes appear from out of nowhere. He bounded from his horse to hug all five children. They clung to him for a full two minutes, and he struggled to regain control of his roiling emotions. Then he simply gave in and let the feelings flood over him. He let himself love and be loved. He accepted and returned every ounce of affection bestowed on him. In all his life he'd never experienced anything quite like this. He'd never been so openly demonstrative.

"How come you're dressed like that?" Flora questioned as she cuddled against his shoulder.

"Because this is part of who and what I am, half-pint," he murmured.

The children backed away to thoroughly appraise the bone-and-metal breastplate, the loincloth, leggings, moccasins and the symbolic headband that carried his totem of a prowling wolf.

"You look like the Indian that raided our ranch," Samuel remarked.

The comment forced White Wolf to grit his teeth against the frustration and rage pouring through him. Knowing Raven had taken Tara for his own protection infuriated him. Everything inside him ached to give chase.

"I need all of you to help me," he stated. "The sheep and horses are scattered around the canyon. The mustangs we were training escaped to return to the stallion's herd."

"Do you want us to round them up again?" Samuel asked.

White Wolf shook his head. "There will be time for that later. The livestock will bed down for the night, so you can sleep here in camp. Tomorrow I want you to herd the livestock back to Paradise Valley while I follow Raven. He took Tara with him."

Silence descended. Five pair of eyes widened in alarm.

"That Indian who hit Tara? He's still alive and he took her away?" Derek asked angrily.

John felt another wave of outrage splash over him. Raven had struck out at Tara? Damn him! Raven had been thoroughly corrupted by those desperadoes and now behaved exactly like them.

"What happened to the other bad men?" Calvin asked as he glanced around the dark canyon.

Five pair of curious eyes lifted to White Wolf. He had no intention whatsoever of going into detail about how he'd pounced in silence, ensuring not one sound erupted to alert the surviving bandits that he was close at hand, and that he'd come to exact the full measure of revenge. White Wolf didn't want to expose the children to the lethal methods he'd used to eliminate the murderers who'd left a trail of terror and destruction. How the outlaws met their end didn't matter, only that no other innocent lives would be lost at their ruthless hands.

"Danger no longer exists here in the canyon," he said simply.

"But what did you do with the outlaws?"

Damn, leave it to Flora to ask the difficult questions.

White Wolf met the inquisitive gazes focused on him. After a moment he stared directly at each child, knowing they would fully understand there were times—like now, especially now—that he became judge, jury and executioner of expedient justice. He wanted to spare them from discovering this vicious side of him, but the ordeal wouldn't permit it.

"The outlaws who captured you died as they lived," he told them grimly. Before the children could pry for the gory details, White Wolf knelt in front of them. "I'm proud of the way you used Apache savvy and went to ground. You made my rescue much easier."

"It wasn't hard," Derek said. "We disappeared into the grass in nothing flat, just like you taught us to do."

White Wolf noticed that Maureen hadn't uttered a single word. She stood back, her arms wrapped around herself, her eyes glistening with tears she was desperately trying to hold in check. He had the uneasy feeling that her traumatic experience had triggered flashbacks from her secretive past. He wanted to draw her aside and reassure her, but time was running out. Raven was putting distance between them, and White Wolf needed to mount up and ride.

"At first light I want you to drive the livestock back to the ranch," he requested. "I can't concentrate my efforts on rescuing Irish if I'm worried about you being out here on your own."

Five chins elevated to determined angles.

"You can count on us, just as we counted on you to find us," Samuel declared. "We'll go back to the ranch and put it in order while you find Tara."

White Wolf opened his arms once again and the children rushed to him—even Maureen, who had yet to speak. She hugged him to her, and he could feel the tension rippling through her taut body.

Damn, he needed to stay here with the children.

He needed to find Tara.

This mental tug-of-war was tormenting the hell out of him.

"Now, dust off the bedrolls and place them by the campfire so you can settle in for the night." White Wolf gave them one last family hug. "Samuel, will you tether the five saddle horses before you turn in?"

"Not to worry, I'll take care of it," the boy promised faithfully.

When White Wolf strode toward his horse, the children wandered off to gather the sleeping pallets. He didn't dare look back, couldn't afford another distraction. His adopted brother had headed northwest, and White Wolf intended to set a swift pace. He wanted to keep Raven in his sights and decide the best location for a confrontation. Tara would be much safer in Raven's clutches if he knew White Wolf was breathing down his neck, waiting to take advantage of the slightest delay.

Chapter Seventeen

Tara roused to consciousness by groggy degrees. Slowly, she became aware of the powerful horse moving beneath her, of the firm grip on her arm. Her head hurt fiercely, but she didn't make a sound to alert Raven that she was awake. She was determined to regenerate her strength before attempting escape. Even if her escape was unsuccessful she knew she could slow Raven down. She also knew John would be searching for them as soon as he'd ensured the children's safety.

There was no question in her mind that John would deal quickly and effectively with the rest of the outlaws. He was too alert, too clever and too cunning not to. She also knew John well enough to realize he shared her protective concern for the children. It greatly relieved Tara to know they were in competent hands. It also inspired her to do whatever necessary to make it easier for John to overtake Raven.

Keeping that in mind, Tara bided her time and discreetly surveyed her surroundings. She could tell by the terrain that Raven had reversed his southwesterly direction and had circled Paradise Valley while she was unconscious. In the moonlight Tara could see the silhouette of Superstition Mountain looming in the distance. If that was Raven's destination, Tara vowed he wasn't going to reach it—not if she had anything to say about it.

The jagged peaks of the mountain formed a natural fortress with stone lookout towers. From there, Raven would be able to see John coming long before he arrived. Tara promised herself that Raven would have no advantage whatsoever.

John was no longer confronting white men who didn't possess his acute awareness and expert survival skills, she reminded herself. Raven was his equal, trained by Gray Eagle's experienced hand. The fact that Raven was desperate, driven by bitterness and poisoned by resentment, made him a worthy opponent. To Tara, it was like trying to predict the outcome of a clash between two omnipotent, mystical Greek gods. She expected hell to break loose when these two men engaged in battle.

Tara had to devise a way to give John the edge and force Raven to alter whatever murderous scheme he had in mind. Despite her hellish headache, she forced herself to relax, to think, to rely on the element of surprise. While she lay slumped over the horse she tried to recall every self-defense tactic John had shown her. Her mind racing, she appraised the landscape again, noting the faintest hint of dawn glowing against the horizon. The rugged ravines that tumbled northwestward forced the horse to step gingerly. Tara knew this was the time and place to attempt escape.

She waited until the horse gathered its hindquarters to scrabble up another rocky incline. When she felt Raven shift his balance to make the climb easier for the pinto, Tara surged upward. She jabbed Raven in the jaw, then hit him in the midsection good and hard with her elbow. She shrieked like a banshee, purposely startling the horse, causing it to rear up, then clatter sideways to regain its footing.

Leveling one last blow at her captor's nose, Tara

pushed herself away from the staggering horse. Raven snarled viciously as he struggled to keep his balance. Tara landed on her feet and skidded frantically, sliding down the rock-strewn arroyo. Her bound hands closed around a nearby stone the size of her fist. She lurched around to launch her makeshift weapon as Raven swung from the back of the horse. The rock slammed into the side of his head, momentarily knocking him off balance. His roar of outrage broke the stillness of the night and prompted her to set a faster pace.

When she noticed a clump of cedars to her left she veered in the opposite direction, certain Raven would expect her to seek the obvious shelter. What she needed— and couldn't find—was a thick clump of grass to bury herself in, giving her a chance to catch her breath. But she had chosen such rugged terrain for her escape route that grass was scarce and cactus was in abundance.

Panting for breath, Tara dived into a narrow, eroded wash that wasn't much bigger than she was. Then she prayed for all she was worth that dawn wouldn't come streaming into the ravine before she could put greater distance between herself and Raven.

"You waste my time and your energy, paleface," Raven growled in the darkness. "No one can outwait or outsmart an Apache. It will be light soon and you'll have nowhere to run or hide. Then you'll be dead...."

Tara strained her ears, noting that Raven was moving in a circular motion as he spoke, for the sound continued to change directions. Her hands folded around another stone the size of her foot. She waited tensely for the anticipated attack.

"White Wolf is no match for a full-blood Apache," Raven growled. "My so-called brother is a fool and he will be until the day I kill him."

She knew he was closing in on the area where she'd gone to ground because his voice now came from her right. Even worse, it wouldn't be long before the darkness no longer concealed her.

"Since childhood, White Wolf wanted to take my place as Gray Eagle's true son. He tried to outdo me, to prove himself the better warrior so he could earn my father's praise and gain influence. I pretended to accept him, but I hated him for interfering."

Tara winced at the venom in Raven's voice. He was roiling with deep-seated resentment and, no doubt, blaming White Wolf for his own failures and shortcomings. It saddened her that White Wolf had been deceived by Raven's pretended acceptance in the family, that John made undeserved allowances for this vicious, traitorous man who warranted no sympathy whatsoever.

"Did you lie with him, paleface?" came the taunting voice. "Are you his *puta?* Perhaps you'll be mine, as well, after I kill him once and for all."

Tara knew Raven was trying to terrify her, hoping she'd break and run. She refused to give the bastard the opportunity to pounce on her. She tensed when she heard the crunch of pebbles beneath his moccasined feet. Any moment now he'd notice her shadowy form wedged in the narrow gully. Heart pounding, Tara raised the stone and hurled it sideways. She needed to distract the demon warrior long enough to give herself a sporting chance.

Time and darkness were running out.

When she heard Raven moving away, she knew this was her last chance to find a new hiding place. It would take him only a moment to realize she'd tricked him, and he'd head straight toward her.

Tara bounded to her feet and tore off in the opposite direction, running as fast as her legs would carry her. She tried to ignore the throbbing pain at the back of her skull, but dizziness and hunger had her floundering to remain upright. She forced herself to keep moving, told herself that she was granting John valuable time to locate her.

God! She wished he'd materialize from nothingness because her exhausting ordeal was taking its toll. She felt as if she were moving in slow motion as she struggled up a slope to reach higher ground, hoping to locate the pinto and make her getaway.

Her breath gushed from her lungs when an unseen body blindsided her, knocking her to the ground. Damn, so blasted close to escaping, yet not close enough!

Raven yanked her abruptly to her feet, intensifying the dizzy sensations that plagued her. He wrapped his arm around her throat like a vise, cutting off her air supply. Tara tried to send up a cry for help, but she couldn't catch her breath.

"Try that stunt again and you'll be dead," Raven snarled. "I have no more patience with you, *puta*."

"Let her go, Raven."

The bone-chilling voice came from the ledge that Tara had been trying to scale when Raven pounced. She glanced up to see a powerful, formidable figure looming in the slanted rays of dawn. Her eyes widened when she recognized the warrior dressed in full Apache regalia.

It was White Wolf, not John Wolfe, who'd come to rescue her. Tara was never so glad to see anyone in her life, though the cold, forbidding expression on his rugged features was utterly foreign to her. This, she realized immediately, was the legendary lawman and bounty hunter that ruthless criminals dreaded and feared—and with good reason. There was a dangerous aura emanating from him. He was poised like a vicious predator prepared to pounce. His eyes glittered with deadly intensity as he focused absolute concentration on Raven.

White Wolf looked so dark, threatening and unapproachable that Tara honestly wondered whether, if she'd initially met him under these conditions, she would've had the chance to know the good and decent man he was inside. This definitely wasn't a facade that invited friendship, she realized. This man lived in a harsh and violent world and was accustomed to using harsh and violent means to insure his survival.

"I said let her go...."

His growling voice reminded her of a rabid wolf. Although Tara would've been thoroughly intimidated if White Wolf were staring *her* down, Raven didn't seem the least bit fazed by the threat or the presence of the six-shooter trained on him. Of course, Raven was using her body as his shield, so he probably assumed he was safe for the moment. Tara, however, wouldn't have assumed anything of the kind if she were Raven.

"I see that you have as many lives as a cat," Raven said with a smirk. "But your *puta* does not. I will trade her life for mine, White Wolf."

Tara didn't believe for a moment that Raven planned to bargain her life for his. She'd spent enough time in this devil's presence to realize he wasn't the man White Wolf *thought* he knew and could trust. And for the first time, she fully understood what a difficult task John faced—more difficult than he ever realized.

He was hounded by guilt because he had his freedom, and he was tormented by a sense of betrayal of the Apache—Raven in particular. White Wolf was willing to forgive his blood brother, to make accommodations and excuse his vile behavior. But Raven had no fond sentiments to cloud his thinking. He was merely maneuvering to gain the upper hand in this confrontation, just as he had during the showdown in Paradise Valley.

"Don't trust him," Tara squeaked, despite the intense pressure on her throat.

She could see the uncertainty sweeping over White Wolf when he spared her a quick glance.

"Shut up, *puta*," Raven muttered, giving her a hard shake that did nothing to improve the dizziness making her head swirl. "This is between my brother and me."

Tara refused to tolerate Raven's deception and was determined to point it out to White Wolf. "Raven doesn't consider you his brother," she wheezed. "He never has and he's preying on your sympathy to gain an advantage. He resents your favor with Gray Eagle. He told me so himself. To *you,* Raven represents a fallen nation struggling to survive the best way it can, but he's done nothing to guide and assist the captive Apache, while you've tried to ease their plight for five years!"

"Do not listen to her lies, White Wolf," Raven snapped. "She is trying to turn you against me. I only did what I had to do to escape and survive when we met in the Canyon of the Sun. I need to be free!"

White Wolf felt frustration and torment channeling through him while he stood poised on the ledge, his pistol trained on Raven's head. Tara was asking him to alter his entire perspective. He reminded himself that her concept of Raven was distorted because she was his captive, that her own anger and resentment were dictating to her.

"*I* saw Raven with the outlaw gang, you didn't," Tara insisted breathlessly. "It was *he* who was in charge. He was not a reluctant accomplice. He's as cruel as the rest of them. Even worse! You have but to look at my face to see how he mistreats his captives."

Yes, White Wolf could see quite plainly how Raven reacted to Tara's defiance. John hated that she was both a witness and victim in this vicious world where he resided. He would've spared her this traumatic torment if he could. But because of her dealings with Raven, White Wolf wasn't sure she was capable of making a fair judgment. She'd known him less than a day, and White Wolf had lived with him for two decades.

"Raven told me that he resents your favor with Gray Eagle. Raven wants you dead because he's jealous of you, has always been jealous of you," Tara declared.

"Lies!" Raven thundered. "You are my brother. We

are family, even if you have forsaken the Apache to enjoy your freedom, just as I have found my freedom by fleeing from San Carlos to join the outlaws. I am only trying to survive!''

White Wolf felt the conflicting emotions tugging at him again. He wanted to believe Raven, but that meant he had to disregard Tara's pleas. She had always been open and honest with him. But then, he believed Raven had been honest and sincere, too. Damn it to hell!

"Look at him," Tara pleaded. "Really look at Raven. Don't you see the bitter, jealous, ruthless criminal that has taken lives in the name of revenge? He's the one who truly abandoned his people for the sake of his personal freedom. He chose a path of evil and destruction and aligned himself with cutthroats, while you chose the path of justice. Raven could've remained on the reservation to bolster his clan's spirit and become their spokesman. Instead, he's preyed on innocent victims. He's stolen, lied and murdered. He's lied to you as he is lying now. He has no code of honor—can't you see that?''

"This white woman doesn't understand," Raven countered. "Only you can, White Wolf. You are Apache. She is not!"

White Wolf swore under his breath. Logic, sentiment and confusion entangled his thoughts. To believe Raven was to forsake Tara. To believe Tara was to forsake Raven.

"Come back to San Carlos with me," White Wolf requested. "Gray Eagle needs to see that you are well. He needs you with him."

"I can never go back. It would be easier for me to turn white, and we both know that is impossible. I am Apache at heart, White Wolf. The question is where is your heart? Will you betray your own brother, sentence him to a life of captivity, just to have this woman?''

"Raven is trying to manipulate you again," Tara

panted. "He isn't a credit to the Apache. He's given them a bad name with his marauding and murdering. You don't want to look clearly at him for fear of what you might see. The truth is he secretly despises you, and he's been careful to conceal his feelings so he can use you to get what he wants. But this time, White Wolf, really look at Raven. Imagine that he's neither Indian, white or Mexican. Then tell me if he measures up as an honorable, trustworthy man in *any* culture."

"Is she right, Raven?" White Wolf questioned grimly. "Have you betrayed me and my feelings for you all these years?"

As the sun climbed higher on the horizon, casting its light on Raven's scowling face, White Wolf looked into eyes that glittered with hatred and resentment. He looked past the color of his blood brother's skin, forced himself to recall those times when Raven had insisted his cruel comments were no more than a form of playful teasing. John remembered those times when Raven had gone behind his back to denigrate him to Gray Eagle and other members of the clan. In White Wolf's eagerness to make a place in Indian culture, to be wanted and accepted, he'd overlooked Raven's character flaws. But now he could see the truth seeping between the cracks of those manipulative lies.

Finally, White Wolf acknowledged the truth of Tara's words. Raven was not his brother or friend. He had tolerated his presence all those years because he'd been forced to, at Gray Eagle's insistence. It was true that Raven was bloodthirsty and merciless, for White Wolf had seen the evidence in raids, in his treatment of captives. White Wolf couldn't help but wonder if Raven used the white captives to vent his suppressed feelings of hatred for his blood brother.

As much as White Wolf wanted to defend Raven, he could no longer do it. Tara was right. Raven wasn't a

man of honor and courage like his father. His soul was
tainted with resentment, hatred and bitterness. Raven was
not his friend, but rather a clever, cunning, self-serving
enemy.

Something in White Wolf's expression must've given
him away, because he saw Raven stiffen, saw the boiling
fury seep through his carefully controlled demeanor.
Years of training alerted White Wolf that Raven had cast
aside all pretenses and intended to take his best shot.

Raven jerked up his Colt, aiming straight at White
Wolf's heart.

"No!" Tara shrieked, then slammed her fists against
Raven's arm.

Reacting instinctively, White Wolf dived to the ground.
He snapped the pistol up in front of him, levering onto
his elbows to gain a better angle for his shot. Thanks to
Tara's interference, Raven's first bullet sailed over his
head. When Raven fired a second time, White Wolf rolled
sideways, brought the Colt into firing position and
squeezed the trigger.

To his horror and dismay, he saw Raven shove Tara
directly into the path of the oncoming bullet. In that terrifying instant, White Wolf knew without question that
every word she had spoken about Raven was true. The
man would stop at nothing, would sacrifice anyone, to
save himself.

When Tara crumpled to the ground, White Wolf fired
again, a split second before Raven could get off his third
shot. The repetitive report of the pistols shattered the
dawn. Inexpressible torment pummeled White Wolf as he
watched Raven stagger backward, clutching his belly. The
pistol cartwheeled over his hand and clattered to the
ground as he dropped to his knees, then teetered sideways.

White Wolf bounded to his feet and sidestepped into
the ravine to crouch beside Tara, who lay facedown on
the ground. Hearing a faint sound behind him, he glanced

back to see that Raven had retrieved his dagger from his moccasin and was preparing to make his final strike.

White Wolf bolted up, then slammed his heel against Raven's hand, thwarting the oncoming attack. Raven didn't have the strength to move, for the gunshot to his midsection was rapidly taking its toll. Even as his life-blood spilled away, he glowered murderously at White Wolf.

"You were never my brother," he said in a hateful growl.

"But you were *mine,* Raven. I would've spared you, remained loyal to you, but it was *you* who betrayed *me,*" White Wolf whispered. "Gray Eagle had enough love for both of us, but you were too selfish to accept that. I pity you, Raven, for you could've been so much more of a man than you are."

When Raven slumped, his clenched fist fell away from the dagger and he stared sightlessly at the sky.

His heart heavy with grief and regret, White Wolf turned away. It was bad enough that he'd been forced to kill Raven. But even worse, he had to break the bleak news to Gray Eagle. The agonizing thought of informing the old chief that his *true* son had perished at his adopted son's hands tied his stomach in knots.

Again White Wolf knelt beside Tara. He hesitated to touch her, for fear the shot he'd fired had been fatal. Praying to every deity in the heavens above, he gently eased Tara onto her back to examine her wound.

Bloodstains soaked the left side of her shirt. Her skin was deathly pale. His hand shaking uncontrollably, he checked her pulse and half collapsed in relief when he felt her shallow, erratic heartbeat beneath his fingertips. Hope rising, he worked frantically to stem the blood flowing from the wound below her collarbone. His heart twisted in his chest as he closely appraised the bruises and scrapes that discolored her face.

He knew he was responsible for every physical and emotional torment she'd endured. Raven had vented his hatred for White Wolf on Tara. He'd used her body as his shield in an attempt to save himself. And worst of all, White Wolf mused as he bandaged the seeping wound with strips of cloth from the hem of Tara's shirt, he'd exposed her to terrors he'd never wanted her to witness, much less experience. She'd been dragged into hell and she'd come face-to-face with the harsh realities of his world.

Grimly, he gathered her motionless body in his arms and carried her up the rocky incline to his horse. He struggled to mount up behind Tara without jostling her more than necessary. Pie didn't object to carrying double weight as he walked carefully from the rock-strewn ravine. It was as if the steed sensed White Wolf's despair, understood the gravity of the situation and was aware of Tara's precarious condition. There was no impatient prancing to stretch out into a run, just a steady, even gait that carried them toward Paradise Valley.

"I'm so damn sorry, Irish," White Wolf whispered brokenly. "I'd give anything if I could spare you this."

He remembered that he'd assured the children he would return Tara to them, but he hadn't intended to bring her back fighting for her very life! It seemed that no matter how hard he tried to set this cursed world aright, things turned out all wrong. He'd broken his promise to Gray Eagle, to the entire Apache nation and to five orphans who trusted him implicitly. He'd failed time and time again.

He would gladly sacrifice his own life, subject himself to all the torments of the damned in the furthermost reaches of hell if he could magically wave his arms and restore Tara's health, grant the Apache nation freedom to roam over the land the whites had taken from them.

Tears clouded White Wolf's eyes as he clutched Tara

possessively against him, praying she'd survive the trek to the ranch so he could treat her injuries properly and allow her to rest comfortably on her bed. If there was anything to that business about Irish luck, he sincerely hoped it was at work, here and now, because Tara needed all the luck she could get if she was going to fully recover from having White Wolf shoot her down.

He wondered if there was some kind of irony, some moral in here somewhere. Unfortunately, he was too over-whelmed by grief, torment and regret to figure out what the hell it was.

John was relieved when he finally reached the ranch, but he dreaded the moment the children spilled out the door and raced toward him. Alarm registered on every face as he leaned out to hand Tara into Derek's and Samuel's uplifted arms.

"What happened to Tara?" Flora wailed, on the verge of hysterics.

"Oh, my God!" Calvin bleated. His thin face drained of color the moment he clapped eyes on Tara's lifeless body and waxen features.

John's gaze darted to Maureen, who didn't speak at all, just stared at Tara with haunted eyes.

In the space of a heartbeat John had another situation on his hands. Not only had Tara been exposed to the violent life he led, but the children were reliving their own traumatic experiences while being forced to deal with Tara's injuries. John cursed himself soundly for bringing more fear, pain and grief into their lives.

Hurriedly, he dismounted, scooped Tara from Derek's and Samuel's arms and strode toward the cabin. "I need medicinal herbs, roots and mesquite bark...now," he ordered. "You know where to find them in the canyon. Hurry!"

The children sprinted off while John settled Tara in

bed. He was bound and determined to cleanse her wound and discard her bloodstained shirt before the children returned. They didn't need to see Tara at her absolute worst.

Working swiftly, he rinsed the wound, then breathed a grateful sigh when he realized his bullet wasn't lodged near her heart, but had exited through the meaty flesh of her shoulder. Knowing that was the case, he couldn't figure out why she was still unconscious. She should've roused at least briefly by now.

John brushed his hand over the side of her head, then examined the back of her skull. "Well, hell," he muttered. There were two swollen bumps at the base of her neck. He couldn't be certain, but he suspected Raven had knocked her unconscious so she wouldn't cause him trouble during the cross-country trek. The blows to her head, compounded with her painful wound, likely prevented her from regaining consciousness. It was probably a blessing, John decided. He knew firsthand how painful a serious wound could be. Remaining unconscious for a few hours definitely had its advantages.

It was a tremendous load off his conscience to know Tara would survive, though it would take time for her to recover her strength and the use of her left arm. Unfortunately, she'd forever bear a scar—a grim reminder that she'd entered his hellish world of cruelty and violence and hadn't walked away unscathed. By his own hand he'd marked her for life.

Damn it to hell!

When the children returned a half hour later, John left them to sit with Tara while he brewed and mixed the ingredients for the poultice. He wasted no time in applying the healing herbs, then gave instructions to the children, requesting that they change the bandages and replace the poultice every four hours.

Leaving the children in charge, John ambled outside, then glanced around the peaceful canyon. Although this felt like home and the children felt like family, he couldn't remain here for long. Not after what had happened to them all. Especially to Tara, he mused as he raked a shaky hand through his tousled hair. He wasn't sure he could face her when she roused. They both knew that the bullet that brought her down had come from his pistol. God, from *his* pistol!

Frustrated energy put him in motion and kept him there. John worked with fiendish haste to finish the job the children had begun of cleaning up the homestead. He wanted the ransacked ranch to look exactly as it had before disaster and tragedy struck. This, after all, was Tara's paradise. This was that special place set apart from the evil and corruption found in the outside world. This was where comfort, reassurance, peace, security and close family ties reigned supreme.

Or at least they had until John contaminated paradise with the wrath of hell.

He was doing a dandy job of wallowing in misery and regret—until he saw Maureen dash off the porch and race past the triple sandstone spires that divided the valley. He set aside the saw he'd been using to repair the corral the desperadoes had practically ripped to pieces in their haste to steal the horses and herd them from the canyon.

He wasn't sure he was in the right frame of mind to track Maureen down and offer comfort, but the girl was definitely battling unseen demons. John couldn't leave this ranch until he'd done his best to console and reassure her.

He found Maureen at the nearest spring, crying her eyes out. She was coiled up in a tight ball in the grass. Tears rolled unchecked down her flushed cheeks. The moment he knelt beside her she recoiled, refusing his gentle touch, staring at him as if he were her enemy.

"No!" she shrieked.

Well, thank God she could speak, he thought in relief. It was the first word he'd heard out of her all day.

"You know I'd never hurt you," he murmured soothingly, wishing he could say the same thing to Tara and know she'd believe that. He'd never, *ever,* forget how it felt to be the cause of her pain. "What happened, Maureen?"

She didn't pretend to misunderstand the question, just stared right through him as if he wasn't there. He waited for what seemed an eternity, wondering if she trusted him enough to share her torment with him. Finally, the dam of buried emotion burst forth like an erupting geyser.

"They killed Mama like that awful man tried to kill Tara!"

Her high-pitched screech made the hair on the back of his neck stand on end. "Tell me what happened, Maureen," he whispered compassionately.

"Mama and I were running through the rain during a thunderstorm to get home. A gang of men suddenly appeared from the darkened alley. They dragged Mama from my arms. She fought them just like Tara fought and—" Her breath hitched on a shuddering sob. "They...m-murdered her and I didn't call for help, d-didn't try to s-stop them. I couldn't s-speak or move at all. And when that wicked Apache took Tara away with him, I saw them on the ledge above me, but I couldn't shout to the other children. I didn't help her when she needed me most! Now she's going to die, too!"

When Maureen flung herself into his arms, John nearly toppled over from the impact. The girl wailed hysterically. Her entire body shook, as if she were releasing pent-up emotions that had been tormenting her for years. A child's nightmare had been reborn, recreated, revisited, and it held her in its merciless clutches.

John hugged her tightly, letting her have her much-needed cry. Maureen was spilling enough tears for both of them, so he ought to feel better, shouldn't he?

Yeah, maybe in about a thousand years.

"It seems to me your mother loved you so dearly that she purposely distracted attention away from you so you'd be safe from harm," he murmured soothingly. "Now that you're older, you probably realize that Tara did the same thing when the raiders attacked the ranch. You know Tara loves you, that she'd do anything humanly possible to protect and defend you and the other children. Just as your mother was willing to make the ultimate sacrifice, so was Tara. She'd willingly put herself in harm's way to spare you. She wouldn't have wanted you to confront Raven when he made his getaway," he insisted. "And Tara isn't going to die, Maureen. Her wound isn't fatal, but she'll need you and the other children to tend her while she recovers."

"She'll need y-you, t-too," Maureen stammered brokenly.

John brushed his hand over the girl's strawberry-blond head, and then gave her an affectionate squeeze. "You are Tara's family. You're all she needs. I have to ride to San Carlos. What I have to do there cannot wait. I wish I didn't have to go at all, but it's my obligation."

"When are you leaving?" Maureen queried softly.

"In a few days, as soon as I'm sure Irish is doing better."

"You'll come back." It wasn't a question, he noted.

"Yes," he assured her. He still wasn't certain he could face Tara again, not after what he'd done, not after the pain and horror he'd caused her. But for the children's sake, he'd return to help make life easier for them.

Maureen placed her hand trustingly in his, and John swallowed the lump that formed in his throat. When the girl stood up and turned toward the ranch, John walked with her, holding her protectively at his side, offering comfort and support. Well, maybe he'd done one thing right in his life. He'd helped this sweet, tormented girl face and conquer her demons. But it was Tara who had provided the loving reassurance that gave Maureen the faith and strength to overcome her tormented past.

Ah, Irish, he whispered silently to the image floating in his mind. *You've accomplished amazing feats through your love and dedication. How I wish I could've accomplished as much!*

Chapter Eighteen

Tara lifted heavy-lidded eyes to see five anxious faces hovering above her. She tried to smile reassuringly, but excruciating pain caused the expression to wobble on her lips. Now she knew exactly how John had felt when he'd been laid up in bed, battling to recover his strength.

The thought of John sent a vague memory sweeping through her. She wasn't sure if she'd been dreaming, but she vaguely recalled him whispering to her in the darkness, sheltering her in his arms and providing warmth to combat her chills.

Tara tried to swallow past the unpleasant taste in her mouth and then found herself niggled by a fuzzy recollection of being force-fed something that left her drifting in a surreal world for hours on end. Peyote buttons…

"I thought you'd never wake up." Flora sidled closer to Tara. "Are you hungry? Zohn Whoof said to feed you broth and water every time you woke up, just like we fed him."

Tara nodded agreeably. She was famished, come to think of it. "How long have I been asleep?" Was that her voice? It sounded as if it had rusted.

Calvin inched closer. "Four days. John said not to

worry about it, 'cause you're extremely fatigued and rest is the very best thing for you.''

"He should know," she murmured. "It hasn't been that long since he was the one who was bedridden...." She frowned. "Where's John?"

"He left," Maureen replied. "He helped us put the farm in order, then he rode to San Carlos."

Tara inwardly winced. She didn't envy John that journey, for she knew its grim purpose. Although she'd remained conscious only a few minutes after she'd been shot that fateful day, she'd managed to catch the gist of the final conversation between John and Raven. She knew Raven's death weighed heavily on John's soul. He'd gone to Gray Eagle, bearing the worst of all possible news— that the blood of his adopted brother stained his hands.

Though Flora spoon-fed broth to her, Tara's strength eluded her. Keeping her eyes open demanded more energy than she could muster. She fell asleep, serenaded by the children's voices assuring her that they'd keep the ranch running efficiently while she recovered. She'd have told them that she didn't doubt their capability for a second, but she was too weary to speak.

John entered the wickiup to find the old man sitting cross-legged on his buffalo quilt. Gray Eagle looked every day of his sixty-two years. Braided hair once as black and shiny as a crow's wing had turned a tarnished gray. Deep creases that testified to years of turmoil and hard living lined the old chief's face. His dark, soulful eyes lacked their usual sparkle and his thin-bladed shoulders drooped noticeably.

"Did you find Raven?" Gray Eagle asked in the Apache tongue. Not one for small talk, he cut right to the heart of the matter.

John sank down across from the aging chief. "I found him twice. The first time I tried to be lenient with him, but he shot me and left me for dead in the Canyon of the Sun. I caught up with Raven after he and his gang of desperadoes raided a farm, captured a woman and five orphans, stole their livestock and ransacked their home.''

Gray Eagle dropped his head, his expression bleak. His gnarled hands clenched into fists. ''So he refused to come back with you.''

''Refused twice,'' John said grimly. ''He wouldn't listen to reason.''

Very slowly, Gray Eagle lifted his head to stare John squarely in the eye. John knew the wise old chief understood what hadn't been said. He silently thanked Gray Eagle for making this torturous conversation a little easier. But then, it wasn't the Apache way to speak of a warrior's moment of death. Gray Eagle knew he'd lost one son at another son's hands.

It was a long, anguishing moment before the old chief spoke. ''He could not accept you into his heart as easily as I could. Since childhood, he measured himself against you and found himself lacking in strength, character and cunning. I hoped one day he would see that you were not a threat, that constantly finding fault with you did not make him the mightier warrior.''

''Yet in the end, *I* failed *you*…and him,'' John whispered, tormented. ''I left here, vowing to make life more tolerable for the Apache at the reservation. I promised to bring my brother back to you, but I've failed in both endeavors.''

Gray Eagle sighed audibly. ''We have prayed to the Great Spirit to deliver us from bondage, but our enemy's numbers are too great, their weapons too powerful. We have been stripped of our land and our pride.''

''I have tried every way I know how—''

Gray Eagle lifted his hand, demanding silence. ''We have become hobbled horses and we must accept what cannot be changed. The Anglos have abolished our tribal government, outlawed our ceremonial dances and forced us to adopt the white man's ways. But the Anglos cannot steal the memories of our past, our history or our traditions. The life of the Apache has never been an easy one, but at least we had our freedom to hunt as we wanted, to visit our sacred lands and to pray to our gods.''

''I will never stop fighting for the rights and dignity of the Apache,'' John promised resolutely.

''I know this, my son, but I have not been fair to you. I have had much time to think on this. I sent you on an impossible mission and gave you the difficult task of bringing your brother back to me. For five years you have become the circling eagle that watches over us. For me, you sacrificed your own chance to find peace and happiness in the Anglos' culture. You did all I asked of you. But now I release you from your vow. I ask no more of you, for the sun has set on the Apache nation.''

''Gray Eagle—''

''You are an honorable warrior,'' he interrupted. ''Together we fought our last fight, but our battle is over. Find your place, John Wolfe.''

His place? The only place that felt like home was Paradise Valley. Yet John could admire it only from a distance, savor it in bittersweet memories—because he'd failed Tara. He'd very nearly cost her her life.

He'd been mistaken in thinking that he'd find the courage to face her again. But seeing her lying motionless in bed—brought down by *his* bullet, from *his* weapon—was a torment too difficult to bear. Sweet mercy! He couldn't forgive himself for that—ever!

He'd sneaked into Tara's room each night to hold her protectively in his arms, giving her peyote buttons to counter the pain. But always before dawn he'd left her bed, for fear she'd open her eyes and realize she'd been held and comforted by the very man who'd shot her. The grim fact was that he'd failed Tara as miserably as he'd failed the Apache.

"Your heart, too, is heavy," Gray Eagle said perceptively. "What else troubles you, my son?"

"A woman," he said on an anguished breath that felt as if it had been ripped from his chest.

Gray Eagle nodded sagely. A wry smile pursed his lips. "Ah, this woman with the five orphans. She has your heart."

John gaped at him, astonished, speechless.

"You are very good at masking your feelings, John Wolfe. You had to be when you became white again—at my bidding. But I saw the expression on your face and heard the change in your voice when you mentioned the woman and children. They mean a great deal to you. Since that is so, it is time for you to take your place in that world."

John couldn't bring himself to go into detail about the reasons he was tormented, the reason he'd never be able to make a place for himself in Paradise Valley. If Gray Eagle rested easier thinking John could find peace and enjoy a bright future, then so be it.

"Go now, my son, and may the Great Spirit go with you." Gray Eagle clasped John's hand firmly. "And perhaps one day you will return here so I can meet my grandchildren. It is good and right that the children pass down to each generation the stories of how we came to be, that they remember our traditions. For if the stories die out, then it is as if our nation never was."

John sincerely wished he could walk away from the reservation knowing the dawn of a new day would bring a better life for the Apache. Despite Gray Eagle's bleak acceptance of captivity, John could not, *would* not, turn his back on his clan. He'd always be the Apache's spokesman, fighting for their dignity, calling attention to white corruption and injustice on the reservation. He was an

Apache at heart and he knew that giving up hope was the worst kind of defeat for the Indian nation.

Tara strolled onto the front porch to survey the ranch. The sight of her beloved home had always brought an indescribable sense of peace and security. Now there was something vital missing—John Wolfe. It had been a month since she'd seen him looming like a dark, avenging angel on the outcropping of rock, facing his most difficult battle against Raven—confronting the most difficult choice life could hurl at him.

The children had seen John several times since then, had spoken to him, because he'd taken time from his duties as marshal to check on them. But never once had John ventured close enough to the cabin for Tara to see him.

She knew why he was standoffish, because now she fully understood what motivated and drove the man who held her heart in his hands. All she had to do was close her eyes and she could recall that fateful dawn when Raven had shoved her into the path of John's bullet. She'd seen the look of horror and regret that registered on his face. She knew he held himself personally responsible for her injury and her brutal ordeal with Raven.

Tara wasn't the least bit surprised that John held himself accountable. After all, the man took obligation and responsibility quite seriously. She glanced at the corral he'd repaired, a case in point. The five original mustangs—stolen by the desperadoes—had been returned. Plus five more mustangs had been penned up and were undergoing training.

Tara remembered the day the children had rushed excitedly to her bedside to report the arrival of their new horses. According to the children, each horse had been broken to halter, bridle and saddle. John had left instructions for them to ride the horses regularly. Naturally, the children obeyed; they thought John hung the moon and every last star in the heavens.

"Tara, yoo-hoo!"

Tara shifted her attention from the mustangs to Maureen, who appeared from a thicket of trees. The girl was toting a package and smiling delightedly. Tara frowned curiously when Maureen bounded up the steps to present her with it. Immediately, the other children stopped what they were doing and came running.

"Where did this come from?" Tara questioned, bemused.

"From John, of course," Maureen said, as if Tara ought to know.

Ah, the guardian angel of Paradise Valley had struck again, she thought as she untied the twine. It seemed that John was trying to soothe his tormented conscience. Not only had he delivered horses, he'd brought them sacks of grain and, occasionally, bouquets of wildflowers. In addition, wild game, cleaned and dressed for cooking, arrived before mealtimes. The children often returned bearing gifts after their visits with John. And now this package. About the only thing that *hadn't* shown up on Tara's doorstep was John himself—the one thing Tara wanted most. All these gifts were no substitute for the man she needed and loved.

"Oh my goodness!" Tara gasped in surprise when she spied the dazzling green satin gown, sensible blue calico dress and frothy petticoats.

The girls oohed and aahed over the fashionable garments. The boys quickly assured Tara that she'd be the prettiest and best-dressed woman at the *fandango* scheduled for the upcoming weekend in Rambler Springs.

Tara silently steamed.

Did that idiotic man think fancy clothes, horses, food and flowers would appease her? How long would he harbor the ridiculous notion that she blamed him for her injuries? Tara's annoyed thoughts screeched to a halt when she realized John would *never* forgive himself for what had happened.

"Oh, for heaven's sake," she muttered aloud.

Samuel's jaw dropped when he noticed her irritated expression. "You don't like the dresses? You've never owned anything so fine in your life!"

"Of course I like the dresses," she grumbled. "What's not to like?"

"I was thinking the same thing myself," Maureen commented, smiling.

"I think Maureen and I should buy a green dress like yours so we can be the Three Muskatators, like the boys with their blue shirts," Flora said.

"Musk*eteers,* half-pint," Calvin corrected.

Flora shrugged. "I'm going to buy a green dress with the money Zohn Whoof gave me."

"What money?" Tara demanded.

"John gave us some of the reward money he received from rounding up those outlaws who abducted us," Samuel explained.

"John said he was going to use the rest of the money to buy food for the Apache at San Carlos. He said it seemed highly fitting, since those sneaky desperadoes dressed up like Indians to raid," Derek added.

"John also said he was going to take us to the reservation to meet Gray Eagle someday soon," Calvin reported enthusiastically. "He got permission from the military commander to take some of the Indian boys with us to hunt so we can get to know each other better."

Ah, so John truly had decided to banish the prejudices of the whites and eliminate the bitterness of the Apache one child at a time, had he? She suspected the inspiration came from his attempt to teach these children Apache survival skills, and from his conflicts with his blood brother. It was John's way of turning something harmful into something righteous.

She did admire his clever strategy—even if the man was a complete imbecile!

"John also said we could go to town today, with Maureen and Flora. They've been cleaning those houses and the church you didn't want us to know you were cleaning for extra money," Calvin said.

Tara's eyes widened in surprise as she glanced at Maureen. "How long have you been assuming my job in town?"

"Since the first week you were recuperating. John said he knew you had a part-time job and you'd be expected. He said Flora and I were more than capable of doing the work, because we do such a fine job of spiffying up our cabin. John has been taking us to town every week."

"John said he's made arrangements for Derek and Calvin and me to earn extra money at the blacksmith shop because we've gotten pretty good at working with horses," Samuel stated proudly.

John said this and John said that, she fumed. The man was working overtime behind the scenes, assuming responsibility while Tara recovered. Yet he was a coward, unable to face her because…because he cared what she thought of him. Because he was afraid her feelings had changed after he'd unintentionally shot her. She was pretty sure he wouldn't allow *her* to forgive him because he couldn't forgive *himself*….

The epiphany caused her to jerk upright and scan the rocky precipices of the canyon, knowing John was out there somewhere. "Oh, for Pete's sake!"

"What's-a-matter?" Flora questioned. "Are you feeling ill again?"

Tara forced a smile. "I'm fine." Or at least she would be shortly.

"Since you're going to town with John, I'd appreciate it if you'd put your bedrooms in order before you leave."

The children nodded agreeably.

"Whatcha gonna do while we're gone?" Flora asked curiously.

"I'm going to the spring for a relaxing bath," she said. "Then I'll take a walk and, hopefully, become accustomed to being up and around again."

The children seemed satisfied that Tara wouldn't be too lonely without them. Discussing what they intended to purchase with the money John had generously provided, they trooped off to tidy up their rooms.

The moment Tara was alone she set her gifts on the wooden bench. A folded paper tumbled from the sleeve of the green gown. Frowning curiously, she plucked it up. Her eyes popped when she read the note from John. He'd used his connections in law enforcement to investigate Mortimer Lindsey's death in Texas.

According to the information John had received from Sheriff Thornton in Palo Pinto County, a young woman from the orphan train had been delivered to Lindsey's ranch under misleading circumstances. His death had been ruled self-defense, based on the evidence of struggle and the telltale metal cuffs secured to the head and foot rails of his bed. In addition, the gravesite discovered on the ranch aroused suspicion about the nature of Lindsey's young wife's death. Therefore, it was determined that the orphan, Meghan Kendric—

Tara blinked in surprise when she saw her given name in print. She had the unmistakable feeling that John had ferreted out her true identity from one of the younger children—either Flora or Calvin—and then pursued his investigation.

Anxiously, Tara continued reading.

As to the other five runaway orphans, no charges had been filed. Meghan Kendric was presumed to have taken the children into her care and disappeared from town. The local citizens who'd taken in the younger children had not registered complaints and the case had been closed.

Tara sagged in relief. For two years the incident and the possibility of repercussions had hung over her head like a black cloud. She'd been exceptionally cautious, for fear of drawing unwanted attention and curiosity. Discovering that she had nothing to fear from legal authorities took a tremendous load off her mind and filled her with inexpressible joy.

Tara also realized this note from John was just another of the many deeds he'd performed in his effort to make amends for her ordeal with Raven. He'd made repairs at the ranch, watched over the children, offered them gifts and purchased fine clothes for her. This was John's way of trying to say he was dreadfully sorry he'd shot her.

He obviously believed he was responsible for her injury. Furthermore, he presumed that her feelings for him had changed because of the hellish ordeal. But the idiotic man was sorely mistaken on both counts.

More determined than ever, Tara made a beeline for the Altar of the Gods. She sidestepped up the steep stone slope to the cavern that held the Apache treasure. Huffing and puffing from exertion, she braced herself against the rugged rock wall and scanned the panoramic canyon.

"John Wolfe, I know you're out there somewhere, and I want you to know that I think you are a complete idiot!" Her voice echoed around her. She waited a moment, then railed at him at the top of her lungs. "Do you think my feelings for you have changed because of what happened with Raven? I would've gladly taken a bullet for *you.* Don't you know that?

"Don't you know that I love you with all my heart and soul? Can't you see that I'll love you, *always,* no matter where you are or what you do? I miss you...I need *you,* John Wolfe, not fine clothes and frilly petticoats. Not even my exoneration and the reinstatement of my good name will do, though I'm exceedingly grateful for your efforts on my behalf. All I want is you. *Just you.* Don't you know that you are always welcome here, no matter what? *I...love...you...* blast it!'' she shouted loudly.

Weary from exertion, Tara carefully sidestepped down the slope and headed to the cabin. *There,* she thought as she trudged onto the front porch. If hearing his name called in the wind, hearing her shout her love for him— from as near the top of the Altar of the Gods as she could get, without falling off—didn't convince that blockheaded man that she wanted to see him, needed to hold him, to love him, then she didn't know what would!

John rose from a crouch and followed at a distance as Tara returned to the cabin. Her unfaltering affection and her unconditional forgiveness humbled him, astonished him.

However, he was more than a little put out about that sassy female calling him a complete idiot. Well, maybe he was, but she didn't have to shout it to high heaven and all over creation, did she?

When John strolled up to his tethered horse, Pie laid back his ears and stared at him without blinking. ''What are you looking at?'' John demanded.

Pie stamped his left front hoof, as if criticizing his master.

''Well, I had to be sure I hadn't destroyed her feelings for me, didn't I?'' John said defensively. ''I couldn't just walk up to her right off.''

Pie blinked, stamped his right front hoof and snorted reproachfully.

''I can't do anything about Irish right now, can I? I promised the children I'd take them to town...and stop staring at me like that, you worthless excuse of a horse,'' he muttered sourly. "I said I'd find the nerve to face Irish again, and I will...eventually."

When John tried to mount up, Pie sidestepped. Honestly, John was beginning to think this stallion had become his conscience.

Hands on his hips, John glowered at his contrary steed. "You want my promise? Will that satisfy you? Fine, you've got it. But you're going to help me with this. You'll have to do something you've never done before, either, pal, so don't come whinnying to me when your time comes."

Pie stared at him for another silent moment, then flung his broad head sideways, as if giving his royal permission for John to climb aboard.

"Damn sassy horse, anyway," John grumbled as he swung into the saddle. "You've gotten pushy in your old age, Pie. Real pushy. And don't think I don't know what you think you're going to get out of this. You're going to get soft while you're lounging around this canyon, munching on grass and socializing with the other horses. Then we'll race off for San Carlos and you'll be wheezing like an old nag."

When Pie snorted indignantly, John chuckled. "Well, she called *me* a complete idiot. That's worse than being referred to as an old nag."

After enduring a month of torment, John felt as if a heavy burden had been lifted from his chest. He was at peace with himself. Tara still loved him—even if he didn't deserve her. Knowing he was loved and wanted was a soothing balm for his tortured soul. As soon as he returned from town with the children, he'd approach Tara. No more staring longingly at her from a distance, watching her venture unsteadily to and from the cabin.

Week by week, he'd watched Tara grow stronger. He'd been greatly relieved to note the bullet hadn't caused serious damage to nerves and tendons. She could use her left arm again. He'd seen her brace herself on her injured arm when she'd climbed the spire to yell at him. John smiled at the image of Tara clinging to the sandstone ledge, calling him home.

"Zohn Whoof! I wore my yellow dress so you'd see me coming."

John glanced up the path to see Flora looking healthy and as colorful as the sun. She sat atop the strawberry-roan horse she'd asked—about a hundred and fifty times—if she could claim as her own. Naturally, he'd given in to her. That just showed what a pushover he was when this little girl batted those enormous brown eyes at him and hugged him every chance she got.

Aw, hell, the truth was he'd let each kid pick out a mustang. John had worked relentlessly to ensure that each horse was trained to behave itself with a child on its back. He could always gather more mustangs to sell later. Right now, all that concerned him was seeing these kids happy.

Tara was thoroughly disappointed when John didn't return to the house with the children. Her family arrived, bubbling with excitement over their latest purchases. Sure enough, Maureen and Flora had bought green dresses to match the one John had given Tara, and they wasted no time modeling the garments. Tara noticed the smiles the girls passed back and forth before glancing at her. She had the feeling there was something going on besides their delight over their new dresses.

"Where's John?" Tara questioned as she stared into the gathering darkness, battling her feelings of rejection.

"He said he had things to do. Don't know what, though, 'cause he didn't say exactly," Samuel murmured. His head was bent over the crisp new bridle and reins he'd purchased, and he was smiling for no reason their conversation could account for.

Tara glanced around, noting the other children were

grinning like baked possums, too. She swore they shared some private amusement she wasn't privy to. She might've interrogated them about their odd behavior if she hadn't been so heartbroken over John's absence. She'd so hoped that her entreaty that he return to the cabin would reassure him. What else was a woman supposed to do to let the man she loved know that she was anxiously waiting to welcome him home?

Perhaps the painful truth was that John had been trying to spare her feelings and he thought that keeping his distance was the best way to let her down gently. Despite everything that had happened, despite his concern, his regret and his obvious affection for the children, maybe he simply didn't love her—at least not to the same intense degree she loved him. After all, he'd never said the words—not even once.

Tara's shoulders slumped in defeat. She tried to tell herself that she'd survive the heartache, that this wasn't the first time she'd felt unaccepted and rejected. Good heavens, she'd been passed over so many times at the orphanage that she should be used to it by now. Even so, having John slip away from her was akin to watching her dreams sift through her fingers like stardust, and feeling her heart shrivel up inside her chest, one agonizing breath at a time.

The nicker of a horse caught Tara's attention. While the children were busy entertaining themselves, she walked onto the front porch, then stopped dead in her tracks. John's piebald stallion was hitched to the supporting beam of the cabin. There was a wreath of woven vines and wildflowers around Pie's muscular neck. Tara's jaw dropped when she remembered the Apache ritual John had described to her two months earlier.

All those awful feelings of rejection, inadequacy and disappointment flew off in the wind when she understood what the piebald stallion's arrival implied.

Her bubbling laughter drifted on the evening breeze as she patted Pie's neck affectionately and then impulsively hugged the stuffing out of the horse. She untied the reins and walked the stallion to the spring to drink. Pie tossed his head, glanced sideways and then slurped water.

Smiling wryly, John appeared from the dense underbrush. "Irish, I distinctly remember telling you that an Apache maiden is supposed to leave her suitor's horse standing for a couple of days. If she leads the horse to water on the first day, it makes her look entirely too desperate, as if she doesn't stand a chance of acquiring another interested suitor."

Tara absorbed the long-awaited sight of him. A deluge of immeasurable pleasure engulfed her. Ah, how she loved this man!

"Well, the fact is I am quite desperate," she admitted, unashamed. "For you see, John Wolfe, you're the one and only man I'll ever love, body, heart and soul. Smart as you are, I thought you'd figured that out by now."

All the wondrous feelings John hadn't allowed himself to fully acknowledge or experience in more years than he could count overwhelmed him when Tara walked, then ran, toward him. He met her halfway across the clearing to sweep her up in his arms. He devoured her with a kiss that testified to all the love and affection billowing inside him.

"I thought you'd never come home," she whispered against his lips. "Life without you was unbearably empty. Don't ever do that to me again, John Wolfe, or I swear I'll hunt you down and strangle you for leaving me miserable."

"Well, complete idiot that I am," he said, pursing his lips, "I wasn't sure you still wanted me after what I did to you."

"What *you* did?" Tara shook her head and sighed. "That wasn't your doing. It was Raven's, and you've defended his actions too often already. Not for one second did I hold you responsible. Not even *one*, blast it!''

John cupped her bewitching face in his hands and studied her astutely. ''I'm sorry I haven't come to see you, Irish. I was so damn afraid to look into your eyes and discover that love no longer shone there for me. I couldn't bear knowing for certain that I had lost it.''

''You aren't going to lose me...ever,'' she said, absolutely.

''Good, because I am going to be here with you to help raise the kids, because I love those little rascals, too.''

''You are?'' she chirped, wide-eyed. ''You do?''

He nodded his raven head and smiled again. ''I have changed occupations. Jacob Shore put in a good word for me at the Bureau of Indian Affairs. I've been hired as a part-time advisor, interpreter and consultant whose duty it is to oversee conditions at the Apache reservation.''

''That's wonderful!'' Tara said excitely.

''Of course, there'll be times when I have to travel, and I'll never give up the fight to see that the Apache are treated humanely and fairly. But mostly, I'll be here with you.''

Tara flung her arms around his neck, ignoring the twinge of pain in her left arm. ''I can't wait to tell the children. They'll be delighted.''

''They already know,'' he murmured as he nuzzled his chin against the top of her curly head. ''I told them this afternoon that I was going to ask you to marry me.''

''Marry me?'' she parroted.

He chuckled at her startled expression. ''Well, of course, Irish. We can't live in sin with five impressionable children underfoot, now can we?''

''But you have never once said—''

He kissed her soundly to shush her. ''Said what, Irish? That you're so deeply embedded in my mind, my heart and my soul that I can't for the life of me remember when

I didn't love you? It's true, you know. I never really understood what love was, and then suddenly I knew, because you taught me how to love and to be loved in return.''

Smiling tenderly, he brushed the pad of his thumb over her trembling lower lip, then rerouted the teardrops that slid down her cheeks. ''When I opened my eyes and saw that lovely angel of mercy bending over me, I knew I was in serious trouble.''

''Ah yes, I remember.'' Tara chuckled as she swiped at her sentimental tears. ''You thought you had already winged your way to heaven. But I tell you sincerely, John, being here with you in Paradise Valley is as close to heaven as I'll ever need to get, for you are my heaven on earth.''

''I love you, Irish,'' he whispered as he wrapped her in his arms and held her against his heart.

When he bent his head to kiss her, and she kissed him back enthusiastically, the world spun away and wild, sweet sensations consumed him. The profound need that Tara alone created, and Tara alone satisfied, swept through his body.

There, beneath the vault of twinkling stars that glittered over Paradise Valley, John expressed the full extent of his love for Tara with each gentle caress and soulful kiss. He discovered that special place where he belonged—in the never-ending circle of Tara's loving arms and the fathomless depths of her loving heart.

* * * * *

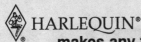

"You didn't have to kiss me at the blasted table!" he erupted

"What good would it do to kiss you in private?" she asked reasonably. "That would defeat the whole purpose of letting the boys know my interest lies elsewhere."

"With that piddly peck on the mouth?" he said, then smirked.

"What was wrong with my kiss?" she demanded, offended.

He swooped down and hoisted her to her feet. Then he bent her over backward and gave her a kiss that was half frustration, half hungry need, half revenge... well, whatever. He couldn't calculate fractions when his brain shut down the instant he tasted her deeply, felt her supple body pressed intimately against his masculine contours. His heart slammed against his tender ribs when she responded rather than shoving him away— which is what she should've done if the damn woman had a lick of sense!